for
D & M

 A M M

A NOVEL

NICK TOTEM

AMM
Copyright © 2015 Nick Totem

Lucen Geist Literary Press, LLC
lucengeist@gmail.com

All rights reserved. No part of this book may be reproduced or transmitted in any form without written permission from the publisher, except by reviewers who may quote brief excerpts in connection with a review.

ISBN: 978-1-943564-00-2

10 9 8 7 6 5 4 3 2 1

Cover design by Conrad Casper
Interior design by Domini Dragoone

*What, then, is that incalculable feeling
that deprives the mind of the sleep
necessary to life?*

—Albert Camus

PROLOGUE

E ven late at night the hospital knows no peace. Floodlights pierce the cold air and illuminate the whole city block, snubbing the stars. Up high beyond the shining lights, dim windows punctuate vast, opaque walls, and enormous modern structures, as if under a false will, inflate toward the sky, stagger against one another in a fatalistic duel, and under the veil of night become a behemoth of concrete with stultifying effects on what little sentience remains. A metallic shine on the new buildings deflects the night's descending cold, while the old brick buildings, much smaller and much too low to the ground, cower in their own shadows.

Presently on the left side of the hospital's main entrance, a white ambulance with its lights flashing red speeds up to the curve, and the siren shrieks, accompanying the flashes of light. Shadowy medics appear, move deftly, and cart out the stretcher with a person already hooked up to an intravenous line and a face mask, and together the awkward mass of people disappears through a sliding door into the building's underbelly.

Waiting for the ambulance to clear the street, Art Sand knows all about what happens next. His fingers tap the steering wheel, and his foot twitches over the brake. The tuxedo encloses his body, giving him the impression of being taller than he actually is when standing, but now that he is fixed in the car seat, it squeezes his chest, and the black tie constricts his neck and makes breathing uncomfortable. Easing his foot and nudging the car forward, he has to get inside the hospital this very minute. He has an emergency of his own.

Seeing the ambulance, he can't help feeling a touch of nostalgia—first as a medical student going for rides inside the ambulance, then as an intern working the night shifts in the emergency room. Years ago on nights like this, always nights like this, he, forgetting himself, walked alongside the stretcher through the same corridor to the operating room and, together with other nurses and doctors, bustled over an unconscious patient. The smell of blood in the air, the shout of 'Code Blue' from overhead speakers echoing throughout the hallway, a young man with a baby face who had been shot in the chest, the cool bright beams of the operating room's lights, the metal chest retractor with its serrated, locking mechanism—Art Sand remembers. He had fumbled with the electrodes, tried to stay out of the way, and in the end watched in admiration the steady hands and even steadier gaze of the old surgeon. Pint after pint of type O negative blood, its color dark red, had been squeezed through the small plastic intravenous tube to infuse the dying; more had been sucked out of his chest, the young man with a baby face; more had been sent swirling through the suction machine, dispersing small microscopic motes into the air to cling finally to Art Sand's olfactory bulb. Raw with slight sulfuric and ureic taste and tinged with life from the sea from where it came, the smell of blood had thickened the air. In times like this and after many years of times like this, the night is redolent with knowledge that can be distilled into wisdom only if he can hone in on the scent of blood and know its primacy, elemental and essential. Even after everything else changes—a young woman with a stony mask of a face awaiting, or an old man accepting, or an infant not yet knowing—only the scent of blood stays and nothing else.

The call had come unexpectedly.

—Dr. Sand, this is Mark. You have to come right away.

—What's the matter? I'm at the department's banquet. Can't you handle it yourself?

—I think you should be here for this.

—What's going on over there?

—David Calweld woke up.

—What do you mean?

—He became verbal, saying all sorts of strange things. I know you're at the banquet, but considering who his father is, I thought you should be here for this one.

—David Calweld is verbal? Impossible. I'm coming.

The mention of the Calwelds had given his heart a jolt. They'd given millions to the University, and the Neural Science Building bears their name. Art still doesn't have a clear idea of what the emergency is, but when the Calwelds are concerned, he knows he must be there in person.

Finally, the column of cars flows into the subterranean parking garage. Art drives to his usual spot. The powerful shining Mercedes hugs the curves, moving swiftly down two floors. He jumps from the car and runs to the elevator. Thick, noxious exhaust hangs in the air. Under the white light of the elevator, the small expanse of his white shirt, his black tuxedo, and polished black shoes are reflected and distorted in the shiny metallic door.

He adjusts his identification badge. His physical characteristics—average height, lean frame, and slightly curly brown hair reaching past his ears—place him squarely in the middle of any male population. If it had not been for his large, brown eyes, encircled by hypertrophic muscles that seem to be in a state of constant contraction, giving him an unnatural focus, his face—marked by the sharp jaw lines, a straight nose, and thin hollow cheeks—would appear conventional. Instead, the thick brows together with the focusing eyes impart the look of a man weighed down by an unknown burden.

On the sixth floor, the elevator door opens. Art steps into the bright white light of the Intensive Care Unit. There are ten separate rooms. Through the cacophony of beeping heart monitors and the chattering of nurses and residents, he hears screaming from the corner. A strong smell of antiseptic, alcohol, and bleach comes from an empty room.

—Dr. Sand.

Mark Phan, the chief resident, calls his name the moment he crosses the threshold.

—Mark, what's going on?

—Well, he started to talk about two hours ago.

Mark comes up to him, his eyes open wide, unmoving as if searching for answers. Another intern and several nurses follow closely behind, their faces having taken on the paleness of the white neon overhead.

—What do you mean "talk"?

—He started to say words. He spoke.

—Spoke? What is he saying?

—All sorts of stuff. Dr. Sand, you've been his doctor for a long time. I was hoping you would tell me. All I know is that he was admitted three days ago for West Nile viral encephalitis. He's been in a coma ever since. He woke up today and started to talk. I mean that would be expected for anyone else but. . . .

—He hasn't spoken much since he was born. Maybe some words now and then, but not any meaningful communication.

—Exactly, Dr. Sand. I went over his records. There's no documentation of his being able to communicate by verbal or nonverbal means.

—Yeah, he was born with severe mental retardation. How are his vitals, blood counts, electrolytes?

Art heads to the corner room from where the screams are coming. Mark follows and reads off vital statistics, one after another.

—Temperature is 98.5, heart rate 105, respiration 27, blood pressure 145 over 94. Oxygenation 100 percent. White count 12.5. Hemoglobin is 33.3.

Once they are inside the room, a nurse slides the door shut. With their appearance the screaming stops, yielding to the quiet buzzing of the intravenous machines, the beeping of David's heart rhythm on the monitor, and his now labored breathing. To the right of the bed a monitor displays greenish tracings of the patient's vital signs, all consistent with what Mark has told him. To the left there awaits a mechanical respirator, for the moment waiting patiently and relinquishing. Bags of electrolytes with their yellowish feigning of human fluid hang from the intravenous poles. Upon the bed David Calweld sits upright, leaning back. Intravenous lines and electrodes emerge from his skin. An odor of stale perspiration clings to the warm air.

Mark pulls Art close and whispers into his ear.

—I have to tell you something.

—Yeah?

—Some of the nurses. . . . they're, you know, Catholics and they think that he's possessed.

—Nonsense, Art says loudly and approaches the bed.

He recognizes the face—light, haphazard blond hair; thinness of skin over bone; the large curving nose; the prominent, outwardly protruding yellowish teeth; and the large sunken eyes with bluish, speckled irises that exude an unmistakable awareness—but he does not know this conscious person behind the eyes, an unwelcome visitor. For all the time that Art has been David Calweld's doctor, he has been treating a physical body and feeling the pulse of matter without a mind, and though never was there any interaction or sliver of communication, still over the last eighteen years he has tested and monitored the growth of this body, the accretion of matter onto matter as if under an obscene law. At the insistence of the boy's father, he has performed encephalograms brain MRIs, CT scans, Pet scans, blood tests over and over but to no avail. All the tests have been normal.

—Doctor . . . Sand, David Calweld says. There's a slight gargling of the words as though a young child is speaking.

Hearing the sound of his own name, Art's heart jumps. So it's true after all, so the boy can speak. But how? His mind swirls with different thoughts compounding quickly—a medical breakthrough, a novel and marvelous neurological process, a revolutionary understanding of the mind, publication of papers, more grant money, and fame. And his father, Hayden Calweld, will be beyond happy, his insistence on the best medical treatment for his son finally vindicated.

—Do you know me?

Art feels David's eyes on him, an irresistible tug of the bluish, speckled eyes.

—Doctor . . . Sand. I know you. . . . Let me out.

Only now does Art see the restraints, thick leather straps that bind David's arms and legs to the bed.

—I thought it best to put him in restraints, just to be safe . . . until we figured out . . . until he calmed down, Mark says.

—I've seen you all these years and you never spoke, Art says.

—I couldn't. . . . before.

—But how? Why now?

—I don't . . . know, says the gargling voice.

All eyes look to Art, waiting for expert judgment.

—Hmm. Well. It's only a theory but perhaps the infection that you had, the viral encephalitis caused some sort of reorganization of your neural pathways, reconnecting different parts of your brain. Since you recognize me, that means that your memory is stored in a part of your brain that's functional. And since you can speak, somehow you've gained consciousness. It's remarkable. I've got to think it through. We need to perform some tests.

—Let me out. I have to go. . . . you will be sorry.

—Please calm down. Let's try to figure out what's going on. Then I'll take these straps off.

—Let me out . . . You don't know . . . what . . . what . . . you're doing.

—Your father will be very happy.

—My father, Hayden Calweld . . . You do whatever . . . you need for him . . . Cost be damned. . . . I know he is not retarded . . . my son is not retarded, David says and gasps.

During their last meeting only two weeks ago, Hayden Calweld had said exactly that as they stood over his son. David has repeated it verbatim.

—It's incredible. How do you remember that? Art says.

From behind him come suppressed voices, whispering, like the background chorus of a Greek tragedy, and Art turns and glances at the interns and the nurses, who stiffen.

—Let me out . . . now. You don't. David screams and yanks on the restraints, twisting this way and that with his face contorting, showing the large protruding teeth.

The beeping of the heart monitor quickens.

—Calm down. David, I can't let you out if you behave like this.

—Let me out . . . You don't know . . . you know . . . you don't . . . You'll be soooorry.

—If you're referring to your father, he'll be happy to know that you can talk, you're awake.

—My father . . . has nothing . . . to do with it.

—How is it that you know how to talk?

—I remember . . . I don't know . . . Now let me out . . . Now, now, now, now.

David twists and yanks on the leather straps. The bed sways.

—We should give him a little Versed, Mark says.

—Hmm. Art contemplates, knowing that sedating a combative patient has always been the automatic response, but this case is full of uncertainty. A smoldering sensation, a fear of the unknown, the fear itself a mystery emanating from a place as inscrutable as David Calweld, tugs at him and grows stronger, hinting at something great and terrible and of all humanity, encompassing and inseparable.

In the waiting eyes of the interns and nurses, he must forfeit a decision, and suddenly he feels the black tie tightening around his neck and the warm, stuffy air inside the room.

—David, you need to sleep, Art says.

—No, no, no. Please, please . . . Arthur Sand . . . 5660 Canyon Drive . . . Los Angeles, California 90272.

—You know my address. Unbelievable. Where did you get that?

—I don't want to sleep . . . I don't want to sleep.

—You'll feel better tomorrow, Art says, though he can hardly hear himself.

—No, no, no. Don't make me sleep . . . I stay still . . . still. His voice sounds more high-pitched and gargled.

—You'll be OK. I promise.

David's head nudges to the side again and again, while his eyes stare into Art's, signaling him to come closer. Following an irresistible power, Art stoops down, turning his right ear forward in anticipation of some secret revelation David has chosen to confer on him. But abruptly his neck is pulled forward, and David's gangly fingers clutch his collar, pulling him closer, so close that he can feel David's breath on his ear. With all his strength he pushes against the bed frame trying to stand up, but he doesn't move an inch, as if a superhuman strength has transformed David's stick-like fingers into steel, into fateful protuberances to deliver Art so that his ears are within range of David's stuttering breaths, the whispering of disjointed words, the choked pleading from a world timeless. While struggling to free himself, Art hears David's whispering in his ear over and over. A second of collective amazement passes before the nurses and the residents grab David and pry open his fingers.

—How did he get loose?

—Oh, my. What the . . .

—Put his hand through the straps.

—Tighten the other one, too.

—I'm sorry, Doctor.

—Are you OK?

OUTSIDE THE ROOM, ART TAKES DEEP BREATHS; HIS HEART IS still pounding, his palms tingling with sweat. Behind the closed door, David's screams are muted. Art examines the chart and tries to think logically, but the harder he tries the more incoherent everything appears. Why would a person with mental retardation suddenly become intelligent? Why this person and not the thousands of other people with a similar mental capacity? Why now? He has never come across anything like this in the medical literature, and if he hadn't been here in person, he wouldn't believe it. Certainly, the medical journals are filled with cases of comatose patients suddenly regaining consciousness after being in a coma for as long as thirty years, but never before has a mentally retarded person gained consciousness and intelligence. Could the viral infection somehow have rewired his brain?

As with many other things in life, he'll never know the whys, yet his mind will not relent. Seeking the answer to the whys must necessarily lead beyond reason, to the realm of superstition and religion. If he were superstitious, he would sooner worship David as a prophet than treat him. But, as a scientist, he will have to settle for the hows, and tomorrow he will start with all the tests: MRI, EEG, blood tests, spinal tap.

Mark comes up to him and speaks softly, perhaps trying to convey an air of privilege under the watching eyes of the nurses.

—Dr. Sand, I'm so sorry about that. I guess he's so skinny he could pull his hands right through the straps. We got him into tighter ones.

—Don't worry about it. I'm fine.

—Have you ever seen anything like this before?

—No.

—Dr. Sand, what do you think he meant? You know he said we'll be sorry. I mean, you know his father. Was he threatening us somehow?

—I don't know, but I don't think so. As long as we're doing our best, you don't need to fear anyone.

—Right, but no one will believe us. I mean without hard evidence. You'll write up this case, won't you?

—Mark, I'll do more than write it up. I'll find out how he has suddenly become conscious. It's incredible. It will change neuroscience.

—Dr. Sand, I don't want to be forward in asking . . . But do you think I can help you with this case? Be a part of it?

—Of course, Mark. We'll need to run all the tests tomorrow.

—Thank you, Dr. Sand. This means a lot to me. What about the Versed?

—What about it?

—Should I start it? I mean just in case he becomes agitated again, only as needed. I hate to call you in the middle of the night.

—Hmm . . . I don't know. I'm not sure about sedating him or what it will do to him now. He's different. His brain is different than the average person's. We know that. We'll have to be careful with all medications until we know how he'll react.

—Yes, sir. But I mean his screams and rambling on and on are really scaring the nurses. If we can just keep him asleep through the night, it'll be more manageable in the morning.

—Hmm . . . I don't know. We should just let him be for a while. Something isn't quite right. He just woke up and maybe we shouldn't put him to sleep again.

—What did he say? I thought he was saying something to you.

—Nothing. It's nothing.

—OK, what else can we do? We can't let him thrash around all night long. He might hurt himself.

—Hmm. . . . All right. But only as needed. And keep an eye on his vitals. Let me know right away of any problem. And start with the lowest dose.

—Yes, sir. I will. And thank you, Dr. Sand.

As Art drives away, he sees the entire University Hospital complex on the car's dashboard screen. Its true enormity unfolds; by itself the complex is a city block, a continuous, weaving labyrinth with roads intersecting and cutting into its core and blind passages as winding and weary as any living thing. Four large streets delineate its border. Sometimes he sees a black shining hearse driving into a subterranean entrance leading into the back of the building. For now the street is deserted, and dim streetlights illuminate black asphalt, gray concrete pavement, and manicured lawn. Life cannot be restored in the hospital; at best it is patched up and stitched together, its innocence shattered, its lessons ignored, he thinks. Until it ends. How many of them had prayed with their whole heart, had vowed to change their ways upon coming here, and upon departure had left uncertain, uncertain whether their prayers had been answered and therefore uncertain whether to keep their vows. Sometimes late at night, he would see a solitary figure sitting quietly in the chapel, and if he were to stand there for a moment and observe, his fanciful mind could almost see a halo of devotion coalesce, like the background radiation of the cosmos being channeled and focused by the human mind into a palpable reality. But he always considers himself better than his patients not in any material ways but in a way born out of the cool working of reason.

Leaving the hospital behind, the car speeds along Wilshire Boulevard toward the Santa Monica Beach. He thinks about calling Anna, but she probably went straight home from the banquet, happy to have been left alone there to enjoy herself. Their marriage has entered that unacknowledged state of estrangement where they no longer engage in the same activities they had done together over the years, yet neither of them dares to be the first to acknowledge this estrangement, this state of bare minimum. Being within a few feet of her, sometimes a few inches of unbridgeable space, has taken a loop of ever enlarging, deepening discontentment. A strangeness he feels. It is a strange loneliness to be so close to her he knew so well, enough to know he no longer knows and knows he will never know so well again.

He toys with his new iPhone as various tangential thoughts intrude: He might as well be any of the seven billions others on the planet; the nanny hasn't called, so his daughter Emily hasn't had another seizure. Anna probably has checked up on Emily by now. The traffic light on the Pacific Coast Highway is green, and he steps on the gas to catch it. Turning right to head north toward home, he puts the car into steady cruise, feeling the Mercedes exude a low–pitched, smooth, comforting hum. He lowers the window an inch, and in the distant rumble of the swirling sea air he hears David's recitation of his address again, his whispered pleading, an act and a consciousness existing beyond all his scientific knowledge, expiating and implicating. Perhaps the boy had seen it on a guest list in his father's study. What about calling Hayden Calweld to inform him that his son suddenly has speech, memory, and reason? His finger slides across the screen to unlock the phone, but then he hesitates. At the thought, a tingle shoots down his back, inciting an overwhelming awe that always accompanies the notion of such wealth, estimated to be in the billions, before which a primitive part of his mind seems to bend in worship.

Everything must be in order before he calls Hayden Calweld; a plausible explanation as to how David suddenly became conscious must be formulated beforehand, all possible questions must be anticipated and answered, and most importantly, his prognosis must be rendered. Calweld does not take kindly to trifles or half answers and, like any astute businessman, can detect the slightest hint of obfuscation. Since the diagnosis of his son's mental impairment, he's taken a keen interest in neuroscience and has done his own research, and he probably knows more about the brain than any layman out there, so guesses will not do. What's more remarkable is that Hayden Calweld has always held the delusion that his son is not retarded. He must not call Calweld yet; his professional reputation, in fact his whole career, depends on the insight of his explication and the supporting evidence.

The phone rings and startles him. The short, muffled buzz comes through the car's speakers. He closes the window.

—Yes.

—Art, where are you? Anna says.

—About ten minutes away.

—Was it anything serious?

—No, no, well . . . Maybe . . . I'll tell you later.

—It was really too bad you had to leave. It's a nice banquet. I wish you could have stayed and talked to some of the other people. There's this hedge fund manager from Wall Street. He's looking for investment opportunities; he heard about your work with Alzheimer's, you know, the new experimental drug.

—Yeah?

—He really wants to meet you. I got his business card. Maybe you should give him a call. He's a really charming guy. Very suave, one of those Wall Street types.

—That's great. I will. How's Emily?

—I don't know. I'm still here at the banquet.

—Oh, you are? That's all right, I'll check on her when I get home then, Art says, feeling a sudden disquiet.

—OK, I'll see you when I get home.

—I thought you were leaving.

—No, I thought I'd stick around and mingle a bit. It's really nice. They spared no expenses. Did you try the Russian caviar? It's unbelievable.

—Well, have fun. I'll see you later.

The phone switching off yields a moment of quiet in turn exacting ratiocination and machination, pound for pound; Art reflects. Life for Art Sand has always been relentless, propelled by various activities and expectations, and yet tonight external coincidences seemed to have accelerated it. When things are changing very fast and when one is positioned at the spearhead of that quickening speed, each shape and shade loses its distinction and is perceived as merging into an elongated, monotonous blur, like flipping through a picture album, the images flowing like a moving picture, a deceitful caricature of life. The question is whether he has the power to arrest it, to insert his hand between the pictures so that he can behold his daughter's large eyes and her beautiful smile, showing white, crooked front teeth. He feels the unstoppable magnetic loops of the world propelling his protonic core forward, injecting him into a circularity immune to the shifting of paradigms outside. Accelerated but always in comfort, he sits in the Mercedes' soft leather chair. He dislikes these thoughts more fitting for a college sophomore and always delving into something unpleasant, and so he turns on the radio. Caught in mid–sentence, a woman's voice tells him about the wars in Iraq and Ukraine, and a food riot in Africa. After two minutes, he switches off the radio. He thinks it's better to keep his mind on something more pertinent to his career.

What has happened to David Calweld? Surely this case will launch him even higher, perhaps a prestigious prize, an institution named after him, or even pop culture fame. As the car cruises, he wonders what it would feel like to suddenly be more conscious. Once in college Art had a violent flu that migrated to his head. Prostrate in bed, he felt recurrent onslaughts of shaking chill and unbearable fever, and his brain pulsated painfully with the beat of his heart, going on for hours. When the pain was most intense, he fainted. He slept a dreamless sleep, and when he woke, the fever had broken. It was as though he'd experienced death for one night. Paradoxically, the next day he saw that the sunlight was brighter, the air clearer, the sound more distinct, and things more real, and he was voracious and ate everything left in the refrigerator. A strange yearning enveloped him and ignited something similar to a desire but much more pronounced and with a strong will of its own that pushed him and wanted him to merge with the entire world. But the end of that day also ended those sensations, save for the memory of that strange yearning, a memory that has been never-ending. On separate occasions since that flu, he has tried to resurrect those sensations not just to remember them for reminiscence's sake but to really live like that forever. He has never succeeded. Tonight they are brought to mind again by David Calweld.

The Mercedes rolls smoothly through the tree-filled streets. In the bright sweep of the headlights, Art sees the neighborhood with its big houses with heavy iron doors and high columns. Behind spotless windows lie bookshelves, grand pianos, and twisted sculptures on pedestals. Manicured rosebushes flit by mundanely, fitting a ready-made vision. He pulls into his driveway and waits as the mahogany garage door lifts. The car rolls into the garage. He gets out and threads his way through heaps of toys and out-of-fashion furnitures, bicycles, skis, and other artifacts, all congealing effortlessly and abolishing forms into a conception of a suburban life. He aims for the door. His phone rings.

On the phone's screen are the words 'Unknown Caller' meaning that it can only be from the hospital. He taps the answer button.

—Yes.

—Dr. Sand? Mark Phan's voice screeches in his ear.

—Yes, what's the matter?

—David Calweld. He just. . . . He just. . . .

—Well? What? What happened?

—He coded.

—What?

—I don't know what happened. I gave him the Versed and he went into convulsions. I mean, right away. He went into cardiac arrest. We couldn't get a pulse. We ran the code. Anesthesia, general surgery, everyone came, but he wouldn't respond. Dr. Sand, are you there?

—Yeah.

—We gave him epi, we shocked him, everything. They even did an emergency trach on him. There's blood everywhere. They couldn't intubate. He was biting down, his jaw was locked. They couldn't pry it open. He must have had an allergic reaction to Versed.

—How is he now?

—I'm sorry . . .

The phone goes silent. Art doesn't even realize that he hung up and that the garage's light has already clicked off. In the dim light of the cellphone, he sees a narrow path toward the door.

THREE

YEARS

LATER

1

The world has transmogrified. At the end of a cycle on an astronomical magnitude, a new world convulses into existence. Yet the new must by necessity come from the old, for immutable space and matter remain the same—only their structure is reordered—and into this new world a different sum is formulated from the old parts. A new spirit arises but its form and will are still inchoate.

From a deep gyrus of the man's cerebrum, this odd thought surfaces as he struggles to awake. An absurd rendering is happening to the world, but the man quickly forgets the thought. His days and nights have been conjoined into one long disturbing track, and that which glues these intervals inexorably together is fear, anxiety, and an unshakable sense of doom. What time is it? he thinks and pushes himself up from the bed, while a thick fog embowers the edge of his consciousness. He looks out the bedroom's French doors through the half–drawn curtains to see the sky, blue, clear, and bright. Golden sunlight blankets the air, warming it, and reaches the foot of the bed but does nothing to stir his memories of those happy days, languorous days of him seeking to prolong a state of placid somnolence, of being warmed and lying next to his wife. In fact, in the last few days neither the bed, nor the closet full of his clothes with his bodily residue, nor the hallway of this house with things settled in place by his habits, can arouse his remembrance of days past, as though all his energy must be expended for the necessity of the present, of extending the now into the future for as long as possible. The digital clock blinks rapidly, the flashing green numbers surprising him, and he hears the buzz of the alarm that until now he has not heard at all. The clock flashes 11:06. Leaning toward it, he turns off the alarm and checks to see if there is a mistake, if he has set the time incorrectly. For twenty years, he has awakened at the same time—6 a.m. Even on the weekends when the alarm was turned off, he would inevitably wake at the same time because his brain has been well trained to sleep only six hours a day and for the remainder of the time to busy itself with thoughtful work or idleness, neither consequential.

—Not again, he laments. What's happening to me? Why can't I . . . Arghh.

He has overslept for the sixth day in a row, sleeping longer and longer each day. How could he sleep for thirteen hours and the blazing alarm could not break through that sleep? And he did not want to sleep; his mind has merely given out due to sheer exhaustion, his eyelids heavy with some internal weights have shut down, and he hasn't had the awareness to open them. Until now. What did he dream about? He did not so much dream as cogitate on a subconscious level, holding on not to the substance of his thought but to the act of thinking itself, a flimsy, tenuous grasp for the sake of his own life, and instinctively he believes that thinking is what has kept him from slipping into nocturnal oblivion.

—Think, think, I got to think, he recites loudly as he gets off the bed. Remember. Remember now. Yesterday I got in bed. Here. Climb up. No jump up. No. No. Did I? No. No.

A dull ache pervades his back and a sharp pain sears his head. He pulls on his hair trying to alleviate the pain. Ignoring the dirty clothes, the unwashed towels, and the various books, scientific journals, and papers that he'd somehow dropped along the hallway, he moves into the kitchen. A layer of dust weeks of neglect have allowed to settle. A strong smell of mildew, condensed sweat, and rotting food floods in his nose, but having been exposed to the smell for so long he can barely register it. Over the kitchen counter, at least half a dozen open bags of ground coffee lie carelessly, spilling out their black, grainy content as a fine layer over the countertop and over the kitchen floor. He proceeds to make a pot of coffee and fumbles through all the bags. Only a handful of grounds remains. Without any reference to past custom, one hand begins to sweep all the particles of coffee on the countertop into the other hand, and when done the hand holding the swept–up coffee empties it into the coffeemaker. Knees on the floor now, his hands brush the floor, scooping up black coffee grains, until he can't pick up anymore.

While he sits at the kitchen table and waits for the coffee, a churning is felt in his stomach, ferocious and urgent. Unable to remember the last time he ate or what he ate, he approaches the refrigerator. When he opens the door, foul air strikes his face.

—Let's see . . . what we have here, he says, breathing in the air.

He examines the carton of milk with curds already formed inside and a block of cheddar cheese with the exposed end that has dried and feels hard to the touch. Broccoli, tomatoes, cabbages, a bottle of ketchup, a half eaten stick of salami, and various other items of food are scattered about, all spoiling and withering. He grabs the block of cheese and lumbers back to the table. Using his teeth, he tears off the plastic wrapping over the soft part. The cheese offers no taste, only a soft, chewy consistency that he knows will calm his stomach, still churning wildly as ever. He bites and chews until half of the cheese is gone, and his stomach agreeable and quiet.

Then he sees the coffee pot. He looks at it, and seeing the carafe half full, the dark surface undulating with each drop, he lunges at it. He decants a large cup and brings it back to the table. His lips recoil from the heat but then curl into a funnel as he blows at the rising stream. But after only a couple of blows, he sucks at the scorching fluid again, only to recoil again in pain, like a forgetful chicken pecking at a trough of wheat. Yet he persists, for even when shrouded in a dense mental fog, he knows from the last few days that the coffee will restore lucidity to his consciousness and with it memory of the past and ability to plan for the future. Because of this knowledge, he has been imbibing this precious dark fluid every waking hour, until late into the night when his tired brain gives out and he collapses on the bed. With each attempt, he sucks in only a spoonful of the coffee.

At last finished and now sitting back, he waits.

—Think, I've got to think. How long will it take? It's got to work, it must work, he says loudly. His head bobs rhythmically. It worked yesterday. It must again.

A mystical ether should materialize at any moment to levitate the shroud hanging over his consciousness, an ether abstruse, and only its power can engage and lift this fog, mysterious and intractable, that if he were to cut his own head open, he would never discover it. Soon and surely awake, awareness and memory flooding back to him, he will pick up again, continuing the previous day's work, the pieces of some important work, a great puzzle now left for safe keeping in time.

—Should wake them up too, he whispers to himself so as to remember. The girls. Where are they? Oh, right. They're . . . they're gone to New York . . . Oh, two years now. What day? I should go to work. Pick up laundry. Did that last week, no? No, last . . .

He sits and waits to see how long waiting, and hopes and prays for the end when it ends, but nothing happens. Only a burning pain jabs at his tongue, stretches along his esophagus down to his stomach, along the path that the scorching liquid went. If he had no knowledge of the past, of how his mind worked, of the facility with which he could comprehend words, order, and the structures of things, he would be just happy as a sleepy imbecile, but the memory of his smartness now tears at him because he knows that at the end of this slide down the slope of intelligence and consciousness is inevitably death. The power of the coffee, he thinks. But how stupid, you stupid imbecile, suddenly realizing his own silliness, you should have known better. It's the most basic knowledge that any teenager should have. It's the caffeine, a neural stimulant that has been keeping him alert, but now is useless. Why didn't I realize this before?

A piece of moldy baguette on the far end of the kitchen table, the wax paper wrapping from a stick of butter, plastic bags of all sorts sticking to the floor, dirty towels, a scattering of congealed remains of hastily eaten food—his dull eyes survey his surroundings—these appear like the unintended casualties of a process, great and unimaginable. What was he trying to do? A glint of curiosity fades. He can't seem to dispense even the tiniest effort, the smallest bit of psychic energy to remember, and his mind still slips along an unstoppable decline toward the prison of sleep from which it recently emerged, but the sudden thought of oblivion sparks only the faintest sensation of fear. Fear grows. Suddenly standing up and with all his might he hurls the kitchen table over. He runs to the wall, slamming his body against it, smashing it with his bare fists. Pain quickens his heart. Shaking his head lamely, he turns toward the hallway that leads toward a different room, scarcely recognizable until he is well within it. It is his study, but for now in his mind exists only one flowing blurriness, a variegated mass of the desk burdened by undetermined objects, blending into the floor and curving upward into the ceiling save for the hollow space in the middle into which he toddles.

—Not working. Goddammit, not working, got to think. What else. What else. Think, think, you useless son of a coward, he says. This is it, think, think.

He sits down at the desk. His eyes focus on the words before him, one word at a time, his mind fighting to arrange them into meaning, his eyes chasing one word to another and yet another, until he realizes that he has been reading a sentence that has veered off the boundary of its own page and gone onto an overlapping one.

'A review of psychostimulant–induced neuroadaptation in developing animals.'

Bending his neck down, his eyes inches from the words, he reads. The large bold words are reflected across his retinas, the converted electrical signal discharging into the optic nerves. But beyond that, the sight of the words might as well be pure photons of light, bereft of meaning. Below these words, he sees something, and as though they are beyond his conscious control, guttural cries escape his throat, his chest muscles go into spasms, and he heaves sobs of horrors. Below these words, he sees his name: Arthur S. Sand M.D., Ph.D.

With both hands, he reaches for the phone; his fingers fumble over the numeric pad and he dials 911. He squeezes the phone against his ear. Hello, hello, emergency, emergency, send an ambulance, the voice in his head screams as loudly as it can, so loudly that he can't hear the monotonous scratchy electric squawk of the busy signal. After a minute of not hearing a human voice, he focuses and listens carefully; finally the busy signal enters his consciousness. He hangs up and dials again. The same busy signal vibrates immediately through the phone. What's happening? he asks.

—What's happening? What on earth? he whimpers. Did I overdose the antidepressant? His hands going for the desk and the phone dropping to the floor, the body is propelled forward, and finally standing, he runs to the front door.

Outside hanging overhead and beating down aslant in a uniformity of indifference onto the suburban landscape, the autumn sun is golden. The sharp leaves of grass point needle–like skyward, radiantly green against the sunlight as though nearly exuding color themselves. Cars lie immobile, haphazardly in the driveway, in the streets, with doors open, and trailing from them are objects strewn by people in a hurry to get away. Amid the chaotic scene, an oblivious dog stretches on the sidewalk and gapes an indolent yawn. But from the air and from up high in the stratosphere, a cacophony of distant explosions and the roaring of machines echo down to earth.

He staggers back, nearly falling. Where's everyone? It can't be just me, he pants, and at this moment a terror, dense and heinous, pierces through his mental stupor, jolts his heart, and squeezes the moribund glands in his body for the last drops of adrenaline. Suddenly, he turns away from the door, following a faint idea that the last adrenaline has just sparked in his mind, and totters along the trash–strewn hallway to his bedroom. Through the bedroom door, he turns into the bathroom; he flings open the cabinet and pulls down everything, jars of creams and skin lotions, cologne, canisters of hairspray, tubes of hair gel, and various glass containers of makeup, once belonging to his wife. All of them fall crashing into the sink. Nothing is recognizable, but his mind searches. Next, he pulls open the drawers. A stack of hand towels is found in one, in another a hairdryer, an electric shaver, toothbrushes, tubes of toothpaste. Finally, in the third drawer where he kept bottles of aspirin, anti-depressants, various antibiotics, the sight of the yellowish–green box with green words jumps at him: EpiPen Jr®.

Picking up the rectangular box, he feels the weight of the object inside and claws it open. Inside the transparent plastic container, appearing new and smooth, he sees the long sharp needle. He brings it up close to inspect the words— (Epinephrine) Auto-Injector 0.15 mg. It was meant for his daughter who has peanut allergy and has been biding its time silently in the drawer, holding in its reservoir a promise of life, and in a crisis it would spring out to stave off death, but never before did he think that it would save his own life. Without much deliberation or hesitation, he jabs the needle through his dirty jeans into his thigh. Strangely painless. His hand holding the device trembles. Wait ten seconds, he mumbles. A prickly sensation ripples from the needle and pulses up his thigh, constricting as it goes. A solitary heartbeat jumps against his chest, then a crescendo of beats thuds regularly and quickens into a spry gallop, and finally a maddening stampede of red corpuscles, of nutrient–filled plasma, of an ineffable life force rushes to his head, echoing in his tympanum a fetal beat, heralding new life.

He perks up lifting his eyes to a crisp lucidity. The very air molecules seem to swirl visibly around his eyes. Memories of previous days return, instantaneous and clear. He pulls out the needle and discards the used EpiPen® carelessly. In seconds, he's back in his office. Files, charts, notes are glaring in front of him. He picks them up. Now he knows.

—It was a great epidemic across the globe, he says out loud, partly reading from the pages before him as if giving a lecture. No one knew where it came from, right? It was the gerontologists, first to notice. Rapid expiration of nursing home occupants. Yeah, the old went first.

He turns over the pages slowly, gleaning the printed words and trying to understand but mostly to remember the hardest parts, the parts already thought about and concluded.

—Charting the prevalence and the incidence, he says, continuing to speak loudly. Increasing logarithmically . . . Epidemiologists, infectious disease specialists, hospitalists, and pathologists, cultured orifices, cultured secretions, dissected corpses, and in the end, what is the result? What was it? Nothing. Absence of abnormalities in the blood, vital organs, including the brain. Nothing in the brain, nothing.

And so it went and finally the puzzle had come to him. As an expert in cognition, he'd been sought out and had even received calls from some important politicians in high office, who promised money and prestige beyond his grandest imagination and more than once mentioned the Nobel Prize. But nothing could halt the relentless decline. Consciousness ebbed from the collective human mind, memory trickled away, and with it civilization itself withered at the edges and crumbled inward, since each individual memory, though finite and flawed, overlapped with other memories, constituting the cement of civilization.

As he struggled to delineate the etiology of this great mystery, he found nothing, not where it came from, nor how it robbed consciousness, nor even what it was. There had not been enough time. The advances that he'd achieved with Alzheimer's disease, the papers that he'd published to acclaim, had taken nearly his whole professional life; so how was he to solve this most hellish riddle in a few months? The Death Sleep struck very slowly in the beginning, the old first and the sick, but in the last few months, as though a criticality had been crossed, the disease has been accelerating by perhaps a thousandfold, so quickly that he himself had started to dribble away. Until today, when he discovered the epinephrine.

—It accelerated. Dammit. God damn it. Logarithmic acceleration. But I got something . . . what? What was it I got yesterday? Ugghh.

He flings away the papers suddenly and snatches up his phone. Swelling up from his heart and overtaking his mind, an outburst of palpitating sorrow shakes his whole being. How could he have forgotten? The very thing that had just saved him from oblivion and restored self to body, the answer to the riddle that he has sought tirelessly was in that device, once belonging to her. His darling daughter, whose delicate hands he can almost feel, whose salty scent of sweat after play wafts afresh from a cherished corner of his mind, is thousands of miles away.

Where are you now? he wonders. Are you playing? Are you asleep? The phone rings an interminable series of electronic chirps. He waits. The electronic voice from the phone recording tells him: You have reached . . . He hangs up and quickly redials. This time, at the end of the electronic voice, he speaks, holding the phone directly before him, hands trembling.

—Anna, Anna. Are you OK? How is Emily? Listen. Listen . . .

If you feel sleepy, the disease— it has gotten almost everyone, it's accelerated . . . If you or Emily feels sleepy . . .

He shakes his head. An urgency prods him on, and yet the words that come out of his mouth are not what he wants to say, nor do they convey the message, that glimmer of hope.

—Use the EpiPen®. Or any epinephrine you can get your hands on. It staves off the sleep. Do you understand? Listen to me carefully: Use epinephrine. The disease makes you sleep. If you hear this message, please do as I tell you. It's the only way. Give it to Emily. I love you. I will find you. I will find you both.

When he stops, he can hear the electronic cackle of the busy signal, and since he was holding the phone in front of him when he was speaking, he doesn't know how long that busy signal has been going. His incredulous eyes stare at the phone. He hangs up and redials. The busy signal squawks back loudly, instantaneously.

He drops into the chair. Her cherubic face hovers before him, aglow with a reddish tinge of sunburn, the skin pulled taut as when an impish smile endeared her curious look, and the round, searching pupils hemmed in by a rim of unblemished white. With the vision of the child, a pain stabs at him, and the thought that he missed the chance to save his darling because his wit was dull, his ingenuity blunted, and that he'd missed the chance by per- haps seconds is unbearable; he keels over in excruciation. Where is she now? No doubt, she is lost in the devastation of silent sky- scrapers, where through empty boulevards and ghostly parks echo cold winds and where the amalgamation of concrete and steel now entombs all its once illusory masters.

2

Lucidity recedes with the same vigor and haste with which it arrived. That familiar, unshakable stupor oozes down from the top of his head like thick molasses, pulsation of his blood withers away, and a shadowy opacity horrifies him as he feels it on the inside of his skull. Words on the pages in front of him crimp into tight clusters of inky filaments, and a thought held clear and crisp a moment ago evaporates into a crevice somewhere in his brain, replaced by a hideous fright that he himself will soon be erased.

Art pushes himself up from the desk where he has been sitting, perusing his notes and scientific articles, many authored by him, with underlined passages. He remembers something, a sensation of some sort, a happiness, a moment of breakthrough; perhaps he'd figured out how to stave off the Death Sleep, but now only a faint halo of that sensation floats hazily somewhere around him. The adrenaline from the EpiPen® is being metabolized much too quickly, he thinks, not enough of it for a man of his size. No, no, he cries out. His hands dig into his hair and yank hard, but he feels barely any pain at all, only the sensation of his scalp being pulled, and that stupefying molasses oozes on, reaching halfway down his head, soon to his brainstem, a primitive part of anatomy he has in common with the reptiles. He shakes his head now as though to liberate a cry from within; he feels he must let it out. More epi, he shrieks. The sharpness of the high–pitched sound slices through the air, and from somewhere beyond he thinks he hears an answer, an equally shrill cry coming from the neighborhood. Now he holds still to listen, but there is only a familiar ringing in his ears, and then he drops down on his knees. Inside the bottom drawer of his desk, on the left side, is a trove of drugs: Valium, Norco, Vicodin, and a package of small ampules of epinephrine. Some of these drugs have already expired but he never had any problem with their effectiveness—a Valium now and then to help with the stress, or a Norco with the sleep. Digging through these bottles and packages, he tosses them aside one by one until he grabs the package of epinephrine, the sight of it sending a jolt of relief through him. He tears apart the transparent plastic wrapping and gingerly picks up a glass ampule between his thumb and index finger. Now I can remember again, he thinks. But seeing the ampule of epinephrine between his fingers momentarily confuses him, and he stares at it and shakes it to see small bubbles forming inside the clear fluid. Still nothing. How is he supposed to get that wondrous fluid inside him? He stares at it until his eyes become dry and close and his mind dozes off, yet an instinct, vile and unflappable, holds on to the ampule tightly, perhaps too tight, and the top of the ampule snaps off. The vial's sharp edge cuts across his finger; blood seeps down his hand, and with the sensation of sharpness, an image of a syringe materializes, finally giving the ampule completeness and proper function. The sight of bright red blood concentrates his mind. He bends over, rummages through the drawer, and pulls out a 3 ml syringe with a needle attached.

In a flash, he draws up all the fluid into the syringe, but all he can do is hold it between his trembling fingers, sensing a danger in the same fluid that promises life. Is it 3 ml of 1:1000 concentration, to be delivered right into the ventricle of the heart for cardiac arrest? And 0.3 ml of 1:1000 for anaphylactic reaction? But how much is he supposed to get for the Death Sleep? The wrong dosage can send his heart into arrhythmia or pop a blood vessel in his brain; yes, yes, a stroke, he remembers faintly. He places the needle against the skin of his right arm but does nothing, except try to think. Even in imminent danger with the molasses now at the base of his skull, he sucks in calm breaths and looks at the syringe with dim vision as his surrounding blurs, similar to waking up in the middle of the night. He closes his eyes for a second and jerks them open again. His body sways back and forth slightly as he tries to think; if that swaying had gone on for even a second longer, he would no doubt have toppled over and lain on his side and curled up into a tight ball for a long and much deserved sleep, but that reptilian instinct emanating from his brainstem tweaks and he shoves the needle into the skin. With the force of the jab, half of the syringe is pumped in, and immediately a heat squeezes along his arm and is felt in his chest, tightening it, making his heart throb vigorously. In just another instant, the heat rushes to his head and his eyes regain their focus; he pushes on the syringe and the remaining fluid disappears into his arm. Maybe he was too hasty, because after the fluid in the second half of the syringe enters his bloodstream, that very same heat seems to explode inside his head, an intense pressure pushing outward against his skull, almost forcing his eyeballs out of their sockets. He braces himself for the pop of a blood vessel in his brain, stubbornly holding onto the desk instead of sitting down; so this is the danger he was contemplating. He closes his eyes. Waves of violent thrust shoot up his neck. When that weakens after a short moment, truncated hiccups start up, and between each set of spasms he struggles to breathe; after several minutes the pressure eases slowly, the heart settles back into its cavity inside his chest, but the jerking up along his esophagus continues. A sour taste in the back of his throat gurgles with each spasm.

That stupefying molasses evaporates, disappears altogether as though washed away by a strong disinfectant, so when he finally opens his eyes, reality unfolds before him. The events of the day before come back to him; he remembers studying these papers late into the night and drifting off into sleep, doing different things, perhaps eating, surely drinking that dark coffee and still dozing off. All things are recalled out of sequence and now inconsequential, save for that halo, that glow of gladness; yes, he did find the answer.

—Yeah, yeah, he screams. That's it. We have it, gentlemen. The Death Sleep is countered by neural stimulation. The Death Sleep is similar to accelerated Alzheimer's.

The Death Sleep has accelerated by a thousandfold, he thinks, but I have it. I would like to thank the committee for the prize. I would like to thank my beautiful wife . . .

He sits down at the desk, and before him the scientific papers are strewn about in an order that can only be deciphered by his mind when lucid. But now instead of returning to the papers, his eyes cast a dreamy gaze toward the windows masked by motionless curtains behind which the glow of bright sunlight catches his eyes, and in it a truth beckons, a truth that is somehow more important than the cure for the Death Sleep itself.

In this glow of bright sunlight, he sees a vision of himself being reborn, not as a child, but as a condensation out of nothingness in turn accruing form among countless unknown particles, only a moment ago drifting aimlessly but now gravitating toward a core a purpose. In that swarming mass of particles a consciousness is born—it is he. His eyes roll and the room begins to spin. He marvels at the birth of himself. What does it mean? He beholds the vision he knows can not be a hallucination, since he is not seeing it before him; instead he is merely conscious of it. How strange. Just a moment ago his consciousness, or to be more precise he himself, had nearly disappeared, but now here he is again, his consciousness reconstituted, not very different than falling asleep each night. Then the vision shakes, the particles rattle, and the rattling intensifies until the particles disperse like so many marbles. From his throat, violent spasms roll up and bring him back; the hiccups are intense. He looks down to the papers and immediately sees what it was that he concluded yesterday—the chemical compound he was experimenting on the mice in an Alzheimer's disease study, a modification of amphetamine, should counter the effects of the Death Sleep.

Yes, that's it. On the edge of the desk sits a bottle of the chemical, its glass a dark brown to shield its content from light, and inside the bottle is a fine, granular powder. It is a matter of exceptional luck he has it at all; he'd brought a sample of it home months ago when he first started to test it on the mice, and it had gotten lost among the articles, journals, and books on the shelves —until yesterday, when during his moment of breakthrough, he took it off the shelf.

—Twenty–five grams is the weight of the mouse, he mumbles, holding the bottle. I used a small amount of powder, but how much exactly? I can't remember. Was it one hundred micrograms of the powder, or fifty? I've got to think. Think.

But it's in the scientific paper, he chuckles as he leans in and reads the fine print under Materials and Methods. Wanting to avoid overdose, he picks up a pencil and begins to scribble down the calculation on the margin, noting the ratio of a seventy kilogram man to a twenty–five gram mouse, the ratio never so significant in the first place but now fading into nothingness against the backdrop of this new world. The rhythmic hiccups accompanied by the sour gastric juice in the back of his throat keep interrupting his thought, but at last he has it, the precise amount of powder for a man of his size.

—How am I to measure milligrams of the powder? he asks. What I needs is a scientific scale. Overdose, I can't let that happen. Not good. Not good. Got to think now.

The only scientific scale he knows of is at his laboratory twenty miles away.

A paroxysm of the hiccups abruptly launches his body straight up, only to be brought down again by its own weight, and each time his thought scatters. He tries to anticipate the next one by counting slowly after each onset. Sometimes after a count of six, his whole body is jolted, at other times after a count of eleven or twenty. The frequency of the hiccups is completely random. He thinks of how debilitating and infuriating it is and how he once used Gabapentin and Chlorpromazine to cure several patients of intractable hiccups.

—Chlorpromazine, where is it? he mouths softly.

His mind now drifts off, chasing after the drugs to cure the hiccups, merrily and sedately trying to recall where he might have put them, and thinking of the bathroom, he gets up and shambles along.

Suddenly the walls tremble, the windows clatter, and the floor underneath him is displaced by a fraction of an inch. He is thrown against the door, and he holds onto it to steady himself as the rumbling dissipates. Earthquake, he thinks, and he heads for the front door.

Outside, a flock of sparrows take off, their dark shapes shooting across the sky. A chorus of crows caw, and an indolent dog takes flight down the street. He feels hard, jagged gravel underfoot as he fumbles into the middle of the road and looks toward the horizon.

Unencumbered by gravity, a column of black smoke swirls skyward, and at the edge of the stratosphere races outward. In an instant the black column grows wider and is augmented by an army of smaller columns of black smoke in a blitzkrieg against the clear, blue sky. Blackness mobilizes and unfurls chaotically across the horizon. More horrific than the sky is a shape lying on the lawn several houses away, a body, immobile and partially hidden by the tall grass. At the sight of it, an icy shiver sparks low in his back and quickly envelops his chest, and his mouth involuntarily opens and pants automatic, shallow breaths. Only now can he smell the pervasive odor of decomposing corpses, the pungent stink of death in the air.

So this is the end, he thinks and dashes back inside the house.

The house now strikes him as too spacious so he seeks out a corner of his study to where he withdraws and crouches, cradling the bottle of powder. Time is lost. He can no longer tell how long he has been crouching there; the hiccups were scared away by the explosion and have been replaced by a fearful, uncontrollable trembling. After a while, a series of explosions shakes the windows slightly, followed by an occasional explosion here and there, but the booms are too faint to be close by. This must be Armageddon as prophesied by the many religions, he thinks. At any moment, he expects to see demons with razor–sharp claws materialize out of the air to tear him to pieces and drag him to hell, and despite the scintillation of light bouncing off the curtain—making him see from the corner of his eye serene, pale-faced demons who vanish whenever he turns to face them—he still cannot reconcile the paradox that prohibits the existence of God and secondarily the Devil. The logical paradox, he thinks, is as valid for him now when the world is ending as it was when at eighteen years old he laid out its logical steps as only logic, cold and hard, perceivable and discoverable by human beings but beyond all their petty meddling, can eliminate God and thus its alter ego.

—You can't take me. You don't exist, he says as though speaking these thoughts will insulate them from the chaos inside his mind so he can juggle them now that his life depends on it. Man splits God into two, yeah, yeah, that's right. And then one into three. God is infinite and all-powerful and good, yeah, that's the premise. But evil also exists therefore the paradox. So you don't exist. You can't take me.

So holding fast to the paradox and the bottle of powder, huddling in the corner of his study, he clings to the hope of survival, of the possibility for human intervention and therefore alterability.

—Unless, unless, he says a moment later, nodding to himself. Man never split anything.

As surely as his blood percolates through his liver, the epinephrine in his system disintegrates, and his consciousness seems to diffuse slowly outward in waves, rolling over the floor with its foggy opaqueness. His eyelids are weighed down by the heaviness normal sleep usually brings on, and the sensation he once welcomed as a chance for rest he now dreads. He wrinkles his forehead raising the eyebrows that in turn pull on the eyelids. He knows it's coming again—the Death Sleep. Somnummortisia, what a stupid name, he chuckles, but then lets out a cry and sobs.

—Why? What for? I miss you so much, he cries, remembering the touch of her plump cheeks, the smell of sweat in her hair, her voice and laugh resonating along the hallway. Oh Emily, I've got to live, I'll find you.

He sees the ampules of epinephrine on the desk, but as if wanting a final resolution he uncaps the bottle, wets the tip of a finger, and dips it into the powder. Overdose be damned. The moistened tip catches a thin layer of powder, and he scrapes it against his tongue depositing it there. The bitter taste is dissolved in the saliva, and he swallows reflexively.

There is no more and no less to him. A minute passes and he is as he was, like before, way before the Death Sleep. His heart beats its normal rhythm, seventy times a minute, unnoticeable unless he takes his own pulse. His mind is alert and fresh as it was on countless mornings when he arose from bed after a restful night. Straightening his legs, he rises from the corner of his study where it seems he has been confined for an eternity. He goes straight to the desk and from a drawer gets an electronic wristwatch, one often used for jogging; he sets the alarm to chime every hour.

During the first hour, he listens for the booms of explosions and now and then peers out the window at the deserted street. But mostly he waits and mentally accounts for those things that make up daily existence. He feels thirsty and drinks from the faucet; water is still flowing. He remembers the large water tank on the hill that can be seen from the backyard. And the electricity died with explosions, even the phone.

The alarm chirps, and the second hour begins. He feels no difference. The crows seem louder, and he can hear not just their threatening caws—always something ominous about them— but also the flap of their wings outside the house. The bright light outside lessens, reminding him of the coming night. He gathers a flashlight and goes into the garage. In the corner is a gun safe; in it is a single twelve gauge shotgun his father used to kill himself. After the police investigation, it was returned to him, but that was many years ago before he got married, and his wife knew nothing of its history; in all likelihood she didn't even know about it at all. Why had he decided to keep this morbid memento when he should have had it destroyed? The policeman who handed the shotgun back to him had told him as much, he'd never known a single instance of surviving family members wanting a suicide weapon back. Art takes the gun and a box of shells to the kitchen table. A fine film of gun oil sticks to his palms, and he remembers cleaning the shotgun many months ago after his wife and daughter had left for New York. When the police finally gave it back to him, it was wrapped tightly in plastic, and it had remained forgotten for many years before he opened it up. It was only when he thought he knew himself well enough that he took it out, held it every which way, and imagined how his father had positioned the gun to kill himself; the long barrel went into his mouth, and since his arm could not reach it, his big toe must have pressed the trigger. Oh dear Papa, he utters as the image now recurs in his mind. He loads the shotgun.

When the alarm signals the beginning of the third hour, he is going through his house that suddenly appears to be beyond his grasp, room to room; aside from his own, he has not been inside the other bedrooms for months. The long, awkward barrel of the shotgun clanks against the door before he has a chance to enter. The stillness of each room is disquieting, beds still made, closets closed, curtains shut with no traces of life, and in Emily's room the faint smell of soap and her odor breaks disquiet into sadness.

He saws off the barrel of the shotgun, the part that went into his father's mouth. When he is done, he notices that the alarm is chirping and sees that the face of his wristwatch has been blinking for fifteen minutes into the fourth hour. He resets it. Outside the once blue sky has turned gray. He heads to the kitchen, opens a can of chicken soup, and sits down to eat. When he is finished, he gets up and, seeking safety, goes back to the corner of his study where he sits with his arms folded around the shotgun, with its sawed–off barrel resting on his left shoulder. Stupor descends over the back of his head; he does not know if it's because of postprandial somnolence or of the powder being metabolized and eliminated from his system. Slowly, beyond his control, his eyes close, but he raises his eyelids to open them again, wrinkling his forehead to do so. His eyelids droop back down, and yet again he tries to raise them. He blinks several times. The heaviness on the back of his head pulls down. His head droops forward, he can't seem to fight it, and he dozes off but jerks himself awake again, trying to hold on to an unwinding, tapering track of consciousness.

He jerks awake again, shaking his head. I can't sleep now, he thinks. Is it time for another dose of the powder? I must stay awake and take notes of the changes, the powder's side effects. The high–pitched burst of the alarm—eeee . . . eeee . . . eeee—cuts through his mental haze. He brings his wristwatch up close, and the digital numbers terrify him; an hour and three quarters already passed since he reset it. Jumping up, he leaps to the desk to fetch the powder. So it has been nearly six hours, he thinks— the powder lasts nearly six hours. If I had stayed asleep, it could have been the end of me, he thinks as he wets a fingertip, dips it into the bottle, and then puts it under his tongue.

The fire, somewhere over Los Angeles, burns day and night.

A fiery glow gleams in the sky at night, and during the day black smoke torments the sky overhead, now churning with stormy tempest, now hurdling into mountainous monstrosity.

The nights amplify his misery. Each evening a darkness rolls in until it encases everything in ink. He tries not to move around if he doesn't have to, and if he must, he shields the flashlight with his hand to hide the light so that it can't be seen from the street. Each night, from houses nearby, cries pierce the walls; sometimes screams of disbelief erupt as though someone has awakened suddenly from death's grip and for an instant is self–aware, and sometimes things crash, or a gun goes off, all amid the steady and increasingly loud howling of feral dogs washing down from the hills. During the brief intervals when silence pervades the house, the ringing in his ears takes over, and during these hours he is conscious of his agitation, of the heat in his skin burning from fear. Every little sound reverberates in his ears, and he stops whatever he is doing to listen. A profound tiredness pummels his body, but each night he lies in bed, cradling the shotgun, and tries to keep his eyelids from closing or himself from yawning and to check his wristwatch frequently to see if it's time for the powder. At times a scraping noise from somewhere in the street startles him, or he thinks he hears footsteps right outside his window, which sets him off, waving the shotgun around in the darkness.

And in the interval between checking the wristwatch and being in total darkness, when he no longer has a sense of time, he lives in the only place possible for him—the past.

—Anna, do you remember that time? He whispers to himself and yet seemingly does not know that he's whispering. You remember one early spring in Paris before Emily was born? The sudden rain. We got completely wet, don't you remember? And we ran to the cafe. In Montmartre, wasn't it? Remember how we sat by the window to watch the rain? I still remember the smell of coffee.

He sees everything so clearly now, her dreamy eyes fluttering so lightly with the rain, her red lips, the raindrops on her cheeks, her wet hair tasseled into knots, the ogling eyes of the waiter, a sympathetic nod from an old man nearby.

—How clearly I remember. It's so real to me now, he whispers.

But was that me? he thinks; it must, yet he does not feel that he lived that day at all—a memory borrowed, a life not lived but only condemned to be remembered.

—Anna, Anna, how I wish you were here with me. What did I do wrong? What I wouldn't do, what I wouldn't do, he utters in the darkness and begins to rock back and forth cradling the shotgun. It seems to him truly a deep hurt to have loved her he now regrets not loving enough.

Inevitably, he falls asleep. Sometimes he has flashes of different dreams, but his remaining consciousness seems to have latched onto the beeps of the alarm, set to go off every six hours, that now guide his existence.

EACH MORNING HE WAKES TO THE ALARM AND AN EXCRUCIA-tion similar to a ball of needles expanding inside his head, until a fingertip of the powder goes under his tongue. During the day, the shrieking from the neighboring houses is somehow blunted by the sunlight, and a sense of certainty and endurability is restored. He puts heavy blankets over the windows, nailing them to the wooden frames, so that he can use the flashlight more freely at night. All the cans of food, a reserve for an eventual earthquake—sardines in tomatoes sauce, Spam, chicken noo-dle soup, clam chowder—are arranged carefully on the kitchen counter, and he plans each meal so that the cans will last as long as possible without his having to leave the house for food.

On the third day, he ventures into the backyard. Aiming the shotgun forward, he inches through the back door. The backyard, where Emily once played on the finely trimmed lawn, is now overgrown, and among the long blades of grasses small yellow flowers now mingle. Cold wintry wind customary for this time of year blows steadily, pushing away the smell of death. The air is fresh and has a salty scent of the sea. He looks toward the horizon, in the same direction that for the last three days he has been peeking from behind the curtains and keeping vigil. The fire has burnt itself out, and the sky, serene and indifferent as ever, now reigns over the earth. He surveys the chairs, the fireplace they often sat around on cold nights, the old olive tree whose age is marked by the massive convolutions of its trunk and the twist of its branches, and the wooden fence squaring out the backyard. Beyond the back fence, the land rises up into the distance to a white water tank on top of the hill.

He suddenly hears a scraping noise; he freezes and perks up his ears, trying to locate its origin. Mixed in with the scraping, the gargling murmurs of a human voice reach him from the left; it is coming from the other side of the fence. The noise is all too familiar; he heard it often enough in the past. Between the wooden planks of the fence, his eyes follow a brown figure as he drags a trash bin scraping along the concrete. Is this Wednesday, the usual day for trash pickup? he thinks. In this new world, that scraping noise hurts his ears. It does not belong here and if it occurs at all, it does so through a surreality in which everything is as it was. To continue to hear that noise is to invite madness.

He grabs a chair, puts it against the fence, and climbs up; slowly poking his head over the fence he recognizes that brown figure, the balding head with reddish hair, and the big stomach that bulges beyond the confine of his brown bathrobe. It's Harry Babinski, his neighbor for over ten years who operates a car dealership, and he is dragging a trash bin with his back turned to Art. The last time he spoke to Babinski was three months ago when Babinski asked him about the Death Sleep. Then weeks ago when some people in the neighborhood died in their sleep and the paramedics came in their biohazard suits to remove the bodies, everyone else in the neighborhood suddenly stayed indoors and stopped talking to each other, probably for fear that the Death Sleep was contagious.

—Psst, Psst. Harry, Harry, Art hisses, but his larynx exudes no more than a hoarse whisper. He clears his throat and looks around, no one else is around. Harry, he mutters, so as not to speak too loudly. Harry, it's me, Art.

The figure stops, and his head turns slightly. Unsure if this is Babinski's reflex to his voice or if it's a sign of comprehension, he presses on, speaking. Harry, how are you and Martha? How are you guys doing?

The head slowly turns, the shoulder rotates, and on Babinski's face are bland, glazed–over eyes and a residue of greenish bile and vomitus that has dried around his mouth and neck and stained his white T–shirt. Art ducks down, but gingerly he raises his head enough to scrutinize Babinski again.

Art shudders. What could it be? Is this another disease Babinski is suffering from? If he is walking, has he found a way to stave off the Death Sleep? There are just too many questions.

—Harry, how are you staying awake? Art says. His voice is shrill and urgent.

Babinski resumes his walk and continues pulling the trash bin away as he has done every Wednesday without fail for as far back as Art can remember.

—Harry, Harry, Art says. Harry Babinski keeps on in his lumbering tread, the trash bin scraping and trailing behind, as though between Art and Harry is a separation no ordinary knowledge can breach.

An idea comes to him, but it is displaced by a renewed fear. There is something in the lumbering gait of Babinski, a new clue about the Death Sleep, but he can't risk it. He jumps off the chair and bolts inside the house.

Without conscious effort, he finds himself sitting in the same corner of his study; the shotgun is in one hand, and the bottle of powder in the other. If Harry is somehow awake, he thinks, what about Martha? She was always kind to Emily and often brought her a piece of cornbread, still hot from the oven, and she would often volunteer to babysit. You know you can always leave her with me, Martha had said to him. We'd love to entertain her and have a grand tea party. Her crackling voice rang out from her front door where she would stand, waving to Art, whenever she caught him leaving or coming.

It's not too late for Harry, he thinks; if he is still walking around, then he can be saved. I should jump over the fence and shove the powder into his mouth. But how much is left in this bottle? How many more times can I dip my fingertip in here before it's all gone?

He struggles with the thought, but in the following days when he is too fearful to leave the house the thought vanishes, and he never thinks about it again.

3

At last all is quiet. There are only the sounds of nature. Art Sand listens to the sounds, but he can't quite comprehend them or associate them with a memory. The natural sounds, the quietude of nature, seem new and alien to him, remaining just beyond the power of his intellect. What he hears is completely dissociated from what he sees; the sight of lawn grasses growing thick and wild, extending beyond the confines of the cement pavement, of green vines crawling up walls and piercing half closed windows, so many days after the great catastrophe, still shocks him and puts him into a transient daze. The sight of nature quietly reclaiming her domain contrasts markedly with the touch of the breeze, the rustle of the leaves, and the microscopic humming of the insects and microbes; all because these sights and sounds never coexisted before in his mind, highly cultivated and learned as it is. Before this quietude, the constant drone of machines, cars, airplanes, and the unceasing rhythmic gyration of the modern world accompanied everything—objects as well as animals and plants—and thus his perception had always been accompanied by this drone, most of the time unrecognized by his consciousness. He must now retrain his senses, learn that the grasses rustle differently as they grow taller and that the whisper of their blades is their natural sound, their voice, in the same way that the squalling voice of a human infant would one day become coarse as the infant becomes an adult. No human could exist without a voice, and even the dumb and the deaf, who happen to speak in a vastly different language than that of a speaking person, nonetheless have a natural voice of their own. So no natural thing could exist without an existential resonance, a voice.

—God, it's so quiet, he mumbles through his teeth. Shh, you can hear it all, can't you?

Suddenly he perks his ears, thinking he hears a high–pitched shrill. He thinks it may be the squawks of the hawks, but this sound lasted longer and came from somewhere closer to the ground. He concentrates, but all he hears is the ringing in his head, a ringing that has grown louder as the world becomes quieter, in almost exact inverse proportion. He waits for another shrill, but nothing comes. It sounded like it belonged to the living, soft at first, then louder, as though it tried to convey a message. It is not uncommon for him to hear the sudden screech of horror by those unlucky enough to regain momentary consciousness and wake from the Death Sleep, even for a short time, but the shrieks of the dying inevitably burst out sharply, cutting to his ears, and now they have become rare. Still, a shiver streaks through his body. After a minute, he turns his thoughts back to the quietude of nature.

As Art contemplates, he sits inside a black Hummer with the engine off, all the windows open, and a gentle breeze blows and seems to cool and soothe him. The Hummer has been stopped abruptly in the driveway, teetering at the edge of the street. Cars neatly line both sides of the street, one after another, their wheels had been turned, backed in with precision into their current location by their former owners, but now the overgrown lawn grasses seem to creep out onto the road to ambush the flat tires, threatening to swallow them whole. Dust and leaves have settled into thick layers over the cars, blackening the windshields and clawing into the paint, the plastic, and even the metal itself. It is just a matter of decay; these cars will crumble into themselves. He sees the empty street, he remembers the bustling vitality, the life that no longer exists, and the vision strikes him with the same shocking strangeness as the sounds of quietude. Suddenly his eyes move to the object next to him. These days his mind cannot concentrate for long on anything; it flits from one thing to another, perhaps an innate defense mechanism bent on self–preservation. Next to him lies the twelve gauge shotgun, dormant. He hasn't had to use the gun yet, but he thinks he'll need it somehow, even if at the moment it is heavy as dead weight. He needs it to counterbalance the fear that has multiplied many times over since the world went silent.

—What do you expect? You can't blame me, he whispers to himself. What am I supposed to do? How many can I keep alive? And how long? Weeks, months? What for anyway? Got to face facts. We've had it. We've had it. If it's not the nukes, the wars, it's bound to be something else. It's better this way. Yeah, you got to admit. It's better this way. Not too many will wake up ever again even if only for a few minutes. I'll be done too. I'll be done soon enough, ladies and gentlemen. At least it's quiet now. Some things better will come soon enough.

Only a minority of people, at frightful intervals—twelves hours, sixteen hours, sometimes even eighteen hours—would jerk awake and, as though lunging up from a long nightmare, struggle to know their reality before collapsing again into a forced slumber. Sometimes he saw them wandering; at other times he saw them performing habitual tasks, just like Harry Babinski taking out the trash.

Just to make sure that it's there—the reason why he came here in the first place—his eyes fix on the glass jar lying on the passenger seat, partially covered by the crumbled white lab coat with the identification card attached to the pocket. On the ID is a diminutive picture of him and under that his name: Arthur S. Sand M.D., Ph.D. As if seeing the jar is not quite reassuring enough, he picks it up and shakes it. Through the brown glass meant to protect the content from UV light, he sees the fine powder disperse into a transparent cloud and slowly settle again. It's too early for another dose of the powder, so he puts the jar down.

—Anything else, anything else. Got to remember, he says quietly. Powder. The jar of powder. All that's left. Look in locked cabinet. Look everywhere. No, that's it, all that's left.

He has been waiting in the car long enough so that nothing new comes to him, and he hasn't forgotten anything. Though he is still alive, his mind has nevertheless been affected by the disease, similar to the mind of patients with Alzheimer's, many of whom were his experimental subjects. His short-term memory bungles even the most significant things and is warped with fantasy as though only dreams pass through his consciousness. So he's devised this trick: He sits and waits after each task until he realizes that he's missed something, and thus he has been sitting and waiting in the Hummer, waiting for that uncertain memory to surface, a forgotten task that had to be done. Sometimes, he would write things down on a note pad to remind himself, but for this most important task critical for his survival, he'd forgotten to do just that. These symptoms that he experiences only confound what he knows about the Death Sleep and continue to frustrate his attempt to identify the root cause. There has not been any fever, even a low grade one—no muscle ache, runny nose, headache, or the bleeding from any organs—and so it could not be a new mutation from any of the common viruses. What about a prion? But he'd dismissed that idea long ago—a prion would take years to kill and could not possibly spread that fast.

Casting a glance into the back of the car, he takes inventory of his belongings: ammunition, clothes, blankets, water, canned foods, and two canisters of gasoline. His glance drifts forward and comes to the passenger seat, to the shotgun, and to the jar, an assurance that he'll have enough powder to last for months.

He turns the key. The engine rumbles and sends a slight vibration through the car; the sputtering of the ignition bursts through the air, echoing far away, unnatural and demonic, scattering the sparrows on trees nearby. He cringes every time he turns on the engine. The car rolls forward and turns left into the street. Abruptly he stops. Looking back for the last time across the vast, empty parking lot, he studies the building, all five floors of darkened windows. For eighteen years, he'd toiled in there, working with molecules and elements, things his eyes could never see, but his intellect knew well enough. What remains? No family or loved ones, no friends or acquaintances. Only this jar of powder and his life, the latter dependent on the former. Across the parking lot, he scrutinizes the large sign by the door, and at that distance he can still read the words: Neurophysiology Research.

The habits of a small, crowded world had been inculcated into him, etched into his gray matter, and so by force of habit he lets the heavy vehicle roll slowly down the street lest it causes irreparable injury to someone, while he knows he can as easily slam down on the gas pedal and go flying through the deserted street without anyone ever witnessing. The Hummer nears a stop sign, its red color tugs at him. The warning does not jibe with the empty street, and in this instance the well-formed habits of a law-abiding doctor of neurology crumble when faced with reality. He lets the Hummer roll on and even pushes slightly on the gas pedal, acknowledging his own awareness. The car accelerates.

Passing the stop sign, he hears the noise again, a shrill high-pitched enough to pierce through the engine noise and his tinnitus; it came in three bursts, like the yelping of a wounded seal, or someone who hasn't yet mastered human language. Without doubt, it was made by a living thing, perhaps an animal, a dog, but certainly it did not sound like the common shriek of the dying. He jams on the brakes. The glass jar on the passenger seat flies onto the floor. At the sight his heart stops. He reaches down, his fingers enveloping the jar, its glass still smooth, the jar still whole. He leaves it there on the floor, sits up, and looks outward, inspecting the buildings facing the street.

In the shrill there is a staggering importance his mind recognizes, but the details and the logic of that fact remain fuzzy.

Even when idling the engine is too loud. He turns the key and the rumbling stops. In one motion, he grabs the stock of the shotgun and opens the door. He jumps off the Hummer, steps in front of the car, and listens intently. The gun rests on his left shoulder pointing skyward, while his left hand holds the stock, his index finger feeling against the trigger guard. His heart contracts forcefully, sending blood swishing past his ears, making it difficult for him to hear. The only good thing about being scared, he thinks, is that his body is releasing natural adrenaline, supplementing the powder. For now, his mind seems like its former self, awake and alert, like the intervals of those former days when he'd been truly awake. He walks forward, listening.

Again the shrilling shoots across the air. His ears catch the sound and instantaneously his head swivels, responding, directing his eyes toward the source. It comes from somewhere high up in the building in front of him. His eyes strain against the bright sky. Now that his mind is more lucid, the logic comes, one proposition connected to another and then another, in an orderly queue of 'If this is, then that must follow'. The shrilling, more like a speaking voice of some sort, tells him that there is life there; if it belongs to a living being, then that being is alive, and if that being is human, chances are that person does not have the powder and yet he lives. The wispiest hope glints through his mind: a natural immunity to the Death Sleep. Without doubt, it will help him pinpoint the cause of it, but more importantly for humanity, it's a chance for the species to continue if there are those who are naturally immune. His heart beats even faster now, not that he becomes any more fearful, but that the realization, the first glimpse of a future life after all these days, shoots through him, buzzing his senses.

From one of the windows, a certain light flits, a shadow moves, a reflection is altered; he notices all this from the corner of his eye. His feet stumble backward, away from the building as his eyes scan the windows on the third floor. Then he sees it clearly: dark fuzzy hair tops a head, thin arms rap feebly on the glass, and from the mouth the same sound shrills again, reaching his ears. Dark hollow eyes, disproportionately large for that face, stare down at him. His right hand rises slowly like a balloon, and he waves.

—Hi, he yells as loudly as he can. Do you need help?

The hollow eyes move sideways. The arms start rapping on the glass again, more feebly, and the mouth moves but this time no sound reaches him.

—Stay there, he calls out. His palm pushes upward through the air, signaling. I'll come up.

The hollow eyes look at him. He doesn't know if the person understands.

He launches himself toward the building but then halts abruptly. A large sign made of marble with large, dark etched letters stops him.

SILVER SPRING INSTITUTE OF PSYCHIATRIC REHABILITATION
ADULTS AND ADOLESCENTS

He hesitates. What type of people are locked up in there? Most likely they're very disturbed, sometimes beyond reason, and since the Death Sleep's manifestation, he can only venture a guess at the condition of their minds, those still alive. And obviously, that person who has been shrilling is alive. He grips the shotgun's stock. Think now, he commands himself, urging on the old scientist in him, his dormant logical self who would know exactly what to do. He approaches the building's front door; through the glass, he sees only a shadowy opacity. Leaning his forehead against the glass and covering the sides of his face, he peeks inside. All is quiet. As though the old scientist awakes, he says to himself, It's biology, not psychology. That's right, he says feeling elated. The biology of that person is what's important; somehow the nervous system has survived the Death Sleep. Saving that biological organism for later study is what he must do. To cement his conviction, he says to himself, Humanity depends on it.

The front door swings open easily. A stinking, putrid smell strikes his nose, and he jumps back in revulsion. He has come to know it well. Without question, it's the most malodorous of all scents in the world, equal to the concentrated vapors of a thousand sewers and yet having its distinct mark, the mark of organic decomposition; immediately it awakens a primitive part of his brain as if that part of his brain has been evolved solely for the task of detecting this smell. All the muscles in his face contract as he instinctively tries to close his nose and mouth. He pulls out a handkerchief and squeezes it against his nostrils. After some time he moves forward, passing the threshold.

Beyond the front door is a small waiting room; four chairs line the walls, a coffee table occupies the central space, and magazines are neatly stacked on the table. Also on the coffee table is a vase of daisies, dried and shriveled to brownish filaments, their petals having fallen circumferentially around the vase. Replicas of Van Gogh hang on the wall.

Finding it difficult to breathe through the handkerchief, he takes it from his nostrils and the scent of death floods in again. He grabs a chair and jams it against the front door to keep it open. After a moment, the smell seems to lessen.

In the distal wall of this small waiting room is a wooden door, and to the right of the door a small glass window. He goes to the window and looks inside. Directly in front of him, a figure slumps over a keyboard as still as the other objects around it. The figure is dressed in a white uniform, and long hair drapes the face. The arms dangle like sticks from the shoulders. He sees the familiar appurtenances of a medical front office: computers, printers, phone, clipboards, pen holders, and other objects strewn over the counter, just as inert as the figure. He slides the glass window open and watches the torso closely; the rhythm of a living person—moving, rising and falling—is not there. Pointing the tip of the shotgun at its head, he prods. No movement. He prods harder, and the body suddenly twitches as its full weight collapses onto the floor. He jumps back. A fine dust rises. He stuffs the handkerchief quickly over his nose again as he moves away from the window, seeing it's too small for him to climb through. He grabs the door knob, but it's immobile and slippery, and his fingers slide round and round without catching on.

Standing back, he levels the shotgun's barrel at the lock, only three inches away. Squeezing his eyes tightly shut, he pulls the trigger. The bang echoes in that small space and strikes his ears; the tinnitus bursts out ringing, cutting into his head. Dropping the shotgun, his hands fly to his ears, but it's useless, the noise already inside his head. He falls on his knees; the muscles of his face pull the lips away to show brown, stained teeth, and the eyebrows wrinkle into deep furrows. Gunpowder fumes fill his nostrils. The noise in his head whistles with a high pitch then slowly tapers off. After a minute, he looks up and sees the door swinging open. With the tiredness of one who has just done hard labor, he picks up the shotgun, stands up, and enters. He proceeds down the dark hallway; whatever thoughts or plans he'd concocted out on the street seem to have scattered with the shotgun's blast. He stops and thinks.

—Yes, he says to himself after a moment. Yes, yes, third floor.

He will try the third floor. He pulls out a flashlight from the pocket of his jacket; the circle of light illuminates the stair door and he goes into it. The stairwell leads from the basement below, from where an earthen smell rises. Directing the light in front of him, he climbs the stairs, passing the door marked 2. He breathes harder as he climbs, and his heart beats forcefully and sends rhythmic pulses up into his head. At the door marked 3, he opens it a crack and lets the light through. He puts the flashlight on the floor, at the edge of the doorway to keep the door from shutting after him and to free up his hand. With both hands holding the gun, he pokes the barrel through and nudges the door open a little more. He can't see much, only the opposite wall where there is a framed print of an Impressionist painting, different tones of blue merging with green, outlining the shapes of trees and lily pads. He recognizes it from somewhere and remembers that he'd thought it beautiful.

He steps into the hallway, about four feet wide. Numbered doors line both sides, and in each door is a small glass window. There are boxes, papers, plastic wrappers, clothes, shoes, and many other objects scattered haphazardly everywhere. The odor of human feces is thick in the air, but he presses on, finding the smell weirdly tolerable, for though it's foul, it's still the odor of the living. He inches forward, following the sunlight reflecting off objects and dispersing through the air.

Who is here? he thinks. What will I find? Psychiatric patients were kept here. He comes to a door and peeks through the glass window. Inside, he sees a small room, a small bed, and a person lying very still, and next to the bed another door, probably leading to a bathroom. Fixing his eyes on the still body, he watches for movement, any movement at all, the rising of the chest, twitching of the toes, any sign of life, but sees none. Toward the end of the hallway is an open door with light flowing through brightly; he heads toward it.

—Hello, he calls out and turns his ear forward to listen. He moves on and calls out again. Hello.

In his mind he goes back down the stairs, through the hall-way, and into the street, so that he can visualize the building and his current position in it. Despite his ever–quickening pulse, his mental gears still seem decrepit and rusted and churn on dully. Before the Death Sleep, he'd have known even without thinking that the side of the building facing the street is on his left, but now he has to think hard to distinguish one side from the other.

He hears a shuffling sound coming perhaps from the end of the hallway in front of him. The ringing in his ears still buzzes and obscures any sound coming in so he can't quite pinpoint the source. But it's unmistakable. Perhaps the creature he saw earlier is making noises.

Eeee. . . . Eeee. . . . Suddenly a shriek bursts out behind him. He turns to see a creature in a white uniform with dark blotches staining its front like the dripping of blood or vomit. Dark eyes on a thin, hollow face stare at him. His heart jumps. His breathing seems to synchronize with her shrieking. He raises the gun at her. His legs stumble backward, stepping on things and pushing them out of the way, but she continues to stagger toward him as though moving on crutches. Her teeth grind as if chewing a piece of meat, and her arms flop across the space in front of her as if searching for something to grab.

This is his worst fear. His call or the gunshot must have awakened her. Up to now, he has been very good at avoiding direct contact with them.

Is this still a person? Who's here to judge him? He takes steady steps backward, putting more distance between them. If he can stay out of her way, he's certain the Death Sleep will reclaim her soon enough; whatever burst of energy that allowed her a brief awakening will soon dissipate and she will enter oblivion for the last time. She's already dead anyway, he thinks. And there is no time to wait.

He squeezes the trigger. Nothing happens. He's forgotten to reload it after the last shot. He pumps the shotgun quickly and pulls the trigger again. The blast propels her backward, and she lands flat on the ground. A gurgled noise comes from her throat. Running his hand over his face, he checks to see if her blood has splashed onto him. He doesn't want to take the chance of getting blood in his mouth, nose, or eyes. Nothing on his face. He turns round and round waving the shotgun in the air, his hands shaking; his breath is too quick and shallow. The blast makes the ringing in his ears surge again, though not as bad as the first blast. I must hurry now, he thinks; the blast could very well have awakened others.

Yes, that person I saw was on the left, he thinks. He walks along the hallway, looking inside the small window of each room. At the third window, he glances inside, turns away but abruptly stops. He puts his face to the glass to look again. He can make out, at the end of the small bed, dark hair just visible above the bed frame. He knocks on the door. Upturned eyes edge up slowly into his view, rising past the straight line of the wooden plank of the bed.

—Hello, he says. Moving unconsciously, he opens the door and pulls it outward. At the entrance, he stands, and his face lifts into an awkward toothy smile.

Whimpering noises come from the corner, scuffling feet pushing against the carpet as though trying to burrow away. The gunshot must have scared her, he thinks. The eyes now appear focused, unmoving; gray irises are surrounded by the frightful white of the eyeballs.

He fumbles inside his pocket and takes out a chocolate bar. He tears off the wrapper and waves it. The chocolate has partially melted and sticks to his fingers.

—Are you hungry? Come, take it. It's good.

The thin face rises a little more, a delicate nose next to pale cheeks. A hand reaches out, the whole body stirs forward, and the eyes must be seeing something familiar, nourishing, for they open, wide and expectant.

He steps into the room and closes the door. He breathes easier now. His heart slows, but half of his mind is still outside the door, in the hallway, keeping vigil on the others in Death Sleep, who might at any moment awaken and act out their worst nightmares.

—Come. It's chocolate. It's good. Come. Take it.

The figure crawls forward. It's unmistakable, a girl, perhaps twelve years old. Dark, straggly hair hangs down to her shoulders; she wears a white, long–sleeved gown that has small blue roses on it and reaches to her feet. On the gown, darker brown patches are encrusted into the fabric. He freezes, and his eyes glaze over as if he were witnessing an epochal vision his dull brain does not quite understand.

Her hand snatches the candy, and like a spring, she pulls back into the corner. She stuffs the candy into her mouth; the melted chocolate smears in large blotches over her mouth and fingers.

Anxiety abruptly tugs at him, arousing him from the daze. I must go soon, he thinks.

—What's your name? He holds out his hand, beckons as gently as he can. What's your name?

She chews and swallows in quick movements and begins to lick her fingers, while staring at him. Her timid demeanor reassures him. She hasn't gotten the disease after all. But what if he were to give her the disease, because without the powder, he would be just like the billion others sleeping. No time to debate now, he thinks. I'll just give her the powder too if she ever falls into the Death Sleep.

—Come. We have to go.

Her fingers dart into her mouth, one after another in rapid succession, and come out nearly clean of chocolate.

—You're hungry. Come with me. You can have more to eat. Do you understand? Come on, let's go.

She looks at him as though he hasn't spoken. He approaches her and kneels to be at her level. He reaches for her hand to lead her out. Abruptly, a slight shrilling noise, at the same pitch he heard earlier, comes from her throat. Reflexively, she puts up her palms.

—It's all right, he whispers. Come, come to me. I'll keep you safe.

Her head shakes from side to side.

—It's all right. How can I make you understand? It's all right . . . Come . . . come to Papa.

Suddenly her eyes shine and focus on him, the face changes swiftly to recognition. Her lips part.

—Papa, she utters and springs forward, colliding with him. Her arms tighten around his neck. Papa, she says softly in his ear.

He doesn't know what to say. A foul odor is in her clothes, but he does not mind. The strands of her hair are filthy with dust and rub against his cheek. He hears her breath next to his ear. She could very well be his own daughter, who is now thousands of miles away and probably also in Death Sleep and whom he can never help. At the thought, his stomach squeezes, his face contorts.

—Yes, darling . . . It's Papa. His own voice surprises him. It's the crackled voice on the verge of crying. We have to go now.

He holds her hand, and in the other, he grabs the shotgun as he leads her out of the room.

Down the hallway, nothing moves. He shuffles through the papers, clothes, and other debris. As they near the body of the woman he shot, he moves along the wall and tries his best to conceal the corpse from her.

Two minutes later, they stand by the Hummer. He opens the door and lets her into the passenger seat. In the back of the car, he rummages through the provisions and finds a protein bar and a bottle of water.

The girl sucks at the bottle of water, drinking so strongly that he has to take it away.

—Not so fast, he tells her and sees the puzzlement in her eyes. Not so fast, darling. Your body must adjust. Do you understand?

He tears the wrapper from the protein bar and gives it to her.

She takes it and puts it to her mouth, but now her movements are slow and methodical.

To his amazement, the sun has sunk much too close to the horizon. Sunlight filters through the leaves at a sharp angle. Surveying the building one more time, he feels there is something he must get from there, but the urgency of the setting sun forces him to go.

The car speeds along the street, passing darkened streetlights. He glances at his watch; it's five thirty, almost time for another dose of the powder, though he feels none of the dullness, the sensation of a curtain draping over his mind, or the dense fog emanating from an ignored pit of consciousness that he often feels. It must be the scare he had earlier and the resultant adrenaline coursing through his brain, keeping him alert.

He turns onto Wilshire and heads toward the beach. Driving along the street, he sees banners and signs flowing past his peripheral vision, endless words that at one time informed him of the services available. Japanese restaurant, Liquor Store, Cleaners, Italian Cuisine, and on and on. Now they are the only evidence that there were people once living here. Now they are only words, mere decorations placed by a cruel artist to commemorate the end of a species. There is Maruki coming up, tucked in a corner of the small street mall. He remembers the cloudy cold nights when he stayed in the lab late to finish an important experiment or sometimes to edit one of his many scientific papers, and he would stop by Maruki on the way home, a small charming restaurant with no more than a dozen seats. The host was always the head chef, Mr. Akira, who would immediately greet him by his first name and place before him a delectable creation, perhaps a hand roll of spicy tuna with smelt eggs. He would always eat whatever was placed in front of him; often he stayed late into the night, drank warm sake, and tried to decipher the wisdom that Mr. Akira dispensed with his archaic, accented voice.

The car flies past Muraki, now dark and lifeless. Mr. Akira sleeps somewhere. Now and then, he can spot a dark figure inside a car along the road, slumped over the wheel; no doubt the drivers had felt a creeping drowsiness and had pulled over for a quick nap before getting on the road again, but they never did.

Glancing over at the girl, he sees that she has fallen asleep. Her head leans against the door. Wilshire ends at the Pacific Coast Highway. Here he brings the car to a full stop; his hand moves over her chest, and his palm feels it rising and sinking, the signs of breathing. With her eyes closed, the graceful gentle features of a child return to her face.

Over the ocean, a wall of fog is rolling in, and though the sun is still above the horizon, a grayish murk tinges the atmosphere. Far out on the sand, he sees dark figures scattered about, lying still between the fog and the sand.

Pressing on the gas pedal, he turns the car sharply and heads north.

4

By the time they arrive at his house, the waning light of late afternoon has given way to a winter night's cold gloom. There is a stir in the air, a difference from other nights in years past. The air possesses an altogether different taste; its very essence is scented with a moldering foliage, and into the atmosphere the rapacious pheromones of a newly hatched species have diffused. Though being nearly unrecognizable, this air encloses him, swirls around, and at the same time agitates old sentiments as though there exists in him a kindred spirit; the air of this new world awakens a feeling of sweet doldrums, a tendency toward remembrance, and he sees his daughter's little feet pushing the pedals of her bicycle as she sped along the street not so long ago. He stands by the car, staring at the darkening street, seeing chimeric visions, and is lost in the convergence of the two lines of trees along the street.

—Papa.

Her gargling voice brings him back. She sits upright with a stiff, straight back; her round, serene eyes wait for him. He walks

around the car, opens the door, and lifts her down. Next, he grabs
the shotgun, now a vital, organic excrescence, and, of course, the
jar of powder.

—Darling, we're home.

He doesn't know her name, and his daughter's name, habituated by a million flicks of the tongue to the roof of the mouth,
resides squarely at the pink soft tip, waits to be resurrected, but
he's ashamed of the sacrilegious thought. Seeing the plastic band
around her wrist, he twists it carelessly, enough to glimpse the
dark printed letters under the car's light: Maya Cahn.

—Let's get you something to eat first. Then you can wash up.

Taking her hand, he leads her up the stone steps to the large,
heavy wooden door. The single-story wooden frame house—its
stucco painted russet almond, its high ceilings, arching windows
and tall entrance, and its deep brown wooden garage doors—had
been his wife's pride. It invited the sun and was often filled with
his family's joy in the summer. In the winter it resisted dank
and gloom. But as soon as his wife and daughter left, it had been
reduced to no more than an assemblage of building materials.
Now, he glances upon the façade once more as he leads Maya
toward the entrance and feels again the fire inside, the warmth of
a family, the precise reason that it could repel the dank of winter,
be it day or night.

—Home, sweetie.

Don't you remember? he thinks about asking. But such questions are bewildering, not questions at all but mere threads that
can only lead to a tortuous labyrinth without end. He can't do
that to her, to himself, or to the memory of his daughter, and yet
something elemental urges him on, goads him to at least contemplate such a thing, and seems to promise him that all will be
made whole, that a new life awaits on the other side of the veil of

hidden truth. He shakes his head to dispel the slightest possibility of deceiving her; there will come a moment when he must tell her the truth. For now as a study subject, she embodies the last great hope for mankind.

Through the door the darkened space echoes with the voice of the child who once lived here, whose "Hello" resounded with a distinct raspiness from having screamed too much during play and whose words took on a timid timbre whenever she was about to leave. He switches on a battery–powered lamp and brings it with him as he shows the way. Instantly expanding to the tall ceiling, the bright white light pushes away the darkness and shows them the upholstered sofa and chairs, the crystalline coffee table covered with glossy, decorative magazines, the painting of the sun hanging over the mantel, the lamps on the set of end tables; they were the fashions of the day that his wife had gleaned from the dozen or so magazines and had proceeded to duplicate. The style is eclectic and transitional, deriving from a mixture of ornamental curves, straight lines, and angular simplicity. But style no longer matters, is dwarfed and made obsolete by the lamps, batteries, flashlights, canned food, bags of charcoal, jugs of water, and countless other objects he'd looted from abandoned stores.

—Sit here and wait for me. He indicates the sofa to her. I'll heat up a bowl of chicken soup for you. You should eat very light food at first.

As he moves toward the kitchen, he feels a tug. Like a floating kite tethered to him with an invisible thread, she is there behind him, her delicate fingers pinching his jacket.

—Oh, he says as he stops and turns to her. How thoughtless of me. What you have been through. You shouldn't be alone. Come with me then.

The two of them moving like a man and his shadow, they go to the kitchen where a trove of canned food is stacked a foot high along the walls. His hand grabs a large can of chicken soup as he passes.

In the back yard, bundles of logs make a disordered pile next to the fire pit, and a trail leads to the side of the yard where he'd discarded the ashes. Pots, pans, forks and spoons are scattered about. Chairs had been arranged around the fire pit, and an overarching umbrella begins to blend with the encroaching darkness. Further out, overgrown grasses with long, sharp blades and flowering stems, render all previous attempts at their domestication inutile; long, smooth stems and thin, verdant blades are deceptively tender and delicate, but always straightened themselves out after each time he trampled upon them. Still further out, the fence separates the back yard from the vegetation of the sloping hill. At the top, the water tank stands, still providing the house with water even after the electricity went out. But he does not know for how long it will last.

Soon a fire crackles inside the pit, and the smoke and the smell of burning wood rise. He opens the can, pours the content into a pot, and places it directly over the fire.

—Sit down here. He points to a chair. We'll let it boil first, then . . .

First we'll boil it, then we'll let it cool down before we can eat; he finds it strange to think about things like that. She sits in the chair next to him and automatically pulls a blanket from the back of the chair over herself. The changing shapes of the flames scribble resplendence across her face and show her oblong eyes bright, expectant, but steadfast as if those eyes had been exaggerated by a devout artist intent on ascertaining the very nature of the human soul. The distant vacuousness on the faces of retarded children who populated the mental asylums he'd known well is absent from her face. Not even a faint inkling, not even the fuzziest fog of its imprint can be discovered on her now that he sits near her, and his curious eyes scrutinize her thin cheeks, full eyebrows, and those probing oblong eyes. The eyes tell it all, and from them a focused beam of awareness and intelligence searches her surrounding, absorbs things, not merely witnessing but palpating the texture of objects, the very fiber of their existence.

Warmth from the fire radiates outward and envelops them; behind them shadows warp and at times merge, blurring reality with memory in which superimposed moments from so many nights like this somehow conjure up the image of his daughter's delirious giggling and of his wife sitting next to him, exuding her usual superior serenity while acknowledging them both. Happiness once existed under this very umbrella on countless nights like this and on other nights with the winds cold and vigorous or at times when the air was hot and humid as though the sea itself had evaporated and invaded the land.

His wristwatch chirps and startles her.

—Don't worry, darling. It's just the alarm.

He unscrews the jar of powder, licks his left index finger, and sticks it into the jar. Powder adheres to his fingertip. He places it under his tongue, and the powder dissolves quickly. Reflexively he swallows. Every six hours, he performs this ritual. It has become methodical but not yet routine, for every moment of his life, awake or asleep, anticipates and leads to this instant when the cycle is reset and life is extended by another six hours. An acute mental energy immediately rises to the top of his head; he feels the sensation but knows that it must be his mind playing tricks on him, and that the effect of the powder cannot be that fast. In any case, another six hours of life is assured.

The chicken soup boils and spills over, and the liquid sizzles in the fire. He grabs the pot and places it on the side of the fire pit. He pours half the soup into a bowl for her.

—Eat it slowly. It's hot.

He eats out of the pot, swirling it and blowing on it. He sees that she imitates him; she cranes her neck over the steaming bowl, stirring with the spoon while glancing at him. She puts the spoon to her lip but has to yank it away immediately. Perhaps it's his age and the callousness that comes with it, his hot soup full of homely smell tastes warm only, delicious, and even precious in contrast to the cold air descending around the edge of the umbrella and wafting over them.

—Let it cool down a bit first, he tells her.

She swirls the spoon round and round, the rising steam moistens and tickles her nostrils, and she giggles and scratches her nose. The lips pucker, and a long breath pushes the steam away from her face, but at the end of the breath, the steam returns. Her giggling, clear and sharp, full of surprise and delight, seems to dance with the wavering flames.

Looking at her, his face swells into a smile, coming from a happiness deep within his chest, something he hadn't felt for years even before the Death Sleep. In the past, he'd frequently chastised his daughter and told her not to play with her food, to eat her food quickly, and then to tend to her homework. But now he sits back and takes in the giggles, the unmitigated happiness, and the reflection of light bouncing off the young cheeks and somehow being further purified and refined. Her face isn't so different from his daughter's, which in all her days had shown the same keenness and inquisitiveness, whether they sat at the breakfast table or took a walk along the beach. A child's face is she one and whole for so long as she is a child, while he wears his, at the moment happy. In all the days that he'd seen his daughter's face, true happiness was there in front of his eyes, but he only saw unending work, filling up volumes of now unusable knowledge, and social events from which he would go away drunk and forgetful. The most delectable essence of existence was before him all that time, yet a cursed hurrying rushed him to a future with everything being the same, down to the same hurrying that would hurry him to another future with him in it hurrying in the same way, save for the singularity of now evaporating.

The fire dwindles. He pulls himself up, adds more wood to the fire, and places a large pot of water over it.

—Eat up now. Let's get you a warm bath.

Under the light of the lamp, he leads her into the master bathroom. Thick curtains have been nailed to the window frames to prevent light from escaping. Dirty clothes are piled in the corner. A strong smell of sweat fills the air. He pours the boiled water into the tub and turns on the faucet. The water level hasn't quite reached a quarter of the tub when he turns the faucet off. He splashes his hand through the water; it's still warm enough.

—Come in before it gets cold. He beckons her.

She comes into the bathroom.

—I'll get some clothes for you. I'm right outside, OK? If you need me, I'm right outside.

He gauges her size and thinks that his daughter's clothes will fit her. He tells her, I'll be right back. I'll put on another pot of water just in case you get cold.

Then he pulls a knife from his pocket, cuts off her wristband with an almost careless flick, and puts them both in his pocket. He turns on another lamp and sets it by the night stand next to the bed. He heads to his daughter's bedroom. He goes out and pulls the door behind him.

How many times he'd sorted through his daughter's clothes—their nightly ritual. Before giving her a bath each night, he would follow her into her bedroom and wait impatiently as she searched for the right colored pajamas, the right shirt, something she hadn't worn during the week before. She liked thin, short sleeved cotton t–shirts and pants in the summer. In the winter she preferred long sleeved, tight fitting shirts and thick pants, and she liked her bedroom cool, almost cold as she lay warm under the thick blankets and breathed in the cool air while she slept. Often he had lost his patience and descended upon the drawers himself, pulling out whatever he found and shoving it into her hands as he told her: Just wear anything. I don't have time for this. Just let me take care of you.

The admonition now reverberates in his ears, seemingly from the walls themselves; now he hears those words, the same words repeated countless times, distorting the way he remembers her face, at once calm and amused, undisturbed by his fits of anger. As he walks, guided once more by habit, he knows that he doesn't want to fall into another routine. Each episode of the past congealed with the next, all the nights blurring together into a nameless memory. When he reaches her bedroom, he is immersed in total darkness, but he knows exactly where the pants and the shirts are. His hands feel the hard knob of the drawers; they plunge into the soft clothes, pull out a pair of pants, and finally stretch it to measure its length. Yes, this will do, he thinks, it'll fit her. Then the shirt, the same long sleeved, tight fitting cotton shirt will do very well.

He heads back, following the slightly shifting light. Silence from the bathroom alarms him. He pushes the door slowly, while calling her—Darling? No answer. He peeks inside. In the corner by the tub, she sits, her knees drawn to her chin. The dirty institutional gown draping her front becomes a sort of protective barrier. He moves toward her but very slowly, for his legs are impeded by an emotional devastation as thick and real as anything between them.

—Why aren't you taking a bath? I got the clothes for you. He looks at her. He kneels down to be at her level. What's wrong?

In her eyes, the sharpness and the same unerring steadiness remain.

—Why won't you say anything? He reaches for her, and gingerly she uncoils and rises to stand before him. Let Papa help you, OK?

Only now does he see that the gown hangs lopsidedly over her shoulder; the gown is too big, and the space around the neck nearly encompasses all of her clavicle. He lifts the gown, and it gives off a dusty stench. The pale skin of her chest appears serrated by the ribs underneath; how ghostly thin she is. As he kneels before her, he notices the wings of her pelvis bulging against the skin and the ends of her femurs enlarging into bony knees.

A wetness smears down his cheek, focusing him. He feels her fingers touching his cheeks, trying to wipe away the tears. I'm crying, he thinks. What vestige of memory surfaces to bid her to soothe him when she doesn't even know enough to take a bath?

—Get into the tub before the water gets cold.

She climbs over the side and settles into the water. He scoops up the water and pours it over her. Then he lathers the shampoo into her hair. He rubs the bar of soap over her, just as he did with his own daughter, thousands of times. Her hands catch the soap bubbles, and at the same time her giggles break out with the spontaneity of first discovery.

—I'll make you a big breakfast tomorrow. We'll get those muscles back on you in no time at all. Yeah. You'll be fine. You'll be fine.

Words are spoken, though he makes no conversation. She seems to listen and, by her movements, she seems to understand, but she utters no intelligible words. So he continues to talk as he's been doing since he regained consciousness and found himself alone. At least, his words no longer bounce off inanimate furnitures, echo into empty halls, disappear off his tongue into the passing winds, or reverberate only in his head where he can't be certain if he spoke out loud. He takes comfort now that his words enter her ears where they will push beyond dark alleys and reconnect loose synapses. So he continues to talk, to pronounce every action and to attach them with words.

—This is the bed you'll sleep in. I'll sleep on this side. Here. Are you thirsty? Drink some water from this glass. This shirt fits you very nicely. Are you cold? Put the blanket over you. You'll be warm in a minute. I'll sit for a moment. Go ahead and sleep. You see I'm tired too. It's been a long day. A special day. I found you today. I found you today. Isn't that something? You know I was going to my work to get the powder. That's all there is in that bottle. I wonder if I can make more.

—I'm not a chemist. I just used the stuff for my experiments on mice. I studied their brains, how they responded to different chemicals. How did I get it in the first place? My collaborator sent it. Yeah, just like that. From a lab in Berkeley. I wonder if I can make some more. All the ingredients are there in the lab. You just have to mix them together in the right proportions. Sleep now. I can't sleep just yet. I have to wait till midnight. I have to take the powder at midnight. That way I can sleep six hours because that's how long the powder will last. I'll set the alarm.

Now and then he looks at her as his mind tries to formulate from his knowledge of neurological development a plausible past for her. But he'd seen it all before; it was the same with David Calweld. A mental disorder of some sort, probably a congenital disorder, had consigned her to the mental asylum, where she spent all her years, most likely in isolation and bereft of human interaction. Thus she never learned to talk.

She lies still, asleep. Her hair is still wet and is cold to the touch. He places a dry towel over her head.

—But you don't need the powder, do you? You're something new. Your mind may not work so well, but you will live, he whispers. There must be others like you and we must find them for your sake. You will bear children and they will live on. They will make use of all that we built.

As the night deepens, cold air descends from the hill overlooking the house and rustles the branches outside the bedroom windows. There are other sounds he does not recognize, but the shrieks of people transiently waking from the Death Sleep are too infrequent.

He looks at his wristwatch. In six more minutes it will be midnight. He sticks his fingertip in the jar and then places it under his tongue. His back collapses against the bed's headboard, and he closes his eyes. Somnolent reprieve, like a portal, appears from deep within, and his consciousness crosses it into another reality more real to his senses than the world he's just left behind. He feels his daughter's presence nearby. He remembers that she's sleeping. He must check on her, and through the dimly lit hallway he moves toward her room whose door appears to be no more than a small darkness at a distance of infinity.

5

Through the small holes in the windows' curtains, the tentative morning peeks in when the alarm on his wristwatch chirps. The ensuing minute is now the most difficult in his life and is marked by dilemma and confusion, by his inability so far to differentiate between gladness that his consciousness has once more escaped the Death Sleep and regret that he hasn't slipped permanently into its hold and gone on dreaming—an end and an enduring peace. What makes the whole situation even more confusing is that he can't seem to remember the actual dream, something to do with his daughter, an intuition of her hovering about him, her presence in his mind but only fuzzily and always out of grasp.

Automatically, he gropes for the powder, uncaps it, and sticks in a moistened finger. Then the finger goes under the tongue. He lies still in the bed and wishes that he could sleep more. The Death Sleep seems to have grasped him tighter than usual, a mental languor dulling his senses. The veil lifts slowly and memory, like rising water, percolates into his consciousness.

Can it be true? Yesterday, he found another person who still survives after all these days and is naturally immune to the Death Sleep. How can it be? And a girl, like his daughter. No, he shakes his head. Like his daughter? The thought strikes him violently. What are the chances of that? No, no. He shakes his head. It must be a hallucination, a very elaborate multi-sensory hallucination. Perhaps a deep recess of his mind has given up on reality even if he hasn't done so. After many days of being by himself, talking to himself, and thinking to himself, his mind must have created for itself a companion in the form of a little girl like his daughter. No doubt, a mental defense mechanism.

He turns on his side mournfully. Seeing the jar of powder, he realizes that hallucination might be a side effect. Very likely. What medication doesn't have side effects? And to remember that he gave her a bath and that he felt her emaciated torso that brought tears to his eyes—how cruel and weak the mind is. Then he notices it. Next to him, a blanket lies, folded upon itself as if someone upon waking up had flung it over. She slept on that side of the bed. But the half-flung blanket doesn't prove anything; he could have done that himself very easily.

The morning sky brightens more, and white light pierces more sharply around the edges of the curtains where they aren't completely nailed down. Nowadays, silence impregnated with midnight's woe and weariness seems to stretch relentlessly into the early morning. Two days ago he heard a dog barking, a gruff growling transmitting a cautious rebuke, and today he hopes to hear the same bark. He hears nothing—the dog must have moved on already; it has the entire city to roam. He turns on his side again, turning away from the curtains toward the door. Languid indifference glues him to the bed; there is no plan to execute today, unlike those few days after he'd discovered that the powder could keep him alive when he'd worked feverishly to secure food and fuel. Now with no urgent desire to do anything in particular, why should he get up? In his mind, he tries to imagine his steps from the bed to the backyard to cook breakfast. Then what? Maybe he can roam the city like a wild dog, or he can skip breakfast and lie around idly, and perhaps he can skip lunch as well. Just another fingertip of the powder at noon, he will be fine until dinner.

Suddenly something drops, just beyond the bedroom door. He hears it distinctly. His heart jolts. He cranes his head toward the door and remains very still. Another sound comes, like the sound of a book falling on the floor. There can be no mistake now. His legs flip off the bed and he swings up, standing erect, his right hand reaching for something. Yes, the shotgun. It's in the corner.

He pushes the bedroom door open with the gun muzzle. He tiptoes softly, trying to avoid the scraps of paper on the floor that make a slight rustling noise against his feet. His heart throbs in his ears. The short hallway seems interminable. He stays still and listens. Faint scratching sounds now come from somewhere near the front door. Perhaps an animal has gotten into the house, and now it's searching for food. He follows the sound toward his study. Just shy of the door, he lowers the gun. His hands shake and his finger on the trigger feels slippery with sweat. His foot nudges the door open. He sees a black head turning toward him, and his mind, presently occupied with the dueling ideas of hallucination and reality, buzzes with confusion. He freezes. He holds his breath and then exhales. His eyes fixate on the girl as though by staring at her long enough he will see through her, and the hallucination will be forced to evaporate. Instead, her eyes tranquil and magnanimous stare back at him, and the strength of her look settles the dilemma for him. There is a familiarity to her face as if she has been living here all her life. In the morning light, he sees clearly her large, gray eyes, the dark hair hanging down to her shoulders, the pale skin where the blue veins are visible, and the delicate hands holding a book. He puts down the gun and smiles at her. Damn, he thinks, I could have shot her.

—Good morning . . . Good morning, darling. What are you doing?

She is sitting on the floor of his study, in front of the bookshelves. The bottom shelf holds all his daughter's books. She is holding a large book with a hard cover, one of those books that teach young children to read. He comes to her and kneels down.

—Yes, yes. That's very good. You are learning how to read. This is A, B, C, D . . .

He sounds off the alphabet for her as she moves her head sideways along the page and turns the pages quickly. At the end, she drops the book and searches for another one among the row of neatly shelved books.

—This is the next one you should read.

He hands her another book, a picture book with simple sentences, and he reads the sentences. She turns the pages rapidly.

—You have to go slowly so you can learn. You should try to remember the words. Then slowly you will know more words. Say this word with me. The . . . the night. Now you say it.

She goes on flipping the pages. Thinking that she hasn't heard him, he puts his hand on her shoulder. She turns to him.

—Darling. Say the words after me. That's how you learn to talk. The . . . night.

She says nothing and turns back to the book.

—Well. You must be hungry. I'll start breakfast. Come and eat when I call you. OK, darling?

IN THE BACKYARD, A FINE DEW STILL BLANKETS EVERYTHING—the stones, the chairs, the leaves. The air is soaked with moisture, and he feels it through his nostrils. An earthen smell rises from the ground. Nothing moves. Such stillness arrests him. Up the hill and beyond, the sky is overcast with a monotonous white layer of cloud. On the top of the hill the water tank sits, barely visible in the mist.

It's still early and the child should sleep longer, he thinks. He turns his ear toward the front of the house to listen for her, but he hears nothing and thinks she might as well have vanished the moment he left her. It occurs to him it's the same as the philosopher's problem of a tree falling in the forest—only he is not in the forest—and though there are corpses all around, enough of a testament to his reality, he might as well be in the forest where no other consciousness exists, where if a tree does fall he can't even tell if it falls for real. He needs other consciousnesses, other independent, feisty minds, who can push back against him and corroborate his reality, even if it means telling him that there is no emaciated little girl with beautiful eyes, that it's all a hallucination.

He throws logs into the fire pit and lights the fire. The wood crackles as the flames rise high. After a while, he opens a can of Spam and holds it over the frying pan. The chunk of meat covered with whitish grease slides onto the pan and immediately starts to sizzle. Right in the pan, he cuts the meat into small chunks. Then a can of black beans goes in. He stirs it until it's boiling; the steam lifts the smell up to his nose. Then he brings it to the kitchen table.

—Darling, come to breakfast, he calls to the front of the house, only half believing himself. Children don't respond right away, he thinks. His daughter used to sit, entranced with her book, and would only come after he called many times. He sits back in the chair and waits for her, not knowing if he should call again. Like a man with endless time, thus infinite patience, he slouches further into the chair, and his hands go into his pants pockets. The tips of his fingers jam sharply against a piece of plastic. He takes it and brings it up to look at it. It reads: Maya Cahn, December 21, 20 . . . He cut it from her wrist yesterday; it is real enough. He reads it again, squeezes it in his hand, and puts it back in his pocket. I will keep it with me all the time so I'll know you're real. You're fourteen, he says softly.

Her footsteps are audible only as she comes close to him. She is holding a different book now.

—Darling, sit down for breakfast.

She sits and starts to eat right away. She looks at him with a cursory curiosity and goes back to the book, holding it with her right hand while eating. Just like his daughter, he thinks; she used to eat like that, reading constantly, and despite his protest he could never get her to do otherwise.

—Even as a hallucination, you sure are hungry, he says and laughs.

Her eyes turn to him, and she stares, her gaze crystalline, unmoving.

—I'm sorry. It's just a joke.

An impish smile breaks out on her face. He holds the pan over her plate and pushes more food onto it.

—Sometimes when you're alone by yourself for so long, you don't know what's real anymore. It would help if you could talk to me. Tell me what you're thinking. I'd like to know what you're thinking instead of just seeing you.

She looks at him, and a subtle smile grows on her face.

He pats her head and feels the strands of her hair against the creases of his palm. Why does she acts as though she has lived here all her life and is so much like his daughter? An eerie feeling comes over him. He wants to know how she will react.

—Maya.

She jerks up and her eyes protrude, showing the whiteness under the irises.

—I'm sorry. I didn't mean to say it so loud. He smiles at her and maintains the smile rigidly for a while to show her that it's sort of a joke. Well, at least you remember your name. How old are you?

She seems to look at him without seeing.

—Do you know how old you are? Can you remember?

Fourteen, he thinks, remembering the year from the wrist strap.

She drops the spoon and puts the book on the table, face down. With a deliberate effort, she points up her left index finger and four right fingers.

—That's right. That's wonderful.

Clasping his hands together, his face beams with the most radiant smile. Though he can't see his own face, he feels the flush of pride overwhelming him.

—That is truly wonderful. Fourteen, right? Not five? Of course not. You know it's fourteen. You're fourteen year old.

He waits for her to answer, but she says nothing and promptly goes back to the food which she quickly scoops into her mouth. Then with her cheeks bulging, she chews.

—I hope you truly know. Anyhow, let me see what you're reading. Do you understand it?

From the cover, he sees that the book is about a horse. His daughter was reading this book only three years ago, and she'd progressed quickly to books for teens when she left two years ago.

—What should we do today?

He clears the table and places the dirty plates and pan in the sink, already piled to the brim. He leaves the girl at the table, goes to the backyard, and looks up at the water tank on the hill. The water pressure has been decreasing, and at this rate maybe in two weeks, there won't be any more running water in the house. But the thought hardly unsettles him. What is truly frightening is the powder. The thought has been creeping upon him in his most lucid moments, when he can confront it squarely. What he knows for sure is that the powder is a neural stimulant, and, as with any neural stimulant— be it cocaine, amphetamine, or epinephrine—its effect can only last for so long, until there comes a time when the effective dose exceeds the toxic dose. That time will be the end of him. He realized this some days ago, and it seemed to have been insidiously grinding him down, putting hypochondriacal thoughts in his head, so now he is not sure if the persistent somnolence he feels upon waking is a manifestation of the tolerance his brain has developed toward the powder. Psychological, he mumbles, it could all be psychological; he should know that better than anyone, but still he fears the day when he has to increase the dose.

Quickly, he springs back into the house. The kitchen is empty. He did not hear her when she left. He runs to his study. There she sits on the floor, next to her a pile of neatly stacked books. He stops in the doorway and moves forward slowly as though she is a butterfly who might fly away.

—We must keep ourselves busy. Well, at least me. I see you have books to read.

He comes to her and sits next to her. The pages of the book appear densely packed with words. Her head moves sideways in a smooth saccadic rhythm.

—I, hmm, I want to go. I want to, hmm . . . We have to keep busy. How do I explain to you? I need this powder, you see. I can't do without it. And I don't have too much of it left. I mean I have enough for maybe three months. But I have to make more. Or try to.

Her still eyes take him in, but it's difficult for him to know if she understands.

—Well, maybe tomorrow we'll head out.

THE NEXT DAY, HOWEVER, WILL BE REMEMBERED NOT AS BEING distinct in itself but a blur in a succession of many days that are all the same: waking up to the alarm, tasting the sour powder under his tongue, heating canned food in the backyard, boiling water for baths, and falling back to sleep, in the end always falling back to sleep.

Then there are times when he talks to Maya, asking her ordinary questions, and tells her about himself. One day he decides to examine her. Through the small aperture of the ophthalmoscope, he scans her eyes and sees the delicate spidery blood vessels like the roots of a tree spreading across her retina, and her blind spot where the optic nerve leaves her eyeball. Under magnification, her grayish irises appear like fine filaments that, when moving, give the impression of being a wave in motion, and when he backs away and looks at her, he falls under the gaze of her large, oblong eyes and feels a strange contentment as though under a spell. Maya, he says to her in almost a whisper, you know that one of my great grandmothers came from Belize? When she was young, she played on the same grassy fields where in ancient times they made human sacrifices. Another one came from Asia to escape the war, he says. Yes, war is a dirty business; at least now there is no war. With the stethoscope, he listens to the da–dup–da–dup of her heartbeats; her heart beats fast as it should for a child and it's much too captivating. As he concentrates on it, he hopes to hear its secret, to know why she is alive and conscious. One of my grandfathers came from England, he says and winks at her. Talk to me, he thinks as he puts the stethoscope over her lungs; tell me something, speak. Her breath murmurs indistinctly. He continues to speak softly as he examines her. Another great grandmother came from France; a great grandfather came from Russia, he had many serfs.

He looks into her ears, sees the large canals and the large eardrums, and deduces that she must have excellent hearing. Then he tests her reflexes but can't understand why they are too brisk or why she is so sensitive for her age, and if he didn't know better, he would think that there is something wrong with her. In the end, he decides that he, in fact, does not know any better. You see darling, he says as he is straightening up. I'm a man who is only possible in this age and this place, I'm a modern man.

Finally he stands back and pronounces, Maya, you're in excellent health.

ONE OF THOSE MORNINGS, HE OPENS HIS EYES TO SEE HER STANDing there, only a foot in front of him, and she stoops down to his eye level, to look directly into his eyes.

—Is this . . . you . . . in this picture?

Her voice is soft. So she stutters; she is speaking to me, she can speak, he thinks. Squeezing his eyes tightly closed, he does not know if he should talk, his mouth is foul with morning breath, and he hasn't yet tasted that fingertip of powder under the tongue, but mostly he isn't sure if he is still dreaming.

—Papa . . . Papa.

She grabs his shoulder and shakes him thoroughly.

—What picture? But you can speak. How?

—I don't . . . know. I could . . . speak . . . all along.

—Just like David Calweld. Someone I knew a long time ago. He was like you.

—Is this . . . you? Maya says, pointing to the picture.

He rubs his eyes, and while they're still blurry from the rubbing, his hand fumbles over the nightstand for the bottle of powder, but instead he feels it suddenly pushed against his chest where she just shoved it. Cradling the bottle, he opens it, dips in the moistened fingertip, and then deliberately places it under his tongue. After a minute, he raises his eyelids, only to stare at himself. Two inches from his face, Maya is holding a picture of him standing next to his wife and holding Emily.

—Is this . . . you?

—Hmm . . .

He moves away from her.

—Papa . . . Papa . . . Papa . . .

The staccato of her voice, firing one syllable after another, sounds so much like his daughter's that he recoils even further, shivering with a superstitious thought that Maya is somehow channeling Emily.

—Yes, yes, darling. It's me.

—Who . . . Who is . . . this?

—That's my wife, Anna.

—And . . . this . . . this girl?

—My daughter Emily.

—Where . . . where are . . . they?

—New York City.

He gets up, goes in the bathroom, and closes the door. Standing over the bathroom sink and avoiding his own reflection in the mirror, he tightens his abdomen and tries to extinguish that eviscerating blow to his gut that always accompanies the thought of his daughter. This time is particularly painful. What is she? That creature out there, just outside the door. Why did he find her? He cringes, bends over, and splashes cold water onto his face.

When he comes out, he sees her sitting on the bed, her legs dangling on the side.

—Papa. . . . Papa. . . . Where . . . am I?

—Where are you? Why, you're home.

—In . . . the picture. Where . . . am I . . . in the picture?

He comes to her, leans down to look into her eyes, and touches her cheek with the back of his hand.

—Darling, you're not. Don't look for yourself in those pictures.

—Yes . . . Papa.

In her eyes, a glassy unflinching stillness as if aroused by a sudden understanding takes hold, and he recognizes it.

—Let's get some breakfast. Let's get to work. We must keep ourselves busy. You know what they say: Idleness is the root of all evil.

—Yes . . . Papa.

6

As the Hummer descends the hill, he starts to see through the fog. The fog has been rolling inland as it usually does on a winter morning and is now evaporating under the warming sun. Far out over the ocean, the fog still appears murky and as dense as the water. Cars line both sides of the street, and further from the street, buildings stand still in the thinning haze; altogether the whole scene impresses on him a surreal sensation as though he is trapped in a painting.

He comes to the Pacific Coast Highway, turns left, and begins to speed. A notion occurs to him that he is wasting his time, he has wasted the last few precious days, and his only objective should be to find more powder and, if possible, to make more. Out of nowhere a sense of panic overwhelms him. He must get to the laboratory fast, and suddenly his foot presses down upon the gas pedal. The car shoots forward, squeezing them both against the seats and leaving behind a chaotic quake of fog. Maya, who has been reading, stops and stares at him. He glances at her and smiles faintly, reassuring her. He turns to her and then back to the road repetitively as he speaks to her.

—It's OK, darling. There's no one on the road. No need to fear. I don't know if you remember the traffic before. There were so many cars that you could hardly move. Stop and go. Yeah. Remember how it was? Stop and go.

—I . . . remember.

Occasionally, vehicles protrude diagonally into the street, but he can spot them a long way off and steer the car smoothly away from them. All the traffic lights are dark. As the car speeds past each one, he cringes a bit; he is still not habituated to the abandonment of the city and the implicit freedom.

Then a dark shape flies toward him from the left, buzzing like a hornet. It comes into the periphery of his vision and triggers an instinctual response. He slams on the brake and at the same time swerves the wheel away from the object. Maya screams. The car spins around, the tires screech, and as it stops in the middle of the street, he sees another car facing him, maybe fifty feet away. It is a large black SUV—a Chevrolet Suburban. Maya's scream and the sight of the man behind the wheel of the other car bewilder him. Squinting, he can make out a large head, almost touching the roof of the car, and broad shoulders. Another person alive, he thinks, and his heart jumps. What can it mean? How is it possible? Indescribable excitement and fear of the unknown flash over him. But very quickly fear takes over, and he finds his hand fumbling over the back seat for the shotgun that flew onto the floor of the car during the abrupt stop.

A silent stillness separates the cars. Slowly the door of the other car opens, and a pair of boots comes out, followed by an old pair of jeans. The man emerges from the car and stands tall; his head extends above the car's roof. He wears a brown jacket and looks at them from small eyes that seem buried deep in the sockets.

—Hello. Hey? the man calls out.

Only now does he hear the quivering moans coming from Maya. He lets go of the gun and grabs her arm.

—It's OK, darling. It's OK. It's OK.

While comforting her, he keeps his eyes on the man.

Aided by the surge of adrenaline, different thoughts go through his mind rapidly. The man appears harmless enough. After all, what can the man possibly want from him that might necessitate violence? Why, all the world is for the taking. They might be the only ones left, and there before him is another man, who survived the Death Sleep. How has he stayed alive?

—Are you all right? the man shouts. He takes three steps forward and leans against the car. By the movement of his torso, he seems to be uncomfortable about something.

—Maya. Stay here.

Art opens the door and looks at the shotgun for a second before stepping out. Waving his hand, he approaches the man. When he is several yards away, he stops. He stares at the man with a strange fixation, and his jaw slackens as though curiosity has taken over. The man, too, looks at him and is breathing heavily.

—Are you OK? I'm sorry . . . I didn't see you.

The man's voice crackles hoarsely.

—Yes. I'm fine, Art says and nods to him for no particular reason.

The man tries to walk toward him, dragging his left leg.

—I'm so happy to see you. George . . . George Cannon. Nice to meet you. You don't know . . . Well you know how it is. Thank goodness for another person.

—Arthur Sand. Call me Art.

Art comes closer. But George Cannon stands firm now and leans on the car as if he is unable or unwilling to move forward. Art extends his hand and they shake. At least a foot shorter, Art looks up at the man and studies the full face with its bulges of deep-creased skin, the brown hair already graying, the thin lips, and the large, downward-turning nose. Even in the cool early morning, a layer of perspiration covers his face.

—How . . . I guess you figured it out too, George says.

—What about you? Art says. He is wondering that very question himself but does not know quite how to ask.

—Epinephrine. Isn't that how you're still alive?

—Yes.

—Do you know what it is? What's causing all this? They just sleep and sleep. And did you see what they did before they fell asleep? Oh, it was awful. Like animals. Not just animals but like mad dogs, mad cows. All that violence. Oh, God, why did it happen? Why?

Spidery blood vessels web George's eyes, and his face appears lividly pale. As he talks, he seems to be struggling with some processes inside him, dividing his attention.

—I don't know. No one knows, Art says.

—It came only slowly at first, then all at once. You know, I started to drink more and more coffee. But it wasn't enough. It got so bad that it seemed like I was drinking nonstop. George inhales and continues. Then I got to thinking, you know, there are other stimulants. What do you call it? Oh yes, sudafed. My doctor gave it to me once and I couldn't sleep all night. So . . . so I started using that but it didn't last long either. You know I've been breaking into pharmacies and upping the dose.

—What about the epinephrine? How did you start using that?

—I figured there had to be something stronger. So I went through the books at the pharmacies. Pseudoephedrine, epinephrine, amphetamine.

George bends over the hood of the car, puts his head down,

and begins to sob. The large hands with the thick round fingers cover his face.

—It's horrible. Every four hours I have to inject myself. My heart just beats so badly, my head is pounding. I can't take much more of this. I can't.

—George, you have to hang on. Maybe it will pass, Art says monotonously, coldly, and automatically as he's said many times before the Death Sleep, when he had to offer condolences to surviving family members of a patient who had died. Only there is neither compassion nor empathy, only logic in the statement—a logic of default, because outside of that no other option exists.

Suddenly George's head pops up, in his eyes, a searching menace. He says, What about you? How did you figure it out?

Art hesitates; in his mind, dull mental processes quicken at a hint of threat, and what he is about to say can lead to some unknown, unfathomable dangers. The steps of deduction are now too difficult. The image of the shotgun flashes through his mind.

—I'm a doctor. . . . I know about stimulants.

—How do you handle the headache? My heart is just jumping. It's hard to breathe, too.

—Different people are different.

—How much are you using? I need five milligrams now. I've been upping the dose. I don't have much more time, buddy. I got cases of the stuff in the car but it's not going to help. My heart will give out soon enough. Or my head. My legs sometimes go numb and weak.

—Five milligrams, that's very high. You should be dead already. But then you're a big guy. You can tolerate a higher dose, Art says.

—I think so.

—What did you do before? I mean your profession.

—I was a lawyer, but don't hold that against me.

—No, no. Of course not.

—Is that your little girl?

Art looks back at the car as though searching for something strange that George has just pointed out, and to his amazement he sees Maya's head on top of her thin neck. An incredible happiness swells over him, tingling his scalp, and enlivens him. His mind, if not actually as sharp and alert as it was before, now feels to be so. You see her too, he almost says. Art smiles.

—Yes, that's my girl. He waves to Maya. From inside the car, she waves back.

—You keeps her awake with epi too?

Art hesitates. His mind still buzzes with the realization that she truly exists. How should he answer or should he answer at all? The silence, like the fog, hangs in the air. Since the emergence of the Death Sleep, human mental processes have slowed drastically, and the silence is regarded as an inability to comprehend or to formulate a response and not as an attempt at subterfuge. George waits for the answer with unquestioning eyes.

—What are you going to do? George says after a while.

—What do you mean?

—When the epi stops working?

—I don't know.

—I shouldn't even bother. I really shouldn't. What's the use? Right? Injecting myself every four hours. Not getting any sleep. I should just let it go.

—No, Art begins but doesn't want to finish with a platitude, and were he to say anything at all, it would be to pave the way for him to withdraw as humanely as possible, to leave this man to his own wretchedness.

—We should stay together, George says, continuing as if he does not hear. There are only few of us left.

—What's the use?

—You're right, buddy. Sooner or later, we'll all be done for. It can't go on.

—Exactly.

—How do we keep in touch?

—I don't know, Art says, not knowing a single reason why they should even keep in touch, but he knows well why they shouldn't.

George takes out a yellow notepad and writes something on it.

—Here's my address. Hollywood Hills. North of Sunset. You know, just in case you ever need something. Anything I can do for you. You can still find paper maps in some liquor stores.

—Thanks. I will.

—Thanks, buddy. Thanks. God bless.

Turning away quickly, Art doesn't want to show his frowning face. Even now, religion incites a sense of dense, unthinking immobility, stifling him; perhaps George meant it only as one would say *good afternoon*, or *goodbye*, a cultural greeting, an unintentional reflex. Art sits in the car, looks ahead without seeing, and is only minimally aware that George still leans over the SUV and seems to be resting. He senses Maya's large oblong eyes on him. Then the unthinking mind begins to stir, different thoughts of how the world has come to be as it is flit through his consciousness, but there are also emotions, mainly sympathy darkly colored with guilt. The human world has died as though the human life force having endured all odds for millennia has suddenly given out. No, that's not right, he thinks; it was snuffed out and that makes all the difference.

His eyes survey the empty street, the lifeless buildings, some burnt out, the abandoned cars, and George standing there with his head slumped over his SUV. Art's consciousness absorbs the vista and finally turns upon itself. Must he also perish? Must he completely change himself to reflect the world? His essence, an abstract construct that even as a teenager he'd formulated with gushing pride, now comes to him like a strange ghost, outside and distinct from him. Honor, compassion, charity, truth, and all other high-minded qualities together made up his essence and constructed the road that, were he never to deviate from it, would lead him to a destination as yet unseen, the ultimate truth of life. Wanting to do good, he became a physician, and wanting still more, he worked to advance the human species so he devoted his life to science. But now he is witnessing the death of his essence, the slumping of George Cannon over the hood of the car, the prototypical lawyer in his despair. No, my essence will remain, he thinks.

Such thoughts ramble on in Art's confused mind, gaining more and more weight, until the heaviness of this thought, as often happened in the minds of men, outweighs the mass of the whole universe existing outside it and even convinces him that the latter is swayed by the former.

Looking at Maya, he smiles a bright and happy smile. He searches on the back seat and finds a small paper bag. Then he uncaps the bottle of powder and pours a third into the paper bag. He jumps out of the car and goes up to George.

—George, listen.

Lifting his morose face from the hood of the car, George fastens his swollen, bloodshot eyes on Art.

—George. Why don't you try this? He holds up the brown paper bag. I've been using this stuff. It's better than epinephrine. You won't get the side effects.

George straightens up; his face enlivens with a sharp focus.

—What's this?

—Diethylamphetamine. It's a modification of amphetamine. A much stronger neural stimulant.

His hands tremble as George takes the bag and slowly opens it; a haze of powder floats to his nose.

—Take the tip of your finger. Wet it inside your mouth, dip it into the powder, and put it under your tongue.

George raises his knitted eyebrows.

—Go on. Try it. You'll feel better.

A tentative finger goes in his mouth and trembles as it moves inside the bag.

—That's right, George. Now put it under your tongue.

As he does so, he turns around and leans against the car, breathing deeply.

—How do you feel? It works very fast. It gets absorbed into the blood vessels under your tongue. Within a minute it's in your brain.

Now swallowing repeatedly with a convulsive spasm, now breathing, George keeps his eyes closed and his head extended for a minute.

—It's so . . . so much clearer.

Finally he opens his eyes, brimming with tears, and looks at Art.

—It's so clear. Just like how I used to feel. Buddy, you just saved me.

—Take it like that every six hours.

—Like a shroud was over my head. It's so clear now. You saved me.

—I'll see you later.

—Wait a minute. Wait a minute, he says, out of breath. How will I find you? I'll need more than this. Right?

—I don't have more.

—How are we going to survive when this is gone? He holds up the bag.

—That will last you at least a month.

—Then what?

—I'll make more.

—You can? Of course you can. Of course you can. You made this stuff, right? You can make more. We're saved.

—I was actually on my way to the lab.

—You dear man, you saved me. How can I possibly thank you? George lunges forward, puts his enormous arms around Art, and squeezes him tightly.

Dusty stale odor from his clothes overwhelms Art who does not wish to offend.

—Don't mention it. It'll take some times for me to make more. Art pats him on the chest.

—How do I find you?

—You can wait for me here. I go this way to the lab.

—Perfect. Perfect. It's so clear.

—Until then, Art says and turns to go back to the car.

—Art, George shouts after him. There are others in central LA. I heard gunfires.

But Art keeps walking, not really hearing what was said.

From inside the car, Art keeps his gaze on George, who stands by his SUV and waves to him. George's eyes now seem to beam with strange clarity and focus, and Art sees a sly machination behind the look. He makes a U-turn and again speeds toward Wilshire Boulevard. George lingers in his mind; that towering frame of flesh seems to possess its own gravity, attracting insatiably toward itself all required sustenance. It is full of life, and it goes along taking what it needs to fulfill itself, using every means, every deception that's available to it until the time when it must end. Why didn't he see that with George? Because of a juvenile abstract notion of essence, Art gave him a third of the powder without deducing the logical end of that insatiability. The image of that enormous torso, the long and powerful arms enclosing him so completely during the hug, and the beaming devious eyes suddenly constitute a life and death struggle. Art dismisses the thought. I can make more, he thinks and feels pleased with himself as though he could do so easily.

Art glances at Maya, seeing her dark, innocent eyes and perhaps recognizing approval in them. Can she possibly understand what went on?

—Maya, did you hear his name? His name is George. Seems like a clever guy. He figured out how to survive. That counts for something, don't you think? Isn't that what it's all about? It counts for something. Maya, I gave him a third of the powder.

Holding a different book, she raises her oblong, indifferent eyes.

—You're reading very fast. Are you sure you can understand everything?

She goes back to the book.

Everything appears as it did a few days ago. The lines of cars along the sides of the street are punctuated here and there by haphazard vehicles that must have careened out of control just as the drivers passed out. The dark halos of heads over steering wheels appear as they were. Near Wilshire Boulevard, as he slows the car for the turn, he sees far out over the sand a figure lying face down; it's the same person he saw. Turning left onto Wilshire, he drives steadily. The sight of buildings, billboards, and worded signs passes unconsciously. Ahead of him is the laboratory where he'll find the bottle of amphetamine in the locked cabinet. On the shelves in his office, he'll find the chemistry books, and he must try to recollect what he learned years ago and figure out the chemical reactions to make the powder. The powder is amphetamine modified ten times over, and its final unique configuration must be exact so that it can diffuse into the brain and stave off the Death Sleep.

Unconsciously retracing the usual route, he drives east on Wilshire, passes Muraki, and turns toward the laboratory. The street and the buildings become familiar, and just as he begins to see the entrance into the parking lot, he suddenly slams on the brake. The car screeches to a stop. Things shift in the back. Maya growls and turns to him.

—I'm sorry, darling . . . but I have to ah . . . ah . . . do something.

An echo of an important thought comes to him. He gazes in front of him; something familiar about that structure—a four-story building with a glass façade—tugs at him.

—There is . . . Art says.

He turns to Maya who puts down the book and also gazes intensely at the building. Seeing her demeanor, he remembers— biology not psychology. Now he sees clearly the sign in front of the building

SILVER SPRING INSTITUTE OF PSYCHIATRIC REHABILITATION.
ADULTS AND ADOLESCENTS

—Maya. I have to get something. Stay here. Nothing to be afraid of. There is no one around. I'll be right back.

Her eyes widen, and both of her hands push against the dashboard. He knows what she must feel, but it has to be done.

—Don't go . . . Papa.

—Don't worry darling. Don't worry, he says and goes out.

Things appear as he left them. The door is still open with the chair jammed against it. A musty stench still lingers, but the thick scent of death is no longer there. Through the waiting room, he enters the front reception area. The corpse that collapsed the day he first went in is lying on the floor, face down, exactly as he remembers it. Along a wall of the reception area are filing cabinets, and he opens them, takes out papers, and flings them away carelessly. They are useless papers, printed forms, instructions, pamphlets, and medical books. Toward the back wall is a door. Shining a flashlight, he goes through. Beyond is a small room with shelves along the three walls filled with charts. The charts are tagged with letters. The Cs are at eye level. Cahn, Cahn, he mumbles as he fingers through.

—Ah, here it is. Maya Cahn.

The manila folder is at least three inches thick, with hundreds of pages between its covers, and the pages are divided into different segments with colored tags—info, history, lab, X–ray, etc.

Outside again, Art sees Maya sitting in the car. He waves to her. He goes back to the car, opens the back hatch, and carefully puts away the chart.

When he is back behind the wheel, he smiles lamely. He squints at her but can't decipher her feelings. Maya keeps her eyes ahead, fixed on the sign in front of the building.

—Now we're off to the lab. You'll like the lab. A lot of interesting things. The best part of all, you'll get to help me make more powder. I depend on it. You don't but I do.

7

That night, after Maya falls asleep, Art takes out the chart. A fine cloud of dust rises from the chart as he opens it; he sneezes several times. He looks at Maya who is breathing rhythmically, undisturbed. Under the flashlight, Art reads:

Silver Spring Institute of Psychiatric Rehabilitation. Adults and Adolescents

Admission Note.
Date: June 13, 20..

History of Present Illness:
The patient is a 14 year old female who was transferred from Children's Hospital. She was not accompanied by her parents or relatives. All medical history was obtained from the accompanying chart notes and transfer notes. She is unable to communicate. Apparently, she was hospitalized for two months for

pneumonia, urinary tract infection, and malnutrition. She was admitted to ICU for high fever and was worked up and treated for possible septicemia. After one week, she improved sufficiently and was transferred out to a monitored bed. There, she continued to improve. After two weeks, she was moved to the Pediatric Medical floor. Chest X-ray, urinalysis, and blood count have normalized.

She was transferred to us for psychiatric disorder, most likely catatonic schizophrenia and mental retardation.

NKDA.
Past Medical History: pneumonia, septicemia, UTI, malnutrition, catatonic schizophrenia and mental retardation.
Past Surgical History: Arterial line placement.
Family History: unknown.
Social History: unknown.
Medications: none.
Physical exam:
Height: 56 in. Weight: 70 lbs. Head circumference: 63 cm
Vitals: Temp– 98.5 HR–94; RR–22 BP–100/59

Nutritional Status:
At Children's Hospital, a nutritionist had been consulted, and attached report was reviewed. She was evaluated to be severely malnourished. Blood test at Children's Hospital showed that albumin level was low; total protein was severely low. Hemoglobin level showed severe anemia. She had enlarged abdomen, extremely thin extremities, washed–out appearance consistent with Kwashiorkor. Presently she appears to be in much better condition.

*Physical stigmata association for malnutrition and labo-
ratory findings have largely normalized.*

Developmental Assessment:
*She is unable to speak, unable to articulate sounds,
syllables, consonants, or vowels, etc. She is able to make
grunting noises. Sometimes she shows signs of understanding when spoken to. Brainstem–evoked auditory response,
performed at Children's Hospital, showed that auditory
pathway is intact. There were normal wave forms.*

*Physically, she is at Tanner stage 2. This indicates
extreme maturational delay for her age. This was probably due to malnutrition, psychiatric illness, and other
social factors including issues of child abuse. Other causes
of speech and physical developmental delay, such as
genetic defects, Tay–Sachs disease, and cerebral palsy, can
not be ruled out without further studies.*

*MRIs of brain have been normal to date, ruling out
infection, brain tumors, demyelinating diseases, or other
organic brain lesions . . .*

06/14
*Patient is adjusting well to the ward. She is able to
tolerate the meals and daily routine without difficulty.
She kept mostly to herself during Yard Time and was
noted to sit in a catatonic daze. She remained uncom-
municative during examination today. But she displayed
a remarkable eye contact—not sure if she is able to
understand anything.*

Seroquel was started.

06/15

Patient had almost immediate side effects to Seroquel. There are tremors of upper and lower extremities as well as body and head shaking. She displayed paradoxical insomnia. The night nurse reported that she was crying and moaning all night long. She did not sleep at all. She refused breakfast this morning.

06/16

Dr. Salzman insisted on continuing the medication despite side effects. He reduced the dosage to the smallest dosage available. The patient continues to have severe extra–pyramidal side effects. She did tolerate some food during breakfast and dinner. She is still unable to communicate or follow commands.

06/17

She was found unresponsive this morning. Her vitals showed hypotension, tachycardia, and tachypnea. She was taken to the ER. Dr. Salzman was notified.

07/04

She was transferred back here from Children's Hospital. Transfer record shows that she had dehydration and electrolyte abnormalities. She has been off Seroquel since 06/17. She seems to have recovered completely from Seroquel side effects. She has resumed eating. She continues to be in a catatonic state. This may be her baseline condition. Dr. Salzman is considering another antipsychotic medication, or a combination of various antipsychotic medications. He hopes to improve her catatonia. Other therapies being discussed are psycho-therapy, behavioral therapy, or touch therapy. However, it is unlikely that she will benefit from these therapies if she is unable to respond.

07/15

Dr. Salzman prescribed touch therapy since side effects and recent hospitalization precluded further use of any medication. Touch therapy has been ongoing for one week. She seems to respond well. She has been displaying characteristic calming signs and making throaty sounds. It may be her way of signaling that she is experiencing stress relief. She has good eye contact and focus during the sessions. She has been able to repeat hand gestures; facial frowns and stressed expressions decreased.

She has been coming to all the reading sessions. She appeared to be listening and was able to pay attention for the entire session. However, she has not spoken a word, even when a question was directed at her. We are unable to ascertain whether she understands anything.

09/01

She does not display any symptoms of the Death Sleep. All workups so far have been normal. On the contrary, she has been displaying signs of being more alert, more attentive. She shows interest in helping the nurses and other patients. The nurses have agreed to allow her more freedom. She is allowed to go into the yard and the kitchen area whenever she likes.

09/15

She was moved to the third floor to be away from other patients. Some have fallen into periodic episodes of somnolence. One of the patients with signs of the Death Sleep, C. K., launched himself at her; however, it was unclear if he was attacking her. She tried to help him get up.

10/03

She is the only patient still awake. The Death Sleep has taken all other patients. Most of the nurses also showed symptoms and have stayed home. Dr. Salzman has died. No one else is coming.

The daily notes stop there. But lower on this page, there is a large handwritten note, words that had been scratched, etched deep into the paper as if with a pen whose ink was running dry. It reads:

We   a Miserable Minority.

Art trembles. Who could have written that? Mostly likely a nurse. Did she survive? Could she have been the one he shot? Curiously the letter A M M had been enlarged to a grotesque proportion as though the hand holding the pen could no longer bear fear and despair. He brings his fingers down, now moving over the surface of the page, tracing out the grooves that form the letters, reliving the intensity of fear and despair. Then suddenly his fingers jerk away, unsure if this conveyance from the past is a condolence or a curse.

Art looks through the laboratory data and the radiologic results, but he finds nothing useful, nothing that can explain how

Maya has survived while other patients with mental retardation, living in the same facility, succumbed to the Death Sleep. Somehow just like David Calweld, disparate parts of her brain connected and gave her a mind, a consciousness.

He glances at her. Why? he thinks. Why should you live and even become smarter when everyone else died? Maya is lying on her side, her legs pulled close to her chest, and from her small frame a profound mystery seems to radiate. And maybe because of their physical closeness, the approaching midnight augmented by the effects of the Death Sleep, and his having read her chart and the handwritten note, he feels hovering at the back of his neck an entwinement of him and her together in that asylum, real and inescapable. He shudders.

Some muffled sounds emanate from her throat as though she is trying to speak, and a sudden long shrill escapes. No doubt a nightmare is making her cry. He wants to awaken her but the noise stops. He watches her for another minute and then turns down the lamp.

8

Six brothers holding hands,
Their bond strengthened by peripatetic spirits swiftly
visiting each in turn.
Joined singly or doubly, perfect in symmetry,
Indistinguishable in mirror image.
So strong is their bond they exist in harmony and happiness
Until out of altruism a hand is extended to the outside,
Beyond their confine, sharing with others the wandering spirit.
The world latches onto them,
Tearing them out of the heavenly sphere of perfection.

—MAYA, THIS IS WHAT YOU BEGIN WITH. BENZENE. THIS IS HOW you make amphetamine.

He says this to her, remembering the poem he once wrote, but she is somewhere out of sight.

Art is flipping the pages of the chemistry book. Upon the pages, chemical symbols combine and form new and different compounds as they would in reality. Long ago, physical matters were deciphered and reconstituted abstractly in the minds of men. Matter could be manipulated to express the will of men. As he's read several chemistry texts over the last few days, these symbols have begun to make themselves known to him again; he remembers how as a graduate student he followed the steps to make different chemical compounds. He doesn't need to begin as far back as benzene. He already has amphetamine, and he only needs to build upon that to make more powder.

The clanking sound of glass bottles precedes her; she is holding a box with several bottles as she comes up to him.

—What have you got in there?

—Hydroxide . . . hah, methylene . . . acetic acid . . . all the chemicals . . . we need to make it, Papa, Maya says with a halting, high-pitched voice as though the connection between her thought and her speech has yet to solidify.

—Careful, darling. You know they're dangerous.

He takes the box from her and places it on the workbench where he has been standing. In the center of the bench are shelves holding various laboratory equipment: a small centrifuge, a Bunsen burner, glass rods, flasks of various sizes, beakers. Behind him are large windows. Sunlight brightens and warms the air.

—Now you have . . . everything you need.

—Maya, tell me again what we're going to do. Luckily we have amphetamine, so we don't have to begin with benzene.

—First, let me see. Cut off ethylamine . . . Next we will add a hydroxide . . . Then add another methyl . . .

She recites exactly what he wrote in the notebook, taking him days of preparation, poring over the chemistry texts and his old notebooks from graduate school. Still, he can't quite get over her progress; silent gazing has been replaced by wide-eyed inquisitiveness, an impeccable memory, and a reasoning ability that can follow any twists, any self–reflection with ease. Just being able to learn the names of the compounds and the steps of the reactions requires a considerable intellect for any age, let alone one as young as she. The wide, dark eyes wait for him when she finishes.

—That's great, Maya.

—But . . . words are not chemicals. Names are not chemicals. They pretend to be, don't they?

—I never thought of it that way. True. They're names. People use names to stand for things. That way it's easier to manipulate things, I suppose. They represent things outside of our minds. Yes, it's true that we will never see their true nature and will never know what they look like with our eyes. I will never know what a benzene molecule looks like. But I know what it is like when I put it through a spectroscopy machine. That's how we see them, with machines.

—How do I know . . . they are true?

—They were made and tested. They do what they are supposed to do, they act as they are expected to. They look as they are supposed to look when you put them through the spectroscopy machine.

—The spectroscopy machine . . . How does it work?

—There's a book about it in my office that you might want to read.

—Thank you, Papa.

—But read it later. Let's make the powder now. Everything has to be done inside the chemical hood, so put on your goggles. We'll close the hood when there is too much fume.

The amphetamine dissolves in a flask of solvent. He stirs the milky liquid, whose particles are at first clearly visible until they are finely dispersed in the liquid and become the liquid itself. Matter changes form before their eyes.

Maya's eyes seem to swirl with the liquid vortex as though witnessing for the first time another world coming to life and acknowledging matter.

—Let it sit while we prepare the next agent. See, we're just going down the list.

—Yes, Papa.

Next a yellow powder goes into the flask, and the milky liquid is transformed into a suspension of iridescent silver flakes. The flask feels warm to the touch. More stirring. Another liquid chemical makes the suspension cool. The flame of the Bunsen burner is applied. More stirring. If it is cold, it is put over the flame; if it's warm, it's stirred in a bath of cool water. The transformation of matter happens inside the flask, and as it does, it reminds him of how it was. The ghostly similitudes of lab assistants and graduate students coalesce out of the air and the sunlight, and there moving about him he sees them. Janet, the lab assistant, is as fastidious as ever. Her red hair is tied into a bundle; her eyes squint sharply at the flask before she measures out the chemical reagent to the exact milliliter. What she lacks in intellect, she makes up with persistence and practical skills. At the other end of the bench, Bob the graduate student wrinkles his forehead and peers at a solution that unexpectedly solidified. His tall frame and large arms appear clumsy among the delicate glassware and equipment, and though he is well versed in theory, he sometimes has difficulty making his knowledge work. Behind them, in the background of his hallucination, Barbara, John, and Ed move about busily. Yes, it was an engaged and successful laboratory, and Art himself was certain that he was on to something great, something that would shift the established paradigm. That something was to awaken patients lost in the nightmares of Alzheimer's disease, and during his most fanciful moments he imagined that it might one day cause the transcendence of man's consciousness and intellect into an ethereal plane.

Maya who has been staring at the whirling liquid says at last, How long, Papa?

—Oh, maybe an hour. Let's set the clock. You can have lunch while I stir. We're halfway through.

Maya sits down to a lunch of rice and fried Spam. She reads as she eats. How many books has she read? He can't remember all the books, but he is sure that their complexity has increased to logarithmic height. On her face, the pink glow of health and life is contrasted by deep blue veins that run along her neck, draining the blood from an unusually large head. He remembers from the chart: Head size is over 100 percentile and workups for hydrocephalus have been negative to date. Inside her large skull, the tightly wound brain seems to suck up all the nutrients, leaving little for the skinny body, and, through the eyes, requires a constant diet of words and ideas. Oh yes, an odd thought suddenly occurs to him: She is growing and must have enough calcium, just as it was with his daughter.

Now and then, Maya looks at the flask and the liquid inside swirling uniformly. Seeing her gaze and in that gaze a strange organization and ulterior machination suggesting something of a higher order, Art suddenly realizes his own thought that has been floating like a vapor in his dreary mind: What are the chances of his own survival, a survival that in turn affects hers? What about the transmutation of her intellect? As everyone else slept she awoke. The diagnosis of mental retardation has incredibly become, in his estimation, that of prodigy. At the end of the known human world, a rare being comes into existence, a being who escaped a common human fate and whose nature and humanity have yet to be determined. Can her existence be more than a coincidence? Can she be the personification of a clear and irrefutable proof of a higher order in the universe?

What about him? Why is he still here? he wonders. Was it because he gave up his medical practice to devote himself exclusively to scientific research even if that meant making much less money? No, that was not entirely true; David Calweld's death had something to do with it.

On the verge of his divorce or was it because of it, he'd decided to resign from a thriving medical practice. His overwrought brain can not possibly contemplate the origin of that decision nor the cause or effect of his divorce. Yet the moment of that decision now appears as crisp as the objects in front of him. That day, the sky was blue and cloudless all morning, and the sun was rising steadily and warming the grass Emily was treading barefoot upon. The white cloth tents had been set up over the grass in front of the lecture hall, and under them were chairs and tables upon which arrangements of orchids, giant strawberries, blackberries, Belgian chocolates, and a bewildering assortment of French pastries had been laid. Bottles of champagne were chilling in large baths of ice, and beside them servers in white jackets stood waiting for the crowd to stream out of the lecture hall. The Neurology Department had put on the best reception for a wealthy donor, a hedge fund manager from New York, who had single-handedly paid for a new building and funded a new research program into human cognition with the aim of curing Alzheimer's disease and other causes of dementia. Art was the keynote speaker and was to deliver an exciting new update on his own research breakthrough, the results of experimenting with new chemical compounds on mice's brains.

When he finished the lecture to enthusiastic applause, he withdrew through the side door and stepped into the sunlight to a vision of his wife and that financier. From far away, they appeared as though they were engaging in deep conversation or even some sort of communion of like-mindedness. Their profiles were locked in a strange diametric juxtaposition of opposing asymmetry, beauty and vivacity against cunning and wealth. The straight nose, gentle eyes, soft cheeks, and full lips, whose suppleness he often felt with his own, were transfixed in the air directly across from the large, bent nose with flanking nostrils, the squinting, narrow eyes, and the tightly curved, thin lips. The financier's head, completely bald and tanned, subdued the sunlight with an odd opacity, and his bent posture made him look shorter than she. Her very light brown hair flowed to her shoulders. How radiant and beautiful she was, Art remembers. About what were they together in communion? Art could only guess; perhaps, it was about the private jets, the art shows in London, the weekends in Paris, or the promise of meetings with rock stars.

Without a precise cause, a sadness at seeing them together crushed him. He wanted to call to her but could not; doing so would have made him small and helpless. Instead, he called to Emily, who was frolicking among the tents and at times giggling to herself. His call did nothing to Emily, who continued as before, but it shook Anna from her trance. She turned to him, and her face displayed an uncharacteristic awkwardness, a startled shyness tinged with an intimation of shame, as though she'd been caught in a terrible act.

On the way home that day, now and then Art glanced at his wife, whose eyes were perceiving something beyond the road. He could only guess where she was and thought that perhaps she was already on that private jet to Paris. That marked the exact moment when he felt that incalculable feeling of absurdity, when he'd decided to leave the practice and to devote the rest of his life to medical research. Six months later, she informed him of her wish for a divorce and her decision to give up her dermatology practice and move to New York with Emily.

THE MID-AFTERNOON SKY IS STILL BRIGHT WHEN ART AND Maya finish. The day's work results in a mere ten grams of powder. Art carefully pours the powder into a brown glass bottle to shield it from the sunlight. As a matter of habit, he cleans up and puts away the equipments and glasswares before they leave.

On the familiar way back, both of them search eagerly for George Cannon. He'd waved them down two days before and questioned them about the progress in making the powder. Art promised he would let George know as soon as he succeeded, and now he drives slowly along the Pacific Coast Highway searching for that big frame, the reddish face that is perpetually covered with sweat.

—Maya, will you look for him too? Your eyes are sharper than mine.

—Yes, Papa. But how do you . . . know it will work?

—Of course, it will. Why shouldn't it? We followed the reactions exactly. At each step, everything was as expected. And it feels the same as the powder I've been using. Believe me, I know what it feels like. I feel it four times a day, every day.

—Papa, are you sure? What about . . . the...hah . . . the spectroscopy machine? Isn't that . . . hah . . . how you see things . . . that your eyes can't see?

—I suppose we could do that. I'm sure I can find a spectroscopy machine and figure out how to use it.

—Papa we should . . . know for sure.

—Maybe for your mind. Your intellect, a rigorous demand

for the truth. I respect that in you Maya. But we don't have that luxury now.

—If it's not . . . the same as the powder you have, will it . . . hurt George?

—Why should it? It's modified amphetamine. Even if it's not the same, why should it harm him?

ART STOPS THE CAR AT THE PLACE HE FIRST MET GEORGE. HIS fingers clasp the bottle of newly made powder in his pocket as he walks along the street and enjoys the crisp cold air. When he's about a dozen yards away, he turns and heads back to the car. Maya sits watching him. The strong sea wind is blowing as it does every afternoon. Sunlight warms his face, and the sensation produced by the mutually effacing effects of warm sunlight and cold sea breeze is quite agreeable and induces a strong sense of nostalgia. Walking along the beach was an activity that he and his daughter often enjoyed; he remembers days like this, when they ran after one another and were completely oblivious of everyone else. Undeniable pride and hope, no doubt instigated by his success in creating more powder, fill him; the success is as much for himself as for George. He hasn't experienced such liveliness and energy since the world became quiet. He walks on for a hundred yards or so, lost in remembrance, but at last worrying about Maya, he turns around and is ecstatic to find her following him at a distance. She is walking on the edge of the sidewalk, trying to balance herself on only the left halves of her feet.

—Come on. Let's go for a walk. We need exercise.

—What . . . about George? Maya screams against the wind.

—He knows our car. He'll wait for us.

On a sudden impulse, he runs toward the sand. Maya squeals and runs after him. The water's edge is farther than he thinks. In the distance he sees the silhouettes of animals trotting in a curtain of dust, too far away to see clearly. Dark figures, partially covered by drifted sand, are scattered on the beach, immobile under the sun as though they're sunbathing, and the whole scene eerily resembles how it was during the winter when only hardy souls would venture out onto the cold sand, seeking solitude. The wind has carved the sand into beautiful ridges as wild and virginal as it was before the first man walked on it. They run headlong toward the water and luckily, they don't come across anything. Maya tries to keep up and kicks up the sand as she runs. Now and then she stoops and picks up a handful of sand, feels the grains in her fingers, and scatters them in the wind.

White foam marks the edge of the water as the oncoming waves crash over the shallow bank and wash up the perfectly smooth incline of sand. Beyond the foam and the surf's upheaval, the water has a faint green tinge. Further out, dark blue water undulates violently. Pelicans pitch high on the wind and fall straight through the water's surface to hunt for fish.

Art and Maya stand just beyond the reach of the water and stare out to sea, captivated by an unseen force. Neither speaks. Several miles to the south, the dark shape of a super tanker that ran aground juts against the sky like a small island.

After a while, Maya sits down and plays with the sand, now sieving it, now picking it up only to let it drop and spread out with the wind. She giggles with delight. What child can resist the sand? Art thinks. Emily was the same and would protest if she was taken away too soon. He leaves her and paces toward the south. He tries to think as he often did after Anna took Emily to New York. Back then, his thoughts were more mournful than penetrating, and an awful hurt glazed all his wakeful moments, benumbing his reason, hemming in everything, and trimming away all sensibilities except for a pointed consciousness. And for all those thoughts whatever they did for him then, in the face of the enormous Death Sleep they now amount to almost nothing, an indistinguishable mark on the brain of an incidental man. What should he think about now? He must think, since the sea has that thought–inducing effect. Denying the material life or taking on an enlightened stoicism—regardless of Anna's mocking manner and insinuation about the cause of his sudden devotion to medical research—led him to where he is today, incidentally alive. Can it be a sort of cosmic karma? If she hadn't taken Emily, his daughter would be here now; if she herself hadn't left, she would be here too. One can always blame someone, especially the dead. They are sleeping now. Or could they still be alive, or at least Emily, by a miracle? Why can't Anna be alive too? Perhaps she must be punished, after all she left him for a life of private jets and luxury. No, he shouldn't judge, but neither can he suppress a sensation of schadenfreude as natural as breathing, and its amplitude is in direct proportion to the hurt he experienced.

Don't blame, he thinks. Not now, not anymore. But most of all have some guts, tell the truth. You were as guilty as anyone, cruel certainly. What did you do? Tell the truth, but where do you find the truth? If not during your waking moments then from dreams. Remember that one dream, that particular dream when you woke up regretting? To regret a dream? It was brutal, certainly. You remember, don't you?

Hitting hard not with his palm but with a closed fist, he punched the face and then went away only to come back, hitting it again and again, yet it remained untouched, bouncing back, hitting back at him with a bemused, stubborn, condescending smirk until the futility of it all overcame him, strong and desperate. In that brutal dream it was Anna's face. His mind couldn't, simply couldn't dream up and stitch together an absurd pastiche from snippets of real life while ignoring the ugly consequences, the connecting segments of reality conveniently scrubbed from his memory, a form of useful amnesia. Could it?

Then he sees the dogs. Their shapes move close to the sand, and as he was preoccupied with his own thoughts, their gradual presence did not arouse the slightest agitation. Now he fixates his eyes on them and can delineate their exact movements. There is something very barbaric about what they're doing. They jump, pull, drag, shake their heads. Oh, how sickening. An intense nausea rises from his stomach. As one bites off a piece, it runs away to a distance to feed, to swallow the chunk whole, and immediately it runs back to join the others. Some collide, brush past one another; their tails are raised high; off to the side are two facing each other, growling and barking. Being upwind he hears only a faint bark now and then. In all there may be a dozen of them of different types—Shepherds, Rottweilers, pit bulls. Without the presence of people, the dogs have shed millennia–old domesticated restraint, and as though seeking vengeance, they now feed upon the corpses. From corpse to corpse, they have been moving closer to them all this time.

Entranced by the spectacle, Art stands there, dazed by mental dullness and voyeuristic curiosity. He can't seem to move or speak until the thuds of his heart pound against his chest. He walks sideways toward Maya and continues to watch the dogs. At a distance of more than a hundred yards, a single dog catches his scent and looks at Art who stands out prominently on the deserted beach; it points his snout at him and barks. Though Art can see the dog barking, he can't hear past the thumping of his heart. Suddenly the reality of impending danger breaks through his consciousness, and he yells to Maya.

—Maya, run. Run to the car.

He sees Maya's wide, bulging eyes, but can't seem to wait for her. He takes a couple of steps.

—Maya, run. Run fast as you can. To the car.

Instinctively, Art breaks into a full run, retracing their footprints. The tall ridges of sand that only moments ago were delightful playthings for Maya become a series of unending obstacles; over them he tries to lift his feet as he runs. How tiring it is to run on sand. His strength is scattered as his feet kick up the silicate particles. He hears howling. The howls of the dogs grow louder, each howl answers another, and in unison they grow in strength, in viciousness. He looks to the north and is horrified by the sight of paws earnestly kicking up sand as many dogs head to intercept him. The dogs are coming from north and south, and having tasted human flesh, they hone in toward its scent.

He screams without looking back.

—Faster Maya.

His legs pound against the sand while he thinks that he must get to the car. The shotgun that has been by his side all this time is in the car. If he has only one shot, that will be enough to scare them off. Their heavy panting and the commotion of their bodies in chase are now audible. Just over there, some dozens of yards away, abandoned cars litter the parking lot. Already he knows what he must do—run through the parking lot, to the street, to his car and the shotgun. He will be in time to save Maya.

Then he hears her shriek. Maya, Maya, what am I doing? he thinks. Turning around, he sees the dogs moving with incredible agility as they leap toward her, their tongues flopping, their teeth gleaming white, and their ravenous eyes delighting in the chase.

In her eyes he sees only dead white. Her mouth hangs open as she sucks in air. Without thinking, he charges toward them, and all at once from his lungs he bellows a piercing, deafening howl. The dogs scatter in confusion; some of them stop, while others move off at a distance and continue barking as though testing and challenging him. The few smaller dogs even yelp meekly, their tails fold between their legs, and they lie flat on the sand. The human howl seems to have reignited the force of domestication.

Seeing them in confusion, he is encouraged for the moment; he growls more loudly, showing them his teeth. His bulging eyes stare at them.

—Keep running. Keep running to the car, he yells to Maya.

—No, Papa. Go . . . They will . . . hurt you.

—Run, Maya. Now.

He is between Maya and the dogs. He backs slowly away from them; a half circle of dogs of various sizes forms. Remembering the knife in his pocket, he gropes for it and pulls it out. The steel blade unfurls with a click. Feeling the hard knife in his hand spurs an enormous relief; he waves and crosses it in the air, hoping they understand its meaning. His teeth grind as he growls at them again.

—I'll kill you all. You filthy animals.

Some of the bigger dogs, refusing to back down, snarl and snap their jaws, sharp teeth dripping with saliva. They move forward in lockstep with him, keeping their heads low and slowly flicking their raised tails.

From a distance, more dogs dash toward them. A German Shepherd charges through and leaps. Art shields himself with his right arm. The dog's jaw catches his arm tightly. He stumbles back, and the left hand, holding the knife, thrusts at the dog's neck. On the second thrust, a squirt of blood follows the blade out. The dog falls to the ground; soft gargling whimpers come from its mouth. Blood continues to pour, soaking quickly into the sand.

Triumphant, Art waves the bloody knife in the air and stomps his feet, kicking up the sand.

—Away, shoo . . .

Instead of deterring them, the smell of blood drives them into a frenzy. They begin to howl and bark more ferociously. The ones closest to him make small leaps with their front paws up high as though preparing to charge in.

Art hunkers down, raises his right arm, dripping blood, and braces himself against another charge. Suddenly, a shot shakes the air. From the corner of his eye, he glimpses the towering figure of George sloshing through the sand. The dogs freeze for a split second and then scatter in all directions. George pumps the shotgun and shoots after them again and again, but at that distance the sound terrifies them more than actual injury.

Maya is close behind George when they come up to Art.

—Good grief, Art. Are you all right? I'm sorry I couldn't run any faster. I'm sorry, George says, breathless.

—Papa, they . . . hurt you.

Maya cries; she tugs at his arm.

Only now does he sense the pain, lacerating, moving up the right arm toward the elbow. He takes off the jacket. On the forearm are two puncture wounds two inches apart, oozing blood.

—It's not so bad, Maya. Don't cry.

—What the hell is with the dogs? George asks. Do you think they have the disease, too? I mean they seem to be getting nasty and violent like people did just before they all slept.

George gasps and looks at the dogs disappearing into the distance; he holds up a pump–action shotgun with a long barrel.

—I don't know, George. The disease may be making them more aggressive.

—Let's get you bandaged up.

His whole body shakes when the alcohol is poured over his arm. Sharp pain seems to screw into the flesh and burrows up to his shoulder. Before George bandages his arm, Art runs his fingers along the length of the radius and ulna.

—Art, are they broken?

—No, George.

—Thank goodness. It's a good thing I saw your car. Good thing you parked right in the street. I knew you were around somewhere. Then I heard the dogs.

—They . . . hurt you, Papa.

—Just two small wounds. I'll live. Don't you worry.

George presses the elastic bandage against the wrist and rolls it toward the elbow.

—A little more pressure. It'll start to swell soon.

—Sure.

—George, thank you. You've got everything in this SUV.

—Yup, you never know what you'll need. I've got first aid, water, guns, batteries, gasoline—anything you might need.

—Thank you, George. We'll get back now.

—No, thank *you*, Art. The powder is a miracle. I feel a hundred and ten percent better now. Headache is gone, chest feels much better, I can breathe. Say, why don't you come with me? I got a real nice setup. Big house with everything you might need. Even a generator. I'll help take care of your little girl while you recover. I'll even prepare you dinner. You can even watch a movie. He turns to Maya and says, How would you like to watch a movie?

—Movie? Maya utters.

—Yes, movie.

—Movie . . . I remember.

—What? You don't know what it is?

—She wasn't allowed to watch much.

—Wow. That's incredible.

—You're very kind, George. Maybe another time, but we'll head back now. I have to start antibiotics soon.

—Well, all right. Maybe another time.

Though his legs are not hurt, Art feels a heaviness in them as he walks to the car. His right arm begins to throb slightly. Then he remembers the bottle of newly made powder. He takes it out and calls after George.

—George.

—Yeah.

He hands George the bottle.

—We made it today.

—You made it? You really made it? We're saved. This is it, huh? Thank you so much. I owe you my life. I don't know how to thank you.

George launches forward and grabs Art in a tight bear hug.

Art drives with his left hand and tries to keep his right arm above his heart. Unnoticed, the sunlight has retreated as the sun approaches its winter solstice, nearing the horizon. The clouded sky is a pasty gray, and the wind whips the car with unrelenting blows. Thinking about the dogs, his mind swirls with what he must do, what he should expect from the injury, and the speed of his thought and the lucidity of his mind all of a sudden enliven him and make him giddy. The vibration of the engine, the acrid alcohol fumes in the air, the darkening road, the whole reality of things seem to be imbued with his consciousness.

—Ha ha. Nothing like a near–death experience to make you feel alive.

—Yes, Papa.

—Near–death experience, that's what we had. Those dogs could have killed us. And when you experience something like that, you cling to life. I've never felt better. I'm so alive.

Far ahead, a dog runs across the street. Perhaps it's a hallucination. He slows the car, and sure enough, a pack of dogs congregates on the far side of the street. Their ears perk up, listening, and some of them bark and look at the car.

—There they are, even if they're not the same ones.

Art stops the car and grabs the shotgun. He flings the door open and jumps out.

—No, Papa. No, Maya screams after him. They . . . are animals. Papa. They don't . . . know.

He turns back to Maya.

—You're right, darling. You're right.

9

At first, a slight chill, almost so slight as to be unnoticed, runs through his body along a well-worn path starting from somewhere low on his back and tingling up to his neck. The arm aches a little more but dinner has to be made, and in the backyard he follows the routine, throwing logs in the fire pit and opening a can of ham, knowing he will need more protein than usual to recover from the wounds. They eat silently under the yellowish light of the lamp. Maya's face shows a curious tension; her cheeks and lips droop morosely, while her eyes gauge his every movement and seem to study the bandaged arm.

—Don't worry, darling. I'll be fine, he says to her.

A fine being, even a profound being, a being with innate empathy and natural sensitivity, he thinks. She will be all that and more; how befitting it is for such a being to begin a new epoch. Naturally she fears that she will be left alone.

The lights dim; they will need new batteries soon. Now that it's quieter and no unknown sources of danger have materialized, except for the wild dogs, he might get an electric generator and restore some of the material comforts of his former life.

—Maybe tomorrow we'll get an electric generator, like George.

—Yes, Papa. And . . . watch a movie.

—Ha ha. Yes, we'll watch movies.

He hasn't laughed like that for so long. The laugh emanates from his whole being and makes him happy as though it's the simultaneous popping of all the bubbles of joy that have been hidden among the cells of his body. The last time he laughed like this was years ago when Emily demanded to ride on his back. How she clung to his hair, pulling him this way and that, her legs wrapped around his chest, and next to his ear she roared with laughter. Finally he'd swung her around, embraced her tightly, and showered her with kisses.

Then another chill, a strong and unmistakable shiver along his back, suddenly awakens the throbbing pain in his arm. He rises from the dinner table to search for antibiotics. The dogs had fed on the human corpses before biting him, and they must carry human gut bacteria in their teeth—Clostridium, Bacteroides, E. coli and other bacterias native to the dogs. Ordinarily, a dog bite is nearly harmless, whereas a human bite deadly. But this is more serious than he imagined. In the drawers of his desk, he finds the bottles of antibiotics; he decides on Clindamycin and Augmentin.

As Art unwinds the bandage, he sees its outline etched into the swollen, red skin. Dark veins pulsate. Yellowish, viscous mucus oozes from the two puncture wounds. When he brings his arms together side by side, the swollen right arm startles him. He pours Betadyne over the wounds, washes them, and wraps a new bandage over the arm. A dizzying heat now hovers around his face and neck, a peculiar thirst dries his throat, and simple swallowing imparts a grainy sensation to the back of his tongue. Unconsciously he moves into the bedroom. He lays the bottles of medication on the nightstand and settles into the bed, fully dressed in his blood–splattered pants. Outside, the wind raps and pushes, the whole house creaks in defiance, and something is scraping against the windowpanes.

Pain roars up the length his arm like an electric zap, and at last feeling around his head a halo of heat dangling dead in the air, he loses himself.

—Maya. Maya, he calls to her when he awakes suddenly. He checks his watch, he has slept six hours.

Under the dim light of a lamp, he sees Maya lying at the end of the bed.

—Come to Papa.

She moves cautiously toward him.

—Maya, darling. Listen carefully. I need your help. The dog bite is more serious than I thought. The infection, my arm is infected and it's getting worse. I'm having chills and fever.

—No, Papa . . . no . . . You will be fine. You'll have to. . . .

—Listen, Maya. You need to be a big girl. You will need to help me. Just in case I can't do it myself. There are three bottles here. Pay close attention, please.

Throbbing pain squeezes up his arm and percolates into the arteries of his head; he feels their pulsation and their fiery heat, and with the throbbing, a pressure builds.

—This bottle is the powder. I need it to live, every six hours, just the tip of my finger. You know how I do it.

His voice strains and Maya nods.

Only now does he feel his heart pounding, pushing rhythmic pulses up. He struggles to expel sounds.

—The next bottle is an antibiotic. I need it. You must give it to . . . and the next bottle . . . go find George . . . if anything happens. . . . Find George. . . . The dogs. . . . Don't forget . . . the gun.

His thoughts vanish. Did I tell her everything? he thinks. Medicines need to be dosed exactly so that the drug concentration in the blood increases with each dosage, filling the area under the curve.

Tears well up in her dark, oblong eyes, and he wants to reach to touch her, to bring his lips to her head, but at the slightest movement of his right arm, a fierce pain jolts him. The hand is now locked in a rigor of its own, the fingers looking like appendages of an alien object. Closing his eyes, he sees the sequence of his life replayed with clarity, and in the same vision the concreteness of objects, the bed he lies on, and even Maya sitting next to him dissolve into the very swish of the howling wind outside the windows, into static indifference.

THE SUNLIGHT PAINTED THE WINDOWPANES IN LONG EXAGGERated shadows on the floor. Through the glass door leading to the garden, he saw the enormous bed of intensely red roses surrounded by a path of green Bermuda grass and the air outside that was saturated with pollen, insects, and dust reflecting rays of the afternoon sunlight. The darting eyes of a precocious eleven–year–old boy observed his father on the sly. Dressed in a dark blue suit with thin, gray stripes and with his hair combed slickly to the side, his father sat at the end of the sofa, reading the newspaper, waiting for his wife, and at the moment his demeanor assumed the role of a partygoer, an escort, a husband, and perhaps most importantly, a man of considerable social standing in a clique, whose eminence would surely be enhanced by his imminent arrival. His father was absorbed in the important news of the day, the stock market, and the editorial columns, and yet something seemed to intrude into his consciousness, interrupt his concentration—something that he was supposed to do. Art would remember that startled look of realization all his life—the look of regret at having lost something irremediably precious, at having traversed through life unscathed yet uncertain if that life still stubbornly possessed a modicum of virtue, a look Art would remember but not understand until it was his turn.

But on that happy afternoon, as they both sat on the sofa waiting, Art's fingers mimicked the musical notes of Bach's preludes until he heard his mother's voice from the bedroom. With much pretense, he moved nonchalantly to the piano, and his fingers fell on the piano keys at the moment the bedroom door opened. He knew that his mother would stand still at the threshold and that his father would quietly lower the newspaper to listen. Discreet joyous sounds of the one hand joined and enriched those made by the other, and together they created a pleasing, flawless melody. Oh, darling. Bach, my favorite. Have you been practicing? she exclaimed. In her dress, light green with a superficial silvery shine, she seemed to glide toward him. She kissed him, her lips barely touching his cheek, but immediately her thumb scrubbed the place her lips had touched, leaving no trace of red lipstick but only red irritated skin. Overwhelmed by the elongated, upward curves of her eyelashes, the perfectly braided hair, the intoxicating perfume, and the noisy ruffles of her dress, he did not hear a word from his father.

After they left, he knew that he'd accomplished his goal and that he would be the subject of their discussion, the source of their pride as they drove to their dinner party. Though his parents often argued, he thought they'd been happy together. His mother died in a car crash five months later. Everything remains frozen in place; the memory of her perfume—sweet, light, gay, intoxicating—remains in his mind unblemished, encasing her image, voice, touch, and even the sofa, the piano, and the light through the windowpanes in its amber rigidity, and by association his father is included.

Paradoxically, the fever, the headache, and the lancing pain in his arm seem to stave off the Death Sleep intermittently and, during these periods, suspend his mind in a sea of alertness so that even with eyes closed he senses his whereabouts, his bodily presence in the bed. Such is the working of the mind, he thinks. One is most conscious when one's mind is whetted by a threat of death and its total focus is directed inward, where a life that was carelessly stored can be retrieved, re–examined with the unerring objectivity of a microscope; and thus this sequence of life, preserved down to the floating specks of dust, is relived so that he can glean a forgotten lesson, a point lost. But what lesson, what point can possibly signify anything against the darkness of a new human reality? Where to next? He has nowhere to go, nothing to do but wait until the pressure in his head builds up enough and an artery explodes, his heart fails, or his lungs drown in their own fluid. A cold liquid touches his burning lips. Mustering all his strength, he raises his leaden eyelids and sees the hazy flickering of a silver spoon being shoved between his clenched teeth. He sucks at the cold water as full of purity and freshness as Anna's lips. Her image comes into view now, crowds out the flickering, silvery spoon, and pulls down his eyelids, already heavy with fatigue. He has no choice but to consent.

Regarding Anna, there was only one problem, in his own estimation, that might hinder her from becoming a good doctor as though there was ever a set of qualities that would make a person perfect for such a profession; it was that she was too beautiful to be among diseases. First of all, her large, languid eyes with their curved lashes and tender lids were something to marvel at, to idolize, and they could not possibly fathom even superficial human suffering, let alone empathize with or diagnose life–threatening illnesses. When she joined him at the table in the library where he'd been studying, he looked up to acknowledge her, but ever since he'd met her, a month into their first year at medical school, he'd never had the need to fully understand the reason for her wanting to be with him, for he merely felt it to be logical without ever actually delineating the steps involved in that logic. There was a vague confidence he had about himself, a sort of superiority not born of reality. To all outward appearances, he was certainly a smart student, having gotten into a combined M.D., Ph. D. program at a prestigious university, but with all things considered, intelligence is relative. Only Art knew that about himself; only he could know how he had to struggle with philosophy and mathematics, with simultaneously holding five objects in his mind and at the same time performing logical operations on them singly and in various combinations so that in the end he could attain a complex spider web of beauty. Time and again, he'd failed. No matter how hard he tried, he could not hold together the tenuous threads; he knew that he would never be a philosopher or a mathematician of any consequence. Only he could ignore the shadow of that failure, a permanent fixture in the corner of his mind, yet inexplicably it never diminished his sense of superiority. Even in the sphere of practical intellectual endeavor that was medicine, he was not the best in his class. That day in the library, Anna had sat down in front of him and proceeded to tell him how she had once again scored at the top of the class, how she had already been admitted to a dermatology residency. So, of the two of them, she was always the more intelligent, and perhaps too intelligent to be a good doctor. How is it that his feverish brain can see it so clearly now? The light he lit for himself has never diminished, like the candle before the eyes that obscures the sun. He never saw how luminous other lights were, the lights of the brilliant minds; even the lesser light of Anna was brighter than his. But what does it mean when they are dead, and yet he remains?

Nebulous air, fuzzy sunlight through the half-open window, shapeless infant toys, a curtain scintillating against the crib in which Emily lay, dark fluidity on the floor hiding his feet, and a strange resistance against his body as though moving inside a fish tank—these things he perceived as he went to check on Emily. The cherubic folds of her face, the curls of her hair, and the fluffy white shirt imparted an angelic aura. But her beautiful, round eyes fluttered. As he stood over the crib, he knew those flutters— an epileptic seizure. Was this the cause of it all? Anna must blame him. For the daughter of a neurologist to have epileptic seizures must denote the end result of some incomprehensible threads of karma. Though he knew that Anna did not blame him for their daughter's illness, being too intelligent to do so, the illusion of his supposed superiority over her and over a great chunk of the world was shattered. He could mark the diagnosis of Emily's illness as the beginning of Anna's bewilderingly contemplative demeanor, her look of being somewhere else even when they spoke, her ques- tioning him about everything when she had never done so before, and the endless carping and petty retorts. After all, Emily's exis- tence could be traced to the very structure of his and her DNA, and if such union was flawed, then their marital union could be no better. Her assuming his worldview, seeing the world through his eyes and applying his logic to it, must similarly be flawed, and the shock of such a realization, like the recoil of a cannon, must have rattled her awake with a disquieting force. At last, when she awoke, she reacted forcefully, as though during all those years of passivity she had saved up the energy of illusion and regret. He never saw any of it until now, but what good would it have done anyway? There was no way to prevent her from leaving, marrying a man in every respect different from him, and taking Emily with her. The only reason it took so long was finding the right opportunity. How clear everything is now.

The oppressive heat of the sun's rays beat upon his head, roasting him slowly. A tall glass of ice–cold lemonade with a slice of lime floating among the ice cubes and dripping droplets of water condensing on the side of the glass would be good now, and he'd love to slide it along his forehead. The heat dissipates. He brings the cold glass to his parched lips, but all he can taste is foul bitterness. The burning sand buries his feet; he looks down and there is a green expanse of grasses; and to his right and left hollow buildings loom, and in their shadows the glittering eyes of feral dogs watch. Which way must he go? Through the faraway windows of these hollow buildings, a small child's dark head suddenly moves, hopping from one aperture to the next as though transmigrating, while her hair wavers like a curtain in the breeze. Struggling to see, his eyes throb with the excruciating pulses of his heart, and his chest squeezes out his breaths. Now he must run, not to the child but away from the glittering eyes. The child is behind him; he hears her pattering feet. The dogs snap at his feet, their growling and barking more menacing than anything, and finally with the bite an incredible pain strikes. Instantaneously, the pain zaps along his right arm, spreads throughout all the fibers of his nerves, and, converging from all these disparate bundles, explodes in his head. His eyelids pop open; consciousness resumes; and he sees that Maya has just pulled off the bandage.

—I won't run in front of you.

What he says to her surprises him. Can he still be dreaming? Her eyes, wide and clear, fix on him, waiting. His fingers move, his right arm appears still swollen, and the two puncture wounds through their black centers stare back at him. He sees black, congealed blood on his pants, and at the sight of dried blood all his senses are restored; he smells the dense foulness of his own waste. Turning away from her, he cringes in disgust. His whole body stirs. His legs curl, his torso bends, and his left arm pushes himself up.

—Papa. You must rest. Stay still. I must bandage the wounds.

She rubs the wounds with Betadyne. How does she know to do that? Then the roll of bandage wraps around the arm. Gently she pushes him back toward the raised pillows.

—Papa, you must rest.

She holds a bowl toward him and shoves a spoon in his mouth. Her movement is natural, without a shred of hesitation as though she has been performing this her whole life. Despite a bitterness coating his tongue, he tastes the salty liquid and sucks it greedily.

—Maya, what day is it?

—Papa, you slept for five days.

10

Three days later as his consciousness and strength hold, he sees things as he remembers them. The two bottles of antibiotics and the bottle of the powder are where he put them. A glass of water, a spoon, and wet towels are on the nightstand. The brightness outside the window tells him it's morning. He moves to the bathroom to discard the clothes soaked in urine. As he stirs, his neck spasms with short spurts of pain, but still he keeps on, knowing that he has to get off the bed before immobility brings on other problems just as deadly, perhaps a blood clot in the legs, in the heart, or even in the brain.

The bathroom floor is cold as melting ice. He steadies himself over the sink. In front of him, the mirror seems to open up an alternate reality, in which his face has two hollow caves for cheeks, the eyes have sunk deeper, and the temples have disappeared behind the curves of the forehead. A sparse beard dots his upper lip and chin and connects with the short twirling hair of his sideburns. Instead of the moan of horror at his own emaciation that surely would have happened in the past, he studies his own reflection as he would study a bacteria or a pig shedding meat and fat if it were denied food, and why should he be any different? In the past, what would he have wanted after a bout of illness? Surely, he would have wanted to feel healthy again, to regain his weight, to swell his face with pink, soft flesh that could cover up the hard facts of existence and help him forget the inevitable, be it loss, death, disappointment, or stupidity. But now he wants none of it back, only to see it for what it is, skin over bone, white eyeballs deep in sockets, disheveled hair, all marks of a bodily passage, perseverance through ordeal. It should stay with him, what he learned when he was near death.

His right arm has nearly returned to its normal size, but the fingers creak awkwardly with each movement. He pulls off his clothes, steps into the tub, and turns on the tap. The cold water sputters out in slow irregular drips, soaks into his hair, digs into his scalp, and runs over his face; it's all very cold and makes him shiver. His muscles feel wasted and feeble. He cleans himself. A moment ago he was warm in bed dreading death; now he is shivering under the cold water, but senses full. What about five days ago? More fright and less life. Four years ago he thought he had a happy life, and now there is only life as pure, cold, and uncompromising as the water flowing over his body. Putting up his palm against the sputtering water, he sees the splashing droplets.

Suddenly the water dribbles and then stops altogether. The tank on the hilltop must be empty. Practical things needed for daily living confront him again. He and Maya must move on, find a new place, he thinks. Or they have to find another way to get water. He steps out of the shower. He realizes with pleasure how he thinks of himself and Maya, no longer any doubt of her existence. His finger runs over the two puncture wounds that have scabbed over and are another confirmation of that reality. She is real, and with an incredible happiness he goes to find her.

In the study, Maya is sitting at his desk, reading. As he looks upon her, he gasps. Altogether she has become another person; the familiar, large, oblong eyes gaze up at him, in them a tranquil, impervious air and an indescribable, endearing warmth. She has put on weight, her cheeks full and vivacious with a natural pink. He moves toward her, still very surprised, but does not know what has induced it, whether it is the visible change in her, the way her wit kept him alive, or the strange, indispensable sense of belonging that only increases in intensity as he comes near.

—Papa, you're up.

—Yes, hah, yes. I'm up. Maya, it's so good to see you. You don't know.

—How does your arm feel?

—Still a little painful. But the worst part is over. I'll be fine. How about you? I'm so sorry I left you all alone.

—I've been reading. I've read all these books. I've been reading mathematics too. It's beautiful, Papa, it's beautiful, she says breathlessly. Pi goes on forever and calculus. It's so clever to sum up small incremental changes as the variable becomes infinitely small. But Papa, Papa, what I love most is prime numbers, a number divisible only by itself and one, going on forever. They can be as large as infinity and yet they are like the number 3 or 5. Don't you see, Papa? All primes can be divisible by 1 and themselves, so they all have 1 in common and yet they all have themselves, their own identity. Don't you see, Papa? It's beautiful. Primes are like living things, each prime can be a living thing, Papa, all having 1 in common, like they all come from a single place. Don't you think, Papa?

Art looks at her and smiles.

—Yeah, I think you're right, he says. I never thought about it like that. You amaze me.

—I read Goldbach's conjecture too. I was trying to solve it. Will you help me?

—I'm sorry, darling. People tried to solve Golbach's forever, and I don't remember much mathematics anymore. You probably know more than I now.

—All right, I'll just read more about it. Prime numbers, they're beautiful.

—How did you know what to do? How did you know to give me the medicines?

—That's easy. You told me you needed the powder every six hours. The Augmentin twice a day. The Clindamycin four times a day.

—But how? There're no instructions on the bottles.

—I read the PDR.

—Physician's Desk Reference. Hah, Maya you amaze me.

—And I cleaned your arm twice a day. With the brown liquid, povidone iodine. The same liquid you used.

—Thank you. You saved my life.

—Silly Papa. Did you expect me to do anything differently?

—No . . . no . . . What else did you do? Amaze me more.

—I did everything just like you. Throw the logs into the fire pit, start the fire. Open the cans. Beans and meat. It was hard at first. You have to hold the can opener tightly. Cook the meat until it sizzles. The same thing with the soup. Don't you remember the soup? Sometimes you didn't swallow. It ran down the side of your mouth.

He listens to her but no memory awakens. During the last five days, he was trapped in his own mind, yet he sensed her voice, her presence about him. Suddenly he realizes the steady, confident cadence, the clear enunciation of the words; her voice is not what it was, and there is no trace of the stuttering interruption, the pauses between words.

—Maya, your voice is different.

—Yes, Papa, I read to you for hours. Don't you remember? Talking is easier now.

—Wonderful Maya. Absolutely wonderful. Well, I'm famished. Let's get some . . . it's too late for breakfast. Let's have brunch.

—Brunch . . . a meal that's both lunch and breakfast.

—Right.

She rises, goes around the desk, and takes his arm. He pulls her close and leans his head over hers as they walk to the back yard.

—Were you afraid? he asks.

—Afraid?

—To be alone.

Abruptly her arms swing around and she squeezes him tightly. A suppressed paroxysm of sobs reverberates against his chest.

—There, there . . . darling . . . sshhh. I'll never leave you if I can help it.

She continues to cry.

—Shhh . . . ssshhhh . . . It's all right now. I'm here. No more crying. We'll celebrate. We'll have something quick to eat and head over to George's. We'll have a big dinner at his place. He has a generator, remember. We'll even watch a movie tonight.

Maya says nothing, only nods. He pulls her closer and places a soft kiss on her head.

THEY PACK THE HUMMER UNTIL THERE IS NO MORE SPACE IN THE back; perhaps he knows that they might not return, or even if they do, it will be an uncertain day in the future. Cans of ham, beef, and soup are stacked to one side along with some cooking and eating utensils. Next to them are two large five-gallon containers of water and finally four five-gallon canisters of gasoline. Medicines, flashlights, sleeping bags, and some clothes go into the back seat, and books of all sizes are stacked neatly on the floor of the car. He wants to be ready for the unknown, partly out of practicality and out of an odd premonition of a long journey ahead.

In between the lifting and carrying, an incredible sadness lurches about in the air, in the corners, over the kitchen table, down the hallway to Emily's room; everywhere he looks, there gut squeezes and tears brim. Turning away from Maya, he wipes his eyes. He wants to take the whole house with him, but here it will remain with its foundation rooted in the earth. Dust will cover all its surfaces; all the metals will rust; mold will consume the curtains, the sheets, and all the remaining clothes; and one day when the termites will have eaten the supporting beams, it will collapse. Of all his personal things, he takes the largest photo album, the one with all the pictures of Emily's life, from the time she was born to two years ago when she left for New York and his personal computer that has remained silent ever since the electricity went out.

ONCE THEY ARE IN THE CAR, HE STEPS HARD ON THE GAS; THE tires screech. He keeps his eyes on the road, staring straight ahead, fighting the temptation to look in the rearview mirror, not wanting to see the vestige of his former life among the majestic trees and the quiet, darkened houses blurring past. Cars on both sides of the familiar road are encrusted with a thick layer of dust that makes the windows opaque, extinguishing all the cars' colors, leaving a nearly homogenous dusty brown. He turns left onto the Pacific Coast Highway and drives to the usual place at the big, burnt-out building. It's nearly mid-afternoon, and though the wind blows a strong, brooding coldness in from the ocean, the sky is bright and clear. Black crows loiter nearby on rooftops and on the pavements, and as they land on the cars, their feet tap out sharp metallic sounds that are cold as the wind and are strung together with their eerie caws into an ominous tune.

They get out and walk about. Reminded by the caws of the crows, he holds the shotgun closely. He thinks he hears the faint yelps of dogs carried on the wind. Maya looks at him and then the shotgun.

—Don't worry, darling. I know they're only animals. I'll just scare them away.

Maya doesn't answer, and she climbs up the nearest car and works her way onto its roof where she twirls around, now peering out to the sea, now up the street from where George Cannon's car had come the last time they met.

Looking in all directions, Art maintains an uneasy vigil over the milieu of buildings collapsing, cars breaking down, and a wilderness encroaching into the city proper with each sweep of the wind bringing sand inland. He sees clearly the firm grip of destruction, and yet, incomprehensible as it may seem, he feels buoyed up, being blown high by the cold wind as if his recent ordeal has vanquished doubt and lifted the veil of ignorance. For the first time since the Death Sleep, he can see the future. He looks at Maya lost in childish play, twirling on the top of the car, and counts one by one the concrete steps of a certain future: the powder, Maya, George, food, shelter, freedom.

—Maya, careful. You'll get dizzy and fall.

—No, I won't. I'm not dizzy.

All right, he whispers to himself, capitulating. He can't wait to see George and know that he is well. An excitement, something like the childish urgency on the verge of receiving an expensive gift, stirs him so that he scuttles around nervously. He felt this way when Emily was born. George, George, where are you? he mumbles to himself. Several times, he hears rumbling sounds suggesting an approaching car, but it's just the vagaries of the wind.

Maya jumps off the car and begins to skip along the edge of the pavement. When you see the substance of a future delineated and want nothing more than that future, you can be said to be content, he thinks. The strange sensation he now feels consists of being fulfilled, being bereft of desire, being satisfied with just being, and this must be contentment. Seeing Maya balancing on the edge of the pavement, he also feels a spark of happiness.

He glances at his watch; only ten minutes have passed, and yet it feels much longer. Circling the car, he tries counting his steps, and after a while he examines his right hand and flexes the fingers, sending twitches of pain up to his bicep. Finally, he hops on the hood of the car and, cradling the shotgun, settles into planning for the future. Along this street and all other streets in this city, cars are rusting, but these cars have tanks filled with gasoline. He has siphoned many gallons from these cars with a plastic tube and gotten a headache from the fumes each time. But how long can the gasoline from these cars last? Even sealed up in these tanks, it evaporates slowly, and how long can it remain combustible? To be prudent, he will need to pump the gasoline into plastic canisters, where it will have the best chance of remaining potent for the longest time possible, and to do that he will need to track down a portable pump; he must be methodical. He'll need George's help.

Not only that, they will have to find a place to live, a source of water and food. What about next year, or the year after that when all the gasoline in the world no longer works? How will they travel? They will have to find electric cars and solar panels, and those things will probably let them go on for some more years, until those too will inevitably break down. Maya will have grown up by then; he'll have to teach her all he knows about medicine and other things as well, and he hopes to find others like her, for her sake, to continue. What about the powder? He'll need to find all the ingredients to make more, enough to sustain them for years to come.

Now closer to the horizon, the sun is veiled behind a bank of cloud, and the air is colder. Art checks his watch; an hour has passed. Lost in thought, he has been sitting in the wind for too long and now senses a coldness creeping from the top of his head toward his chest. Maya has gone back inside the car and is now reading a book. He gets in too.

—Oh, it's so warm in here. Maya, he's not coming.

—Yes, Papa.

—We'll have to go to him.

—Do you know where he lives?

—Yes, I know the area. It won't be hard. Off Sunset Boulevard, he said. It used to be an expensive area. Where did I put the address? Oh, there it is.

The piece of paper with George's address lies undisturbed on the dashboard, tucked into a sharp corner made by the dashboard and the windshield. Art unfolds the paper and reads the directions.

—Yup, just up this way, to Sunset Boulevard, past the 405 freeway. That's quite a distance; then turn left on Bellagio Road. Bel–Air.

He drives east. The road rises gradually and begins to wind into large, expansive curves to the left, then to the right. Soon it merges with Sunset Boulevard, and along the boulevard, overgrown trees and shrubs on both sides of the road hang inward, casting pockets of shadow here and there. After many miles and several switchbacks, they see the jagged blackened edges of rooftops and, in some areas, only the blackened remains of chimneys and concrete foundations; in the driveways some cars appear merely singed and discolored, and yet others had been combusted, their tires melted into amorphous blobs over the pavement. Dotted all along the road, the charred skeletons of trees rise sharply into the air as though inviting hangmen, and an occasional, desiccated human body lays quietly as though sunbathing amid the overgrown grasses. The devastation extends many city blocks, evidence of a fierce fire that swept through until it burnt out on its own, probably because it couldn't jump across a wide street. Ever since the Death Sleep, Art has not ventured this way, and now the sight of this disaster, something he could never have imagined in his previous life, assaults him with renewed brutality, reminding him once more of the enormity of the catastrophe.

—Oh, boy. Oh, boy. It was a fire, a big one, Maya. It must have been weeks ago.

He glances at her and sees that she is looking coolly at the scene. Her feet rest on a pile of books.

—Yes, Papa. She murmurs and returns to her book.

Of course, you can't relate to this, he thinks; can you imagine that people once lived here, thousands of them, in these burnt-out houses that line these streets, stretching toward the foothills. He steps on the gas, picking up speed very quickly, and thus has to keep his eyes on the road to steer clear of the cars and various objects scattered about. Sunset Boulevard soon crosses high over the 405 Freeway; he slows to a crawl, and perched on the overpass he can see far into the distance either way of the freeway. The drivers must have veered onto the freeway's sides, where there are now long lines of cars, and when they couldn't, they piled into one another, leaving a huge mass of mangled metal. In another minute along Sunset, the empty green of the golf course appears on the left, and after he turns left onto Bellagio Road, heading up hill, another world seems to materialize, a world of large houses with tall gates, broad roads, and towering trees. Here a strange tranquility still persists as though preserved by the sheer power of wealth, protected from every sinister menace, even the Death Sleep. At any moment he expects to see around the corner a woman in designer clothes walking her French Poodle or a Rolls–Royce with its darkened windows moving heavily past him. But all the streets remain lifeless except for dozens of squirrels scattering as they approach. When they first decided to live in Los Angeles, Art and his wife drove through this neighborhood and often wondered out loud if they could ever afford to live here.

—Maya, look at these houses. Aren't they something different?

—Yes, Papa.

—You know . . . Before all this, only very rich people lived here, in this neighborhood.

—If you say so, Papa.

—You know . . . but how would you know? How would you know what it means to be rich? I will have to teach you about history. No . . . maybe history is not the right word. Well, it's more like archeology now.

He sees the street sign and turns into it.

—Let's see the house number. It's painted on the side of the pavement.

—There's his car, Maya cries out.

The car stops in front of the house. There is no mistaking the black Suburban sitting squarely in the driveway. Following an inveterate habit, he pulls over and parks the car neatly; somehow leaving the car in the middle of the road is indecent. They both get out. Art takes the shotgun with him and looks up and down the street, at the houses next door and across. All is quiet. In the house across from him, a shadowy shape catches his eye, and he stands still, staring at it until he hears Maya calling. Maya has run up to the house as soon as she got out of the car, and now she stands in front of it calling for George.

—Maya, wait for me.

He runs after her and catches her shoulder.

—Maya, darling. Please don't go anywhere without me.

—But it's George's house. GEORGE, GEORGE. Come out.

—Let's knock on the door.

They come up to the front entrance, formed by a grand arch leading to a door. The door itself is at least ten feet tall, made of black iron, and has an intricate, curvilinear pattern that protects the semi–transparent glass beyond. Maya goes to the door and starts to bang on it.

—GEORGE, GEORGE, COME OUT.

Art puts his face to the door, his hands to the side of his eyes to shade them. He can see along the wall, a singular band of sunlight, coming from a window somewhere in the back. Maya follows him, and they both stand there with their faces against the door, trying to make out any movement or sound in the house.

—Papa, where can he be?

—I don't know. It's a big house. He may be in the back. He won't be able to hear us.

Darkness will come soon, he thinks, and they will need to get off the street. Driving back to his own house is an option, but they have to drive soon since they can't possibly risk driving at night with the headlights on, attracting the unknown. Then he decides that they will stay here even if George is not here. They will just wait for him.

—Let's go around the back. Maybe we can get in.

—It's not our house.

—We'll wait for him. I'm sure he won't mind. He invited us, remember.

—Yes, Papa.

Through the side gate, a walkway leads to the backyard. All along the walkway, weeds have grown and now almost cover the stones. Tall palms line the boundary of the enormous backyard; in the center is a large swimming pool, its surface covered with dead leaves. To the left is a gazebo with large outdoor sofas and chairs. In a corner, a barbecue grill made of concrete and steel shows signs of recent use; dirty pans and pots, tongs, knives, forks, empty food cans, and plastic wrappers of all sorts lie strewn about. A generator sits near the back wall, and there is an electric line connecting it to an outlet; empty red plastic gasoline canisters are mixed in with a large pile of empty plastic water bottles.

Seeing that the back door is open, Art goes to it.

—GEORGE, GEORGE. Are you in there? Anyone home? Art calls out.

He pushes the sliding door, made of thick, heavy glass, and goes inside into the family room. Cases of canned food are stacked high along the wall, and on the kitchen table are electronic contraptions in various stages of being dismantled. Maya follows him, but just as she reaches the threshold she stops and turns her head to listen.

—Papa, Papa. Wait. Wait.

—What is it?

—I hear something.

—What? George?

—It sounds like a car is coming. Do you hear it?

—No.

They stand still, listening.

—I don't hear it, but your hearing is better than mine.

—I hear it, Papa. It's getting louder.

—It's probably George. He's driving another car, probably out getting stuff. He'll be happy to see us. Let's go in and wait for him.

Inside the house, Art observes the high ceilings, the decorative moldings along the edges of the walls, and the variegated tones of the Venetian plaster. A hallway leads from the kitchen toward the front. A gigantic television screen hangs along the far wall of the family room. Through the skylight overhead, light wanes, and a grayish hue reaches into the front of the house. They have barely sat down before Maya starts rubbing her nose and shaking her head.

—What is it, Maya?

—Papa, I smell something. It's really bad.

—Hmm. I smell it too. Foul. Something is rotting.

Taking short sniffs, he samples the air, turning his head toward the front of the house.

—It smells like where I was.

—Where you were?

—Yes, Papa. Where you got me.

—Oh. It smells like that?

As he continues to sniff, a car's rumble suddenly echoes through the backyard, enters the kitchen, and seizes them where they are. The sound of a running engine was something he habitually ignored before, but now it captivates his attention. His heart begins to throb, and he cranes his neck to listen to it, perhaps to see if it is coming closer. They stand still and listen, but it stops. All is quiet.

—It's George. He's driving another car.

—Yes, Papa.

—I'll see what's rotting. It's from up there. Maybe upstairs. I'll get it out of here. We'll open the windows, let the air in. We need to start dinner soon. Wait here. Call me when George comes in. We can watch TV while we eat. Look how big the TV is.

—Yes, Papa.

Toward the front of the house, the odor intensifies abruptly as there is no air movement. The foulness is not simply in the manner of garbage or decomposing organic matters but suffocates as though the air is choked with the most heinous substance, and it clings to his nostrils. It's familiar but somehow Art refuses to comprehend it. He brings the sleeve of his jacket up to cover his nose and climbs the stairs. At the top, it's dark, but he can see the weakening light from the back, from where the master bedroom should be. The foul miasma draws him toward it, and as he approaches the bedroom's entrance, the smell saturates his lungs and his throat, nauseating. Could it be George's dog? he thinks, or worse, a family member who died. George has not mentioned them, but then they haven't talked much. When he gets to the door of the bedroom, he can see the foot of the bed, and simultaneously he hears the rumble of the engine again. The tailpipe belches a couple of pops, sounding very close by, nearing the front of the house. GEORGE, GEORGE, he hears Maya calling from downstairs. He crosses the threshold of the bedroom and looks at the massive bed. In the bleak, grayish light of oncoming dusk, the air seems to stop, a high–pitched buzz shoots through his ears, and he stares at it. A body is leaning against the headboard, its face is a dark bronze and bloated, and the eyelids are swollen and bulge out with tight slits of eyelashes across them. The abdomen has become like a large balloon. Even in the midst of decay, there's no doubt it is George.

—No, Maya, Art utters faintly. His body jerks backward and he runs. He jumps down the last few steps and dashes to the back. Maya is no longer where she was. In the backyard, he hears the rumbles of the car further down the street, and intertwined with the rumbles of the car's engine is Maya's call, striking terror in him. The terror is sickening and trails behind him like that miasma of death as he runs along the walkway, readying the shotgun, unconsciously holding his breath and with his mind singularly on Maya, forgetting fear and ignoring the tall weeds lashing his legs. Through the gate, he sees Maya waving after the car, now at least six houses past them. Maya is walking out to the middle of the street, passing in front of their own car, calling for George. He lunges at her before she clears the car, and pulls her back. They both fall backward onto the sidewalk. She gives out a little shriek.

—No, Maya. Shhh . . . Shhh. No, darling. Don't make a sound.

—Papa . . . What are you doing? It's George.

He turns on his knees and crawls over the grass, pulling her along by the wrist.

—No, Maya. It's not George. We have to go. Please, Maya.

—But it's George.

He crawls three feet to the car's door, opens it, and climbs in. All this time he keeps himself low so not to be seen in the rearview mirror of the other car. He steps on the passenger seat and crosses over into the driver's seat.

—That's not George. We have to go.

Maya stands up and looks at him.

In the side mirror, he sees that the other car is at the end of the street, and its rear lights are lit up red. The pulsation of his heart throbs in his ears, and some sort of bubble seems to encircle his head, leaving him detached. The ringing in his ears buzzes loudly. He turns to Maya and sees her large, oblong eyes staring at him, questioning him, and finally popping the bubble.

—Maya, get in the car now.

—It's George, Papa. Why are we going?

Her voice sounds muffled to him. In the side mirror, he sees the other car beginning to roll, turning right, but then he doesn't quite believe it. That car is stopping again in the middle of the street, and suddenly it becomes clear that it is turning around.

—George is dead. I saw him upstairs. Whoever is in that car isn't George.

As Maya climbs into the seat, he steps on the brake and turns the key. There is no stopping now; those in the other car must surely see his car's rear lights. He presses on the gas and at the same time spins the steering wheel; the tires squeal and the Hummer launches into the street. In three seconds, he sees Bellagio Road and pulls left. The car swerves and jostles, leaning to the right as it turns, nearly colliding with other cars on the street. The street descends. In the rearview mirror, he can make out houses, trees, and cars receding, and above them a darkening sky. At Sunset, he slows the car and takes another look in the rearview mirror. He thinks he sees a flash of yellow light, the headlights of the other car. He pulls a hard right onto Sunset and drives fast. The roar of the engine accelerating is punctuated by the pounding of his heart, and under the darkening sky things are beginning to lose sharpness, but he dares not turn on the headlights. He sees the 405 Freeway coming up, and he turns left onto the curving on-ramp. Around the bend, he slams on the brake; the car slides and stops. The on–ramp is blocked by a Toyota that was left diagonally; its doors are open, and Art can see through the empty car. He rolls the car toward the Toyota, and when his car touches it, he revs the engine, pushing it out of the way. Once the way is cleared, he drives north on the 405 Freeway, all the time concentrating to see and avoid various cars and objects. Several times the car runs over somethings on the road. After a while, a light in the rearview mirror catches his eyes, and he slows the car to look at it. There is no mistake now; behind him, the other car is sitting over the Sunset overpass, parking there and they—whoever they are—are watching him.

On top of the hill to the left, the straight lines of an enormous concrete structure blot out the darkening sky as though they are an extension of the hill itself. Art knows it well; it's the Getty Museum. He has gone there many times before, and perhaps because there is a modicum of safety in a familiar place, he takes the off–ramp, turns right and right again only to stop beneath an underpass. Here he turns off the engine. Now, only the sky is visible, a dark gray. He sees the outline of the road curving around, passing by the pay booths, leading uphill to the Museum.

Maya is crying. He knows that she has been crying since he told her of George's death, but only now does he look at her.

—I'm sorry Maya. I didn't want to tell you. I shouldn't have but you didn't want to leave. I don't know who those people are. You see, I'm your Papa. I have to look after you. I have to make sure you're safe. Maybe seeing George, the way he was, spooked me. Maybe those people had nothing to do with his death. Maybe they could have helped us. But . . . I don't know. I don't want to take any chances. And they were chasing us.

—How do you know?

—They were. I saw them stopping on the overpass and sitting there looking at us. Just before we pulled off.

—You can't be sure.

—I saw them. I'm your Papa. I had to make a decision and I decided to be safe.

In the dark, he barely makes out her eyes, and he puts his hand toward her face and feels the tears.

—I'm sorry. I didn't want to tell you about George. But that was the only way to get you to go. I know it's hard for you. It's hard for both of us. George was a nice guy.

Even as a superior being, whose existence is still an enigma to him, she cries as his daughter did, the spasmodic utterances, the periodic gasps of sorrow escaping from deep within her chest.

He pulls her close, feels her head against his cheek, and kisses her.

—I'm so sorry, Maya. Go ahead and cry as much as you like. I just want to protect you, keep you from harm. And that could be anything. Until I know for sure, I won't take any chances.

She nods.

—We can't get back on the road. Up that way is the museum. We can stay there tonight. It's not safe to be out here. We'll take the sleeping bags, a couple of cans of food, water. We'll decide what to do tomorrow.

Outside the car, a wind swooshes down along the hillside, and the faint light of a crescent moon barely shows the way. They walk up the steep road. In the trees along the road, Art thinks he sees leaves with the color of darkness, not merely shadows, crawling up and blossoming alongside their daytime brethren.

11

At the center of the beam of light, where it is brightest, where shines the whiteness of the solitary flower, the green and the blue are diminished, and an insinuation of yellow tinges everything and binds them all together with unseen decay. Art holds the flashlight on the painting, perhaps the most famous in this museum; he had seen it dozen of times before. Sometimes when he could break from his work, he came here just for it, and at other times, he took Emily, who could never hold still long enough for him to tell her his thoughts, to impart to her the beauty of this masterpiece. He'd read different versions of Van Gogh's biography as well as a litany of publications by a long line of art critics, each version more glowing in its praise than the previous, but the painting's true nature seemed hopelessly trapped behind the final varnish. Tonight, it's no different. He holds the flashlight on it but realizes that his impression of the painting and his awe at its supposed sublimity had been marred by the overwhelming green color of the currency of its price tag, a value that vanished with the people. The museum paid millions for it, but now how is he to measure its greatness?

He directs the light at his wristwatch; it's only ten o'clock, too early, two more hours before he can allow himself a finger lick of the powder and sleep. He knows that under no circumstances should he deviate from his schedule of taking the powder every six hours, a constancy that will keep him alive. Under the halo of the light, he glances at Maya sleeping on the bench, her body unmoving, her hands clutching the sleeping bag, her breath rustling slightly in the quietness, and her stamina probably drained by the scare earlier. The tall white walls and the high ceiling enclose too much space for him, and together with the spotless floor, an eerie sense of something amiss creeps up on him and throws him out of his usual comfort, the cluttered home with walls of canned food, water bottles, and stacks of supplies scattered around. There is so much emptiness here for a person to get lost in. Suddenly he hears something, a sound from something moving, being disturbed in the next room; for a split second the sound shoots through his ears, and he turns to listen. After a minute he hears nothing. He picks up the shotgun and moves to the room. Large paintings along the wall come alive as the flashlight advances. Standing very still for a while he hears nothing at all. It must have been some sort of auditory hallucination, he thinks, the kind he frequently had when Anna and Emily first moved away; for weeks after their departure he would hear their footsteps outside his bedroom door and sometimes Emily's giggles in the dead of night. He moves to the tall glass door at the entrance, switches off the flashlight, and walks outside into the dim light of the crescent moon.

Cold wind, coming in from the ocean, pushes against the hill and once on top races inland. He shivers. In the transparent, cloudless sky, he sees the entire length of the Milky Way. Despite the cold wind thrashing against him, the shroud of the Death

Sleep begins to descend, and the familiar grogginess, the blunting of the senses, and the heaviness of his eyelids converges and deepens. He walks into the clearing in front of the building; he squeezes his right palm and flexes the muscles to feel the pain radiating up the length of his arm. The pain is much less now but still wakes him up. Howling starts far inland, bursts out distantly in an ever–growing concatenation of canine chatters, and echoes against the wind. Upon hearing it he walks backward to the glass door and withdraws inside once more.

He lies down on a bench, holds tight the bottle of powder and, while counting Maya's sonorous breaths, waits. His eyes remain open in the inscrutable darkness, and he tries to hurry toward the moment when he can uncap the bottle and feel the bitterness of the powder under his tongue.

With the chirping of his wristwatch, he wakes up and feels the hardness of the bench on his side. He perks up and looks around. From the skylight above, the early morning sends down grayish rays giving the paintings an illusion of fluttering in space and Maya of levitating and hovering in front of them. He rubs his eyes and pushes himself up with his right arm; it feels nearly normal. The bottle of powder is next to him, and he uncaps it and takes the powder almost automatically. He rises, grabs a bottle of water, and goes to the bathroom to clean himself.

A moment later, he emerges and comes to her. She is standing in front of a painting, scrutinizing it closely, and her fingers slide over the surface, feeling the texture of the paints.

—Good morning, darling, he says and stands next to her.

—Good morning, Art. How is your arm?

—Much better.

—That's good.

—Did you sleep well?

—Yes.

—Any dreams?

—I dreamed of my family, she says with hesitancy.

—Your family?

—Yes.

—Was it a good dream?

—Maybe it was not a dream. Even though I was sleeping, maybe I was remembering.

—What did you remember?

—Their faces, their voices.

—Hmm . . . Do you want to talk about it?

—We're talking about it.

—It's an expression, a question people use when they're not sure if a subject should be discussed further. By asking that, what I really wanted to know is whether it's uncomfortable for you to discuss it. I leave it entirely up to you.

He folds his arms and turns slightly toward her.

—Oh, all right. Maybe later, another time. So this is a museum. I've never been in one.

—Yes, Maya. This is supposed to be a place where the best of arts are kept. Things like paintings, sculptures, ancient artifacts, have been brought together. It's meant to represent the best of human creativity. That's what I think anyway.

—I like this one.

—Joseph Mallord William Turner. What do you like about it?

—It's mysterious, somehow. I see the ship but I see it through what? It's not clear at all.

—What about this one? he says and leads her to Van Gogh's "Irises" in the adjoining room.

—It's a pretty flower picture.

—Maybe when you've read the artist's biography, you'll like it more. It's one of the most famous paintings in the world.

—They try to imitate three-dimensional objects.

—Yes, Maya. Human beings first depicted what they saw thousands of years ago. There is a gift shop downstairs. Maybe we can find an art history book for you.

—Yes, I'd like to learn more about art.

—Art can be very complicated and very expensive.

—Expensive?

—Do you remember anything about money?

—My parents never had enough. They always talked about it. I remember that.

—Oh . . . money was also complicated. It was used in exchange for things, to buy things. But back to art, the better or more famous a painting was, the more expensive it got. There were always plenty of people with lots of money who wanted to buy them.

—How expensive was this one?

—Over fifty million dollars. And just to give you an idea of how much money that was, in the best year when I was very frugal, all I could save was about a hundred thousand dollars.

—You'd have to save for five hundred years to have enough money for it.

—Hah, that's right.

—But some people had that much money all at once.

—Yes, but almost everyone else did not.

Almost unconsciously, he holds his hands together with his fingers intertwined, just as he did when lecturing passionately to residents during hospital rounds. His feet are firmly on the ground, and his body leans slightly toward Maya.

—What did people do with the paintings?

—They'd hang them up in their houses; sometimes they'd

give them up to a museum like this for everyone to see and hopefully to appreciate.

—Who decided that these paintings were the best?

—Art critics, art historians. The people who studied art.

—Do you agree with them?

—Sometimes. I don't know.

—Why don't you know?

One of his hands reaches up and squeezes his chin, while the other goes under his armpit, and he looks up as though at some void in the air.

—You see . . . I don't know . . . Well, the world, you're here, everything changed . . . It makes you think differently . . . The world is different . . . I see things differently now . . . I guess I never really had my own thoughts about art. I read a lot about it and I must have taken what I read for my own opinion.

—Art is subjective?

—It is, and it is not. Maybe I'm not the best person to explain it.

—Art, do you like this flower painting?

—Yes, yes I do. I used to stand here and look at it for a long time.

—What do you like about it?

—Ahh . . . Hmm. Let me think. It's hard to say. It represents solitude, loneliness. See, you have to know something about the artist to appreciate it. The artist was largely ignored when he was alive, only to be worshipped after his death.

—How did he die?

—We're not sure exactly, but people thought that he shot himself. He had a sad life. He was in the asylum for a while.

—Like I was.

—Ahh, not exactly but something like that.

—Please continue.

He shifts his weight from side to side, all the while tugging on his chin.

—What I like about it? The vibrant colors. The simplicity of the arrangement.

—Is this your opinion or what you read?

—Ah . . . ah . . . It's my opinion, or I like to think it's my opinion. Anyhow, let's have breakfast. We can talk more about it later. I will run down to the car and grab some food for us. Don't go far and don't go outside.

Outside a heavy fog obscures the landscape. He can see about twenty yards in front of him, but he knows the way and starts toward the front through a vast quad, where the ground had been constructed with stones and dry leaves have been piling up in the corners and along the edges of the buildings. Luckily, all the doors of the museum seem to have been left open when the Death Sleep struck; perhaps whoever was responsible for locking down the museum did not have enough wit to do so. He goes through heavy front glass doors and descends the stairs, and when he reaches the tram rail to the right, he goes downhill on a path to the left. On the left side of the road, thick bushes with white flowers have grown several feet onto the asphalt, mirrored on the right by more wild bushes, and fallen leaves and pine cones line the entire way down. Last night, he'd parked the car under the overpass, and it took them nearly fifteen minutes to climb the hill. But going down is much easier. A mist cools his face.

Something about the conversation with Maya irks him; perhaps it was the tone of her voice, the cold inquisitiveness, those large oblong eyes that observed him with unerring precision, or the unflattering realization he'd admitted about his own thoughts. She expressed her opinion clearly enough, and even when her opinion was inchoate, her words left no doubt in his mind as to her conviction. He can't say that about himself. Only since last night, some significant parts of her seem to have changed, and he is certain of that, but what? She doesn't call me "papa" anymore, he thinks. Just as well. Children always grow up, or they want to grow up, always too soon. A child is an adult not when she wants to be but when she knows enough to want the moment before, and not a moment sooner.

The Hummer stands as he left it, and he stops, squats down, and looks at it and its surroundings. The car and the bushes are quiet in the morning fog, but instead of seeing them, he sees only Maya's cold eyes on him, questioning and absorbing all he said.

After some time, he moves to the car and gets in. He inserts the key into the ignition, but hesitates. The image of George Cannon's engorged face, the lights of the other car chasing him, and fear of the unknown make this moment more unbearable than ever. He cringes and turns the key. The engine fires, and the rumbling permeates the fog that will carry the sound farther than normal, just as water carries sound farther than air. He hopes no one is close enough to hear. The sound of the engine steadies and settles into a low buzz, and he eases the gas pedal down. The car rolls slowly uphill through the fog.

For breakfast, they eat crunchy bars of oats and almonds mixed together with sticky sweet caramel and drink bottles of warm orange juice. Art sits in front of Van Gogh's "Irises" as he eats, and now and then he glimpses at the painting as if he is afraid that Maya might catch him looking at it. Does it indeed have the vibrant colors, the simplicity of arrangement, as he claimed, or was it something he'd read, the opinion of an art critic, who might have been a quack after all? Maya wanders off to the far side, continuing to examine one painting after another, moving her hands over the canvasses, now putting her eyes close to the paint, now backing up at a great distance while twisting her head to left and right. The "Irises" is behind a glass pane, otherwise he'd love to run his hands over its surface, just like Maya, to feel its textures, to be one of only a handful of humans in the history of this painting to have done so.

After a while, Maya comes toward him with her lips pursed together tightly, making her eyes even larger and her face nearly menacing.

—What's the matter, Maya?

—I don't understand any of these paintings. What are you supposed to get out of them?

—Pleasure, understanding of ourselves, appreciation of beauty—take your pick.

—I am not burdened by your history. Is that why I can't understand them?

—Burdened by history? That's one way to put it. Maybe. But how did children learn to appreciate art? The adults had to teach them. So just imagine yourself a child, so you have to learn. Either from me or from books.

—Yes, I understand. Please teach me.

—OK, it's not my area of specialty, but I'll try. Let's go to this other painting. It was painted by a famous Impressionist painter.

They go to one Impressionist painting and then to another, and they move on to the next wing, where there are paintings from the Middle Ages to the Industrial Revolution. On the walls are the giant portraits of men and women of a long-forgotten age; their eyes appear fixed and yet seem to track them as they move past. Over the centuries they have been observing passersby like this, Art thinks. In front of a large painting, Maya suddenly stops, stands still, and raises her eyes with sweetness, as if she is intimately familiar with that person. The painting was done over two hundred years ago and shows a beautiful woman reclining on her right side, her black hair combed smoothly over her head, split symmetrically in the middle, her dark eyebrows and dark eyes staring straight ahead, and her bountiful bosom exuding health and fertility.

—Do you like this painting?

Hearing no answer, Art continues. This is a type of realistic painting. This was done before the age of photography. Notice the realistic depiction, the simple symmetry of the face. It was meant to capture the likeness of the person.

He looks over at her and is startled to see tears in her eyes.

—What's the matter, Maya?

—She looks like my mother.

—Oh . . . Your mother was . . . is . . . a beautiful woman, then.

—She probably slept like everyone else.

Maya blinks rapidly, dries her eyes, and goes further away. Along the walls, a tall lady in white poses, a drama is played out, the ruin of Rome is laid, and there are scenes of a bull fight, a countryside, and even a forlorn farmer resting. They move along and observe in silence.

—Now what do they think? Art asks suddenly. What do they think of what just happened to us, Maya? Do they even care?

—Who?

—Them, Art says and points to the paintings.

—It's a painting, not a person.

—You're right, but there is something more, something much more. You see, every artist wants to bring his works alive, to make his work live just like a real person, and if he succeeds, the work of art would talk to you, right? And these are the best, right? So what do they say to us. Just look at what happened to us. There is no one left, so what do they say?

He runs back to the "Irises" and Maya runs after him.

—Maya, look at it. Do you think it's alive? Do you think it's talking to us? What do you think it's telling us? Art says.

—It's a painting, Art. It can't say anything.

—Alive, it's supposed to be alive.

—No, it's not. Maybe as a metaphor. I understand what you're saying. It's alive in the sense that it's seen differently by different people. In the sense that it reflects the viewer, similar to the function of a mirror.

—Yes, but also more.

—It doesn't have a mind of its own.

—No, no. You're right, but I sometimes feel that it does.

—It's not alive.

—I was wrong then.

Sunlight, reflecting off the wall near the entrance, now brightens the room a little more, and as Art moves away, he sees his faint shadow. In that shadow, the shape of an amorphous distortion of a man, are combined the concreteness of reality, the flow of molecules with immutable precision, and the inevitable progression toward chaos. He is shaken.

—Maya, we have to go, Art says.

—To where?

From the pocket of his jacket, he takes out the bottle of powder.

—See here? Art says and points to the corner of a paper label on the bottle. It's an address. See? Thomas Ledesma, Ph.D. It's in Berkeley. I've known him for a long time; we should have gone there sooner. We can be there tomorrow or the day after.

—Who is he?

—He's a chemist. He made the powder. We were collaborators in our research. He must have more.

—How do you know he's still awake?

—I don't. Even if he's not, we can go to his lab. There must be more powder there.

—That makes sense. But why didn't you think of that before?

—I don't know. It just came to me.

He checks the time and sees that it's past ten o'clock. It's a good time to go, he thinks. They pack up their sleeping bags, and as they depart, the invisible magic of the paintings that seemed to hold them captive just a moment before dissipates and leaves, remaining on the walls, the fanciful doodling of children. They go downstairs to the gift shop and take several art history books, and then make their way to the front of the museum. As they descend the stairs to the car, going past a large, white statue of a naked boy holding a frog, Maya breaks out laughing.

—Is that art too? she asks.

—Yes, it is. Though I don't know what it means.

—It makes me laugh.

—Which is just as good.

They get into the car, buckle the seat belts, and both look down the winding road.

—Do we have everything? Art says.

—Yes. We haven't missed anything. We took everything with us.

—All right, Art says and braces himself for the ignition. His fingertips touch the key, and he takes a deep breath and bears down to draw up the energy to turn it, but instead he withdraws his hand.

—Is there anything wrong, Art?

—No, no. Not really. I was just thinking, that's all. I have this idea, you know, that I'll never see it again.

—See what?

—The "Irises."

—It will always be here.

—What if something were to happen to it?

—Like what?

—Fire, earthquake, theft. Those people who were following us. They might come for it.

—What do you want to do, then?

—Stay here. Don't leave the car. I'll be right back.

Art makes his way back to the "Irises." On each side, two steel wires hold the painting by way of a metal harness, and the back of the frame is attached to the wall. He takes the knife and pries the frame from the wall, and then he cuts the wires that are attached to the painting, undoubtedly a part of the alarm system. Lifting the frame, he unlatches it from the harnesses, one side, then the other. Finally, his arms enclose it as he would a beloved person. Though the painting is not light, he carries it with a strange elation; his steps are sprightly and happy, for the moment forgetting his own reality and entering into another, more courageous and free.

He wraps a sleeping bag around it and places it in the back. He gets in the car and smiles at Maya.

—Thanks for waiting.

—Should we go now?

—Yes, yes.

The car rolls downhill, goes under the freeway overpass, turns left, and, after about a hundred yards, enters the 405 freeway to head north.

12

Behind them, everything is quiet. Art drives north. The sun rises high behind them and, with the day being one of those exceptional California winter days, shines so brightly as to bring out the palpable concreteness of things. For the first time in many weeks, the abandoned cars with their shadowy interiors, the trees with dark trunks underneath green leaves, and the freeway's divider grab his attention, and their presence warns of physical consequences should they be challenged. Over a swath of open sky, hawks circle. Paying wary attention to them, Art dares not get above fifty miles an hour, for every time he speeds up, he sees some objects in the road, some abandoned cars left randomly on the freeway, and has to slow down to navigate around them.

Maya sits with her feet resting on a pile of books, reading an art history book that she took from the gift shop. After some time, she puts the book down and gazes at the distant dark green hills broken by rows of houses as still as the trees themselves, not a trace of smoke from the chimneys. Her eyes droop slightly and her lips slacken, and he can recognize the look of forlornness and sadness anywhere, even in her.

—You know, Maya, Art says, we used to take road trips to San Francisco.

—You?

—Me, Anna, and Emily. We drove on this very freeway, up to the 101, and took that up to San Luis Obispo. It took longer but it was more beautiful. A scenic drive. We'll do the same thing. We'll stay in San Luis Obispo, at one of the vineyards. You'll like it.

—What did you do at the vineyard?

—We drank wine. Well, not Emily. We ate very well. We went sightseeing and learned how they made wine.

—A vineyard is where grapes are grown; grapes contain glucose and fructose. Fermentation turns them into alcohol.

—Maybe not this time of year. The grape vines go into a kind of hibernation, I think, in the winter. But there'll be plenty of things to look at.

The constant hum of the car somehow exacerbates the detachment on Maya's face so much so that the forlornness is increasingly transformed into moroseness.

—Listen, Maya. You know what we can do? I know a couple of restaurants there where they had dry ham, from Spain, Iberico ham. It's very good. We'll cook a pot of rice or maybe we can find bread from somewhere.

—Did you find anything from my folder?

—Your what? You mean your chart from the Institute.

—My chart. Yes, the one you got.

—Your chart. Yeah, what about it?

—Is there any information on my family? Is there an address?

—No, Maya. There was no address. I was looking for that myself. There were a couple of entries about how they were looking for your legal guardians, your parents, but they found nothing.

—Are you sure? You have to tell me before we're too far away.

Art slows the car and stops in the middle of the freeway. He puts the Hummer into park and turns to her.

—Maya, of course I would tell you. You can look through the chart yourself. It's in the back.

Reflexively she turns her head to look.

—I know it's hard, Art says. You're becoming smarter every day, and I can't possibly understand why you've become like that when everyone else just slept and died. Without the powder, I'd be the same. I know you want to know where you came from, your parents. You must have thousands of questions, but I just don't have answers for you.

—I know where I came from. I remember my parents, I remember everything. You don't need to tell me.

—Trust me when I tell you that there is no address, no name, no phone number that will tell you where your parents are now.

—All right.

—I'm sorry. I've lost my family too. Emily, my daughter, is gone.

A sudden, uncontrollable gasp escapes his chest; he inhales. He closes his eyes, and his hand comes up and rubs them hard.

—I'm sorry Maya. I'm sorry.

—I believe you.

—I know what it means to you. To know where you came from. If only I knew where your parents lived, I'd take you . . . so you . . . even just to see them. Even if they're not alive.

—Thank you, Art. Please, let's go now.

He wipes his face on the sleeve of his jacket.

—All right. Let's go, then.

ROGUE CLOUDS MUST HAVE COME IN SUDDENLY FROM THE ocean, and though things are still illuminated as they were minutes ago, there is now a whitish glaze over them. Beyond the car's windshield, everything looks so still, so static as if almost belonging in a painting. Art has to focus his eyes to make out the gentle swaying of the branches high up the hill. When there were still people and movement everywhere and cars clogged the freeways, he was reminded constantly of motion, and deceitfully that motion, by its very nature fleeting, somehow became a permanent reference. People by the billions had displaced trees, bushes, and animals, and in their place had put up the constructions of cement and steel according to their own thoughts. Only now can he see the still earth, the deeply rooted trees, and the clouds, even though they are, for the moment, static. And how beautiful the scenery is, so clear and real and majestic in the way that only the improbability of the universe that resulted in this earth could be.

To break the unbearable monotony of the engine, Art turns on the music. The CD player squeaks, and Debussy's "Claire de Lune" trickles out. The music strikes a deep melancholic tone in his mind, transporting him into a surreal reverie and probably sleep if there weren't cars strewn about on the road to keep him focused.

—They are all gone Maya, Art mumbles. He remembers the handwritten note in her chart. We . . . a miserable minority.

Without answering, Maya stares ahead.

He continues to mumble but is loud enough to be heard. Somehow, her presence, like the people who were around him all his life, brings out a kind of natural inhibition, a sort of polite stoicism in the face of large-scale suffering, and as it was before, he finds it's best to keep silent, for to do otherwise is somehow obscene. Along this line, shame for his recent maudlin outburst creeps up, grows in his chest, makes him feel hollow, and slowly seems to strangle him, tightening his chest.

There is no one around any more, he thinks; why shouldn't he mourn as loudly as he can. He should shake the earth if he could for his daughter. Glancing at Maya now and then, he wonders what she thinks. She is here, she is a blessing. At least now he can experience grief, for without her here there would be only a vague numbness that bleached the remaining colors out of all things.

—I miss them so much. I miss my daughter, he says finally.

—She is beautiful, Maya says.

—Emily?

—Yes, I saw her picture.

—I think you'd like her, he says; his voice crackles. She was stubborn as a nail though.

—Your wife is beautiful, too. Where are they now?

—We divorced. A divorce is when a marriage ends.

—I know what it means.

—My wife took Emily to New York. It was just a couple of years ago. She shouldn't have done that. Emily might still be here. Sure, she'd need the powder just like me, but it'd be better, wouldn't it?

—Why did your wife go there?

—She married a very rich man.

—Because she was beautiful?

—Yes, something like that. He worked on Wall Street. That's where the business of money was. He made a lot of money and she was going to have a fabulous life.

—I read about it in the book *The Coming Deflation and How To Protect Your Assets*. It's the financial center of the world, the epicenter of the last financial crash that spread around the world.

—Yeah, I remember. I bought that book thinking that . . . I don't know what I was thinking. Maybe I was trying to know more about finance just after she left. They were going to live in a beautiful penthouse in Manhattan.

Far ahead he sees some cars in the middle of the freeway. He shifts his weight in the seat, leans forward to see the obstacle more clearly, and slows the car. As he gets closer, the familiar sight of a corpse leaning over the steering wheel becomes clear, and next to that car are several more cars, overlapping each other and blocking the way. He eases the car up slowly to make contact, and once the bumpers touch, he revs the engine, pushing the other car away. The tires screech, the bumpers scrape with a cutting sound on both sides of his car, and the corpses get shaken and keel over. Once he clears through, he picks up speed again.

—What about your family? Art says. What do you remember about them?

—I lived with them until I was five years old. We lived in a small apartment. There was always yelling. From the people above us, below us. My parents also yelled at each other. I don't blame them.

—It's normal for married people to argue. Maya, trust me I know it very well.

—I could see the freeway and all the cars going past day and night. I stood by the window and looked out. I could hear the noise of the engines all the time.

—Do you remember the freeway?

—No, there was no sign nearby.

—Your mother must have been very beautiful if she looked like the woman in that painting.

—The last time I saw her was on my fifth birthday. After that, they put me in the asylum. Some months later they put me in a different place.

—What about your father? What was he like?

—He looked like you. But he had gray eyes. I remember his eyes when he hugged me.

—You got your eyes from him, light gray like the cloud. Very pretty.

—That's why, when I saw you at the asylum, I thought you were him. I can see his face very clearly. I knew that you were not him. But when I saw you, I must have wanted you to be him.

—Of course, Maya. Who wouldn't? You were stuck in that horrible place. It's a very normal human behavior. It's called projection. It's when you project your feelings, in this case your desire onto other people or objects.

—At your house, I still didn't want to believe it. I had never seen your house before. I saw the picture of your family, you, your wife and Emily. I didn't see myself in there. But I didn't say anything even after you told me. Until today. I should have said something. I should have told you that I knew. I was wrong.

—No one blames you. It's very normal to do what you did. I'd have done the same thing. Look at the world, Maya. Just the two of us now. It's not important any more.

—It's important to me. I'm sorry I didn't tell you the truth when I knew it.

—OK . . . OK. If it's important, then I understand. I get it. Apology accepted. I'm just as much at fault as you are. I thought that it would help you cope if I was your Papa.

He reaches for her hand and squeezes it.

—Thank you, Art. I feel better now.

A sudden thought tickles him, he leans his head toward the window and runs his hand through his hair, and at the same time he shakes his head, trying to dispel the thought. He glances at her and hesitates.

—Maya, you know . . . I can . . . since we're honest with each other . . . I can . . . I can still be your Papa.

She does not answer, but her eyebrows wrinkle and her eyes pierce at him.

HE DRIVES NORTH AND TAKES THE 101 WEST AND, AFTER ABOUT forty miles, turns north. They are entering Santa Barbara County now. The hillsides, once crowded with rows of similar houses with orange tiled roofs, become greener and more wild as the houses are further away from one another. On great stretches of meadow on either side of the freeway, the black shapes of cows dot the greenery. When the car drives close to the fence, the cows set off running along with it for some yards, mooing loudly.

—Whatever causes people to sleep is making the animals very aggressive, Art says as if speaking to himself. At the sight of the agitated cows, he flexes his right arm and feels a dull ache tightening in the muscles.

—Whatever it is, it woke me up too, Maya says.

—Do you remember when?

—One hundred and eight days ago.

—Did it occur suddenly? Or gradually?

—It was sudden. It was like I woke up from a sleep. Exactly like that.

—But you remember everything? You mentioned that you remember.

—Yes, I remember everything. Everything I heard, saw, smelled, touched I remember. I lived and yet I didn't, and then I began to live again when I woke up. I knew how to talk, I knew words. I just couldn't talk very well. Many people in the asylum were beginning to sleep. They were so violent, but I don't think they knew what they were doing.

—No, you're right. Whatever caused them to sleep also caused them to lose inhibition. They lost their minds. What about the nurses? The doctors?

—One day the doctors stopped coming. It was about seventy days after I woke up. The nurses stayed on but they also slept, Maya says and inhales, and her hands clasp together, visibly shaking.

—Poor darling. It's over now. You don't have to talk about it if you don't want to. But it's always good to talk about it.

—Maybe another time.

—Of course, of course. You can always talk to me when you're ready, whatever you want to talk about. I'm here for you.

—Thank you, Art.

But she doesn't have to say any more; the horror of that place—the narrow and darkened hallway with the corpse of the nurse he shot now decomposing, the small rooms resembling prison cells, and the air saturated with fecal matters—hovers before him vividly enough that he would willingly spare the worst criminal the same punishment. No wonder that she is still shivering from the memory of it. While she was in that place, he was in his own house drifting deeper into his sleep each day. He fancied himself putting together all the data, trying to figure out the origin of the Death Sleep; by isolating himself in his own house, he escaped the violence and cruelty and didn't bear witness to the unraveling of the proud claims of civilization and humanity. How flimsy. Yet for weeks after, he still heard their sudden awakening and screaming; he wonders how their bodies managed to continue on for so long.

He reaches for her hand and squeezes it.

—You'll be fine, Maya. You'll be fine.

Beyond Santa Barbara County, the road is better; there are only a few abandoned cars scattered sporadically. Over different stretches of the road where the fog seems to make a dreary dream of the landscape, the ethereal vapor rolls down from tall hilltops, percolates through wire fences, and crawls over the black asphalt, only to swirl in great wakes as the Hummer passes. Then they both sit up and turn their heads in unison to look at the side of the road where freight trucks and tanker trucks, perhaps several dozen in a long column, line up two or three, side by side, one after another. Several have toppled over. Further on, sunlight burns through and lights up the vast patches of meadow green and radiant, where the black cows congregate and feed happily. The visibility is better as the day progresses, and seeing how the road is clear, Art speeds up and holds the speedometer at over sixty–five miles per hour.

—Can we stop? Maya says.

—Do you have to go?

—I want to walk around on the grass. I've never been to the countryside before. I know you want to get to Berkeley as soon as possible, but I would like to walk on the grass.

—Of course, Maya. It's a good idea, in fact. We should stretch our legs. And don't worry about me. I have enough powder to last for weeks. But thank you for your concern.

Art slows the car and pulls over. As they step out, cool mist envelops his face and chills his nostrils. He breathes in, and as he exhales, he sees two streams of vapor flowing from his nostrils. Maya slams the door and runs toward the barbed wire fence. She bends down to clear the top wire and steps through the opening, and she runs up the hill with her arms spread apart and her open jacket flapping about her. Be careful, he wants to yell, but instead he merely mumbles to himself. Something has changed in her, something as ineffable as the fog and yet grow-ing vast, so vast as to comprehend all, as distanced and detached as the sky so as to judge, and at its worst it sees things, him, and his own doings, that are unknown even to himself. She seems to glide over the grass with a familiar confidence, and if she can shoot a gun, she can render him obsolete. There is no need, he thinks, to tell her to be careful.

He opens the back door to get the shotgun, holds onto the edge of the frame of the "Irises," perhaps satisfying a sublimi-nal urge, and finally closes the door. Through the rear window, Maya is visible as she runs up the hill. He stands by the car with the gun hanging on its strap from his shoulder and urinates over the tire like many a dog. At length he heads up the hill and stands tiredly by the wire fence as though unable to over-come a force, mysterious and forbidding. At a distance, he sees her bending over tall grass, her hand reaching toward a small yellow flower. The movement, illuminated radiantly by the moving sunlight and made more real by his groggy mind, con-stitutes a familiar, mutual recognition, a sort of homecoming. From high up the hill, a small herd of black cows scuttle down in a disjointed black mass as though mowing down the wild grasses, and halt near Maya; they look at her, wag their tails, and twitch their tagged ears. Maya straightens and approaches them. He wants to yell out to her, but his words of warning are caught in his windpipe. He looks on helplessly as she lays her hand on the smooth black hide, and a chorus of deep-throated moos and snorts ring across the vast meadow. His heart quick-ens. He grabs the shotgun and aims. Still, he does nothing. As he sees her skinny legs and diminutive frame against the mas-sive bulk of bovine flesh, her elongated fingers caressing the black hide, something yearns to be deciphered, but what? The cows are not violent, he thinks, perhaps because of their lack of human contact or their ignorance of the slaughterhouse. But at last he can only gaze on with an impartial detachment and is walled in and paralyzed by a tacit acknowledgment of its incomprehensibility.

13

At three o'clock in the afternoon, when the air is cold and the sunlight seems already subdued as though the sun had hurried through its apex at noon and its most intense light had lasted for but a second, Art drives along Pismo Beach and aims north for the 101 Freeway. Knowing that the Diablo nuclear reactor is nearby and that there is possible contamination, he races to put distance from it. Up till then, they've crawled along crowded sections of the freeway littered with cars and other objects; sometimes they flew in fits of incredible speed to make up for lost time or in anticipation of more delays ahead. Before noon, Art felt the effects of the powder dissipating and quietly took another finger swipe.

During these hours, they say little to each other aside from a few words of inquiry as to when they should take a break for food, for fuel, or to stretch their legs. Art throws silent glances at Maya, and seeing how she is reading with such focus, he can't interrupt her. He feels he should tell her something about his world, the world that has gone to sleep, but as hard as he tries he can find nothing worth saying, and the things that a father might teach a daughter—pitfalls, treachery, evil, the knowledge of which had been necessary to succeed in that world—have already vanished with its people. Nothing human left to teach, he supposes. Then for a long stretch through Pismo Beach, they see the ocean to the left. The view of the dark gray waves, churned up by wind, lifting high far out and crashing over the beaten sand, mesmerizes them. Slowing down, Art gazes at the watery tempest, and when the car is closest to it, he has the impression that the waves are not just water moving under the power of the wind, according to physical forces, but the manifestation of an enigmatic dark will emanating from the deepest trenches along the ocean floor, trying to exact a just vengeance.

With the waves receding in the rearview mirror, his mood lightens and he steps on the gas. The Hummer roars as it climbs. This stretch of the 101 runs through a valley, and on both sides are sloping mountain ranges. Solitary houses stand far apart, partially hidden under overgrown foliage. Around the bend of the freeway, large buildings suddenly appear.

—Maya, that's downtown San Luis Obispo. We'll take a break there. Another half an hour and we'll see the ranches. We'll stay overnight at one of the ranches. Head out early tomorrow.

—Yes.

—We need more gasoline, too. I'll show you how to siphon gasoline from the cars.

—I watched you. I think I know how. I can try next time.

—Sure, that's great.

What about the gun? he thinks. He takes her forearm in his hand, and his fingers completely enclose the thin bones; her arm lies placidly with the hand dangling as he lifts it. She looks up at him.

—I'm thinking, Maya. I think it's time you learn how to shoot, too. You have enough muscle in those arms to hold the gun. What do you think?

—I don't know. If you think I should.

—Yes, I think you should. Just in case of emergency. We have to prepare for the worst case scenario, just in case I'm not around and you need to defend yourself.

—All right. It sounds logical.

ART TAKES THE FIRST OFF–RAMP AND SLOWLY WEAVES through a scattering of debris. Here and there desiccated corpses, fully clothed, litter the streets; some are missing limbs or heads, and yet others' abdomens are open with intestines trailing feet away, perhaps the work of animals. A cloud of early insects swarm over them. A quick glance informs him that some of the dead are the result of unspeakable violence. Everywhere grasses have grown to a height of several feet and now lie heavy on the ground, aiming to advance over and eventually reclaim all the concrete and asphalt. Brown leaves atop a decomposing brownish musk cover the pavement and the road. An earthen odor mixed with foulness and organic decay float in the air. Over tall buildings inert with rows and rows of darkened win-dows, thick layers of cloud hang low, and in the clouds' folds and convolutions an impenetrable gray opacity appears like a dead weight and imparts to the sky an oppressive and locked–in appearance as though the clouds in cahoots with the earth are bent on making everything between them unbearable. The air is nearly palpable.

The car stops in the middle of the street. Art gets out, holding onto the shotgun, and looks warily in all directions. The constant buzzing of insects strikes his ears, replacing the sound of the engine. From the back, he gets a clear plastic tube with a half-inch diameter, a crowbar, and a red five-gallon gasoline can.

—Come, Maya. Let's get some gas.

Maya gets out and comes to his side.

—First, you need a plastic tube. This is five feet long to reach the gasoline in the gas tank. You need a crowbar, sometimes, to pry open the door or smash the window. You'll see. And lastly, you need this five-gallon gasoline container. All right. Let's go.

They come upon a large truck nearby. Its tires are flat, the windows covered with dirt, and the interior empty.

—First we have to open the door to the gas tank.

He walks to the driver's side and pulls on the door.

—It's locked. I have to smash the window. Watch out for the small pieces of glass. Here we go.

He lifts the crowbar high and brings it down hard. The glass spiderwebs but stays together.

—Car glass doesn't break like normal glass. It shatters but doesn't fall apart. They made it like that so that when there is an accident, the small pieces of glass don't fly out and injure the passenger.

—I understand.

With the sharp end of the crowbar, he jabs through and clears a big hole. Then his arm goes through and unlatches the door from within, while he pulls with the other hand from outside. The door opens.

—See how it's done? Come here and look at this. He points to the button for the door to the gas tank. Push on this to open the gas tank door. Come on.

Maya moves forward, puts her finger against the button, and pushes. Nothing happens. She pushes again.

—Hmm. The battery is dead. It needs electricity to work. We'll have to pry it open then.

He goes to the small square door on the side of the car.

—You have to use the crowbar to pry it open.

Aiming the sharp end of the crowbar at the small door, he jabs at it, pulls out, and jabs at it again. There's a dent at first; then it opens up more, and finally the dent creates enough space so that he can stick the crowbar in and lever it. The small metallic door pops open. He breathes tiredly. He unscrews the cap. Gasoline vapor rises to his nose.

—It smells really strong. Lots of gasoline in there. Do you think you can do the rest? You know what to do?

Maya takes the plastic tube and threads it into the gas tank. Then she kneels down, holding the red gasoline container in one hand and the plastic tube in the other. She puts her mouth around the plastic tube and sucks, while turning her head toward where the tube goes into the tank and watching the tube closely.

—Careful not to get it in your mouth. It tastes really bad.

Gasoline flows into the tube, and as she sees this, she puts the tube into the red gasoline can. The fluid descends quickly and makes a splashing sound inside the can.

—Very nicely done, Maya. You do it better than I can.

Maya stands up and wipes her lips.

—You didn't get it in your mouth?

—No, but the fumes are awful.

—I'll do the rest. So long as you know how to do it, that's good enough.

When they are done, having gone through five cars, they've filled up the five–gallon can five times, and each time he's carried the can back to the car and poured it into the gas tank. The last time, he puts the full can in the back as a reserve. A strong smell of gasoline sticks to their skin and clothes and hangs about them in an invisible haze.

—With the gas in the tank already, we probably have over twenty gallons, he says. This will last us until Berkeley.

From several feet away, Maya looks on.

—How far is it from here? she says.

—Maybe three hundred miles. Let's say this car takes one gallon for twenty miles.

—It will consume fifteen gallons.

—See, we have plenty. Don't you worry. Besides, gasoline is everywhere. The problem is that it won't last too long.

—It evaporates, Maya says.

—That's right. Even if you can prevent that, the chemicals inside the gasoline will break down and eventually it won't work anymore.

—How do you know that?

Her voice is sharp and abrupt, startling him.

—I read it somewhere, he says.

Her questioning look flits in and out of his view as he moves about, closing the hatch, putting the shotgun in the back seat. On the smooth, delicate skin of her young face, the tightened lips, the crinkling of her eyebrows, and the squinting eyes persist and somehow trouble him so that by the time he gets into the driver's seat and turns on the engine, an emptiness squarely occupies the center of his stomach as though he's missed something important, left something critical to their survival undone. He sits still, trying to remember, but nothing comes.

—Why don't you drive? Maya says.

Turning to her, he says, Give me a second.

The moment he turns to her, he is struck again by her frowning, disbelieving face. Yes, that's it, he thinks and recognizes instantly the reason for the hollowness in his stomach; on Maya's face, he sees both his ex–wife's disillusion and his daughter's sadness. The divorce with its forceful effects—estrangement, iso-lation, viciousness, guilt—comes back to him.

He drives the car parallel to the freeway and aims to turn right at the next big street to catch the on-ramp.

—All things must end, he mumbles.

—I don't understand what you mean by that.

—All things must end. I'm just thinking, that's all. You can understand it in a philosophical sense, in a natural scientific sense. For example, in a philosophical sense, it's a truth. It simply states the nature of everything—you, me, the earth, the universe. Or in a scientific sense, every physical thing will break down eventually, decompose by chemical processes, end.

Art drives the car onto the sidewalk to avoid a large truck lying across the street. In front of him he sees a large square with a dry fountain in the middle and just beyond that a court house. The court house has a tall façade of white stucco off which reflects a whitish glare, large wooden doors reaching over fifteen feet high, and a bell tower in the manner of a Spanish mission.

—I understand. What were you thinking about?

—Ha ha. You never assume anything, do you? he says, steer-ing the car toward the empty fountain as though being drawn by a noxious force.

—I don't know if the examples you gave are the ones you were thinking about.

—Your mind is exact and uncompromising. You continue to amaze me. No, that's not what I was thinking about. It's more personal for me—my marriage, my family, being a father. Those very human things end, too.

—You're saying that non-physical things will also end. Nothing lasts.

—Yes, Maya. Relationships to other human beings, being a

friend, a parent, a child to someone. One day you will see, he says and points to the court house. You see that court house? My marriage ended in one like that. I stopped being a father. They made the decision for me.

—Those human things depend on human beings to exist, Maya says. It's logical that they can not last without human beings. They exist only in the human mind. It appears straight-forward to me.

He stops the car, sits facing the court house, and is captured by its white glare and the memory of his divorce proceeding. That morning, the judge, whose fat neck bulged uncomfortably over his shirt collar, was perched high on his seat and gazed down at them with narrow eyes. With a loud bang, the gavel put an official end to everything.

—You know what they say, Maya. It's all about the money. Moving money around. It's not about taking care of Emily. I took care of Emily all those years. I gave her the medications. Me, I'm a neurologist, and yet they claimed she'd be better off with her mother.

—You wanted to keep Emily?

—Yes. A judge sat in a court house like this one and took my daughter from me.

—What kind of medications did she . . . did you give her?

—Anti–seizure medications. She has epilepsy. Doesn't it make perfect sense to you that she should stay with me, the one who is most capable of taking care of her? I knew her, I knew the medications and the side effects.

—Yes, it makes perfect sense. Why did they take her away?

—I fought for her. But it's the system. A judge decided. Their lawyer was very convincing, the best son–of–a–bitch, the most expensive lawyer money could buy. He convinced the judge that

Emily was getting better, was outgrowing her illness. He even had other neurologists testify against me. He convinced the judge that I was no longer a clinician but only a researcher.

—I understand. I read about the judicial system. It was complicated and sometimes flawed. After all, it was an artificial system, so it could be manipulated. The judge . . . a human being.

Strangely, her steady voice, resounding with an undeniable logic and a cold declarative power, conjures up the old world, his world, the mental anguish he harbored when he crawled into bed each night, the helplessness as he bid farewell to Emily, and the overwhelming sadness. Suddenly a burning heat sets his skin seething. His hands shake, and feeling a sudden suffocation, he jumps from the car and inhales deeply. Maya stares at him with wide eyes.

—I've got a great idea, Art says, gasping. Come on. Come with me. He reaches into the back of the car and grabs the shotgun and a box of shells. His eyes beam, and he glares at her, beckoning. Come on, he yells. He walks around the fountain toward the tall wooden door of the court house. Now he can clearly see the carvings: the scales of justice and the sword on the door. He turns to see Maya getting out of the car, and just as she approaches him, he aims the shotgun at the door and pulls the trigger. A loud bang explodes across the open square, and instantly an echo answers from far beyond. The shotgun pellets spatter the door's wood in a disordered circle. He pumps the gun, aims the shotgun at the scales of justice, and pulls the trigger again and again. A puff of smoke drifts from the barrel and disappears. Empty shells fly out and scatter on the ground next to them. A circular area on the door gives way, and they can see the darkened space inside. He reloads the gun and hands it to Maya who is pressing her hands to her ears.

—It's your turn, he says. Here, hold the gun against your

shoulder. He presses the gun into her hands and adjusts the butt against her shoulder. It's loud at first, but if you're going to shoot, you'll just have to get used to it. Now hold it tight and aim straight. When you pull the trigger, the gun will recoil against you, so you'll have to put your shoulder into it.

His voice is fast and his movements seem even faster, so that together they cement her into action; she holds the gun with the butt tight against her shoulder, pointing it at the door.

—Now shoot, he commands.

The slender finger pulls the trigger, and she staggers back. The gun jerks upward, its barrel pointed at the sky.

—Put one foot forward and anchor yourself against the ground with the back foot. That way when the gun recoils the force will transmit through your body to the ground. You saw how I did it. Now pump the gun to reload and shoot again.

With much awkwardness, she pumps the shotgun and aims it again.

—Shoot again, he says.

The shots burst out in regular succession, and she holds the gun steadily each time. Pellets spray out haphazardly over the doors and adjoining walls.

—You saw how I reloaded the gun. Now you do it.

With her hands trembling, she shoves the shells into the gun.

—I got a great idea. I'll be right back, he says as he turns and walks toward the car.

A moment later he comes back carrying the can of gasoline. He goes directly to the door and places the can next to it.

—It's going to be fun, Maya. I'll let you do the honor, he says. Just aim at the can.

—No. Why Art? Isn't it going to burn the whole thing down? Gasoline is very flammable. You know that.

—Don't I know that? Of course it's going to burn. It will be even better than that. You'll see.

—No. No. I don't want to. Why do you want to burn it? It's understandable but it's not logical.

—What's understandable?

—Your anger with the judicial system but that was in the past. That system is long gone, dead like all the people. We don't need to waste gasoline. Please try to be more objective.

—I've lived a lot longer than you. I don't care how smart you are, just don't lecture me about your objective nonsense. I'm trying to teach you a critical skill in this world. If I wasn't there when the dogs went after you, where would you be now? Next time, you'll need to know how to defend yourself. Now shoot.

Maya closes her eyes, and her face cringes into a grotesque twist as though she wants to close off her ears as well. She pulls the trigger but the shot goes high.

—Open your eyes and engage the target. If you can't even hit a target ten feet away with a shotgun, you're in trouble. Open your eyes.

Her eyelids ease open. This time the shot seems to explode from the barrel of the gun, and the explosion instantaneously ignites the gas can, which bursts into flame and scatters a plume of brightly burning droplets. Both of them take several steps back. The flames quickly seize the wooden door and rise high. The burning wood crackles.

—Woohoo, that's awesome. This is exactly it.

Black smoke begins to discolor the white stucco as it rises and expands swiftly in the cold air. The sun has descended to within two palms' width of the horizon, and in the gray sky the black smoke curls upward with a peculiar menace.

As the flames whip high, they take automatic gingerly steps

back; the smell of burning wood and gasoline pushes them away. The door continues to burn, but the loud crackling and the roaring of the fire burst out as if from something sinister inside the building, and soon more black smoke rises from other parts of the courthouse and the bell tower. Flames suddenly blow out from underneath the eaves, all along the front side, and sweep upward, blackening the orange clay tiles, some falling down and smashing against the concrete ground below.

Finally, the heat envelopes and awakens them as they stand there, mesmerized by the fire.

—Let's go, Art says.

They get into the car and drive to the freeway. Once on the freeway, Art can see in the rearview mirror the enormous column of black smoke rising fast, already pooling into a great mass against the low clouds.

—Look, Maya, he says. Have you seen a fire like that before?

She says nothing and looks ahead as if without a shred of curiosity.

—That felt liberating. Don't you think? The one thing I'm glad about in this new world is that there are no lawyers, or bankers, or financiers. They were all about the same thing, don't you think? Maybe we can burn a bank. Or better yet, I've always wanted to burn a gigantic pile of money. That'd be something to see.

—What if the whole city burns down?

—It won't. Even if it did, the fire will end sometime. All things must end, remember. Besides, there are thousands of other cities. I'm sure many of them have already burnt down.

—It will hurt someone.

—How so? They're already dead. There is no one around anymore.

—How can you be so sure?

—I can't be sure. Neither can you, even if you're that smart. And they should know how to run.

THE SETTING SUN GLEAMS RED OVER THE HILL AND SEEMS TO darken objects beyond its reach, voiding the dividing lines between matter and shadow as a shadowy aspect infects them all. At the top of a hill in the distance, they can see a large house, the last sunlight striking its roof. The car rolls up the dirt road toward the house. The road is rank with weeds, on both sides wire fences are nearly hidden by the tall, spiking overgrowth, and beyond the fences, receding rows of dormant, leafless grapevines divide the land and give it order. In front of the house the Hummer stops, the doors open, and they step out. The sounds of wild animals echo across the vineyard; the sudden hoot of a hidden owl comes from the trees. During dusk in the winter, a fine, cold mist pervades the air, and as Art gets out of the car, he takes it in and remembers the mist years ago when he, Anna, and Emily came here for a weekend getaway. They stayed in this very vineyard. For dinner, they were served lamb shanks slow–cooked in red wine alongside a Pinot Noir, Anna's favorite wine. For dessert they shared a large soufflé that had taken the cook thirty minutes to prepare, and Emily couldn't get enough of it.

Art stands by the car and surveys the darkening landscape; in the distance the swaying of trees draws his eyes. He stares in that direction for a while and then shakes his head. He shouldn't have come here, he thinks; he shouldn't let sweet memory lower his guard. It's a strange territory he's heading into. Toward San Luis Obispo, he can still see the red glow from the fire in the darkening sky. Despite what he'd said to Maya, he prays that the city won't burn down; there is no sense in any further destruction than that old court house, no more good done after purging an old hatred he no longer feels. He gets the shotgun and flashlight from the back and approaches the front door. Maya walks close behind him. The tall door is unlocked and creaks loudly as he pushes it open; he goes in and shines the flashlight around. He hears loud scurrying and squeaks from the back.

They enter a large living space with three large couches arranged around a coffee table, in front of an enormous fireplace. The ceiling is at least fifteen feet high with a circular wooden chandelier. Logs are stacked in a neat pile next to the fireplace. There are two tall candles on the mantel, and their light is meant to give the room an ambience of warmth and coziness on a cold night like this. On the left side, opposite the fireplace, is a large dining room with a table that can sit twenty people. He remembers that the kitchen is straight ahead toward the back, and on the right a wooden stair leads up to the bedrooms, where he'd once slept.

He arranges several logs in the fireplace and starts the fire, while Maya brings in the provisions, the blankets, and her books. Soon the smell of sizzling ham and beans spills out from the fire, and in direct response to this temptation, the squeaking of rats from the back calls out loudly now and then. Maya sits on the couch and watches him.

—Don't be afraid of the rats. Country rats are clean. In some countries they eat country rats like any other animals. The rats feed on grain and so they're good to eat.

—I never want to kill any animals.

He only smiles. The warmth of the fire cheers him, and its shadows waver over his face as he jostles the pan and tosses the ham and beans.

He takes down the candles from the mantel, sets them on the coffee table, and lights them. He sets out two plates and divides the food equally. In the kitchen, he finds two glasses and a bottle of Cabernet Sauvignon, and he fills the glasses half way.

—Come and eat, darling, he says. He looks at her and smiles. He remembers how his wife, after each argument, had employed the same tactic with him and had easily won him over, how his anger had evaporated so quickly as though he was never angry to begin with.

The squeaking of the rats seems to come from behind the walls, from unseen spaces, and to wait there patiently.

Maya picks up a plate and starts to eat.

—You can have some wine, too. I think you're old enough. I'm going to have some.

—Wine has alcohol. It removes your inhibitions and decreases your motor ability and cognitive ability.

—Yes. But sometimes that's exactly what a man needs.

—I remember my parents drinking a lot of wine and beer.

—And what did they do?

—They argued. And lost consciousness.

—Ah, but if you do it in moderation, it's a fine pleasure.

—Moderation? Alcohol is addictive.

He picks up the glass, twirls it, and sniffs it. With his lips gently touching the glass, he sips the liquid and feels it dispersing over the surface of his tongue.

—Hm. This is wonderful. You know, Maya, drinking wine is mostly about the smell. That's why you should sniff it first and then drink it. Then you'll get all the flavor and aroma.

Her unchanging eyes watch him as she eats.

—Go on, have a little taste. Try it with the food. It makes the food better.

Suddenly she puts down the plate, swallows the mor-sel already in her mouth, and picks up the glass. Twirling and sniffing the wine as he did, she sucks in a mouthful; then she squeezes her lips tightly, and her eyes become watery as she stares ahead. Finally she swallows and gasps.

—Ha ha. How's that? What do you think? Art says.

—Very bitter. And the alcohol, it rises to my head.

—It's an acquired taste. Then you'll like it more. He picks up his glass and holds it out to her and says, Cheers. You pick up your glass and touch mine.

She does so.

—To our health. May our journey be safe and uneventful, he says with a somber tone.

He empties his glass and pours himself another. Then they eat, accompanied by the constant squeaking of the rats. When he finishes, a warm fluster hangs about his face and neck; he feels bloated and uncomfortable. He gets up and goes outside. A cold wind ruffles the trees, and the sound of the branches bending and thrashing is the only evidence that something still exists beyond the surrounding darkness. In the direction of the city, the sky still glows red; something else must have caught fire. Maybe Maya was right; the city might burn down. Bracing himself against the wind and the occasional howl of unknown animals, he stands for a long time in the darkness. He looks up at the sky where there are small patches of clearing, where the intense dots of bright stars twinkle against the dark sky, stirring in him a curious yearning, as though a part of him had been constructed for this very purpose from man's earliest inception and for a cosmic puppet show that's being orchestrated for a strange purpose across a vast distance.

—Nothing. It's nothing, he mumbles to himself at last and goes back inside.

Maya has already settled into one of the sofas so that the light from the fire lights up the pages of the thick book she is holding. A blanket drapes her feet. His entrance doesn't disturb her reading. He goes to the fire and throws more logs onto it. Then, he goes toward the kitchen, following a faint idea, a sort of abandonment and forlornness that abruptly take hold of him. From the kitchen, he comes back holding two bottles of wine. He falls into the sofa and begins to cut away the aluminum wrapping around the corks.

—You shouldn't read in this light. It will ruin your eyes, he says.

She puts the book on her chest and glances at him. Turning on her side, she rests her head on her right arm, pulls the blanket to her neck, closes her eyes, and lets the book drop to the floor.

He twists the corkscrew into the cork, pulls it out, and puts the bottle to his mouth. The fluid runs almost continuously as he swallows. When the bottle feels light and nearly empty, he lets it drop to the ground, lets his body settle into the couch, and lets his mind be still so that the residue from a lifetime of friction with Anna can take form and flight again in the burning light. In a wondrous fluidity the fire gives life to everything, painting them in resplendent amber as he sees her dancing, her hair confluent with the air, her face untouchably beautiful, her hands with delicate fingers delineating space, her lithe legs twirling and inviting. His bloated stomach thumps with the beat of his heart, pumping harder and harder, and behind his eyes an intense pressure grows and tears begin to pool as he sees her image distorted in the firelight, receding from him. He closes his eyes and falls asleep.

14

First, he is conscious of being shaken, then of the deep–seated throbbing inside his skull where every little movement causes a painful quake. Maya is holding him by the shoulders, shaking him strongly, and as he stirs awake, she stops. With eyes barely open, he sees her towering over him, inspecting him, looking down as if from a podium. Now he tastes the welcome bitterness of the powder under his tongue and feels it percolating through the floor of his mouth. It makes him swallow.

—Art, you should wake up. You overslept. You shouldn't have gotten drunk last night. You lost consciousness just like my parents, Maya pronounces.

He pulls himself up against the sofa. He looks at her and sees she has already washed and changed clothes.

—Thanks, he murmurs.

—I put the powder under your tongue.

—I guess I was really out. Shouldn't have drunk so much.

—Did you take the powder last night? Maya says.

—I . . . I don't remember, he says and looks at his wristwatch; it's six minutes past eight.

Maya must have fed the fire, because it is burning strongly; the warm air seems to close in on him, choking him. He staggers to the front door and goes outside. A homogeneous gray sky obscures his sense of distance. The wind blows harshly and sways the trees at the edge of the vineyard. In the frigid air he feels awake and can focus as he leans against the car and breathes. Toward San Luis Obispo a column of intense black smoke still rises, billowing and swirling in an ever–changing motion, feeding an enormous mass of dark clouds that have gathered there from the day before. The sight shocks him. The whole city must be burning down; the wind must be fanning the fire, he thinks. Well, it's probably the most significant thing he has ever done in his life, but it's one among thousands of cities and not a particularly important one at that. Still, an awful stir, an irritation, and a burning sensation he readily recognizes as guilt begin to bubble in his stomach. Even if he were the last man on earth, must he feel guilt? In the previous world, it had been used by others, and often enough he himself had allowed it to work on him, to pulverize the tiniest resistance, to constrain and incapacitate the slightly raised head. It only requires one pair of eyes watching to induce it, even when that pair of eyes is only a possibility or imagined, but now those eyes are large, oblong, and beautifully gray, eyes that see things truly and are waiting for him inside. More and more, as he stares at the column, the plumes of black smoke draw him in with a strange promise of freedom, dissipating that unruly sensation that ought to go up in smoke. I've no guilt, he whispers.

Strangely invigorated, he turns.

—Maya, he says as he bursts through the door. We should have a quick breakfast and get on the road soon. We have to get to San Francisco and then onto Berkeley before nightfall.

The light through the windows is bright enough, and Maya

puts down the book she's been reading and stands up. She grabs a blanket and begins to fold it.

—You get things ready. I'll use the bathroom and I'll cook breakfast. How about a bowl of chili? It's always good for a cold day like this.

—That will be fine.

—All right. It'll be good, he says.

A moment later, he comes back from the bathroom and goes about opening the cans and cleaning the pan he used last night. Then he puts the pan over the fire and moves it about until it settles into the burning logs.

Soon the chili boils, and he splits it into equal halves.

—Come and eat, Maya, he calls as she's loading the blankets, the books, and the bottles of water into the car.

She comes in and sits down to the bowl. She puts her face over the rising steam and sniffs; she smiles secretly as she brings a spoonful to her lips.

As though oblivious to the heat, Art eats quickly, swallowing spoonfuls while drawing out a plan in his mind. I will continue north on the 101, he thinks, until I get to San Jose; then I'll have a choice of continuing on the 101 to San Francisco or taking the 808 straight to Berkeley.

—I was thinking, Maya, that I could show you one of the great cities of the world. San Francisco. I have many lovely memories there. It won't be the same but we can still walk the streets, go to Fisherman's Wharf, cross the Golden Gate Bridge. And if we're adventurous, we can take a boat and go under the bridge.

—I've seen pictures of the Golden Gate. Yes, I'd like that very much.

He smiles and nods to her. With a new day, he feels a lightness between them, two opposing psychic forces, or rather two different points of view reflecting across no ordinary chasm but a dimensional drift. Yet the more he thinks, the clearer it seems that only one can see the truth, by its very nature universal and unchanging regardless of the vantage from which it is seen. He stops his thought short and listens to the high-pitched hissing of the wind that blows in now and then through the small cracks under the windows and the front door.

Strangely, a low rumbling is mixed in with the hissing, and before he can comprehend it, it freezes him as though unconsciously he already knows what that noise is. Hearing that low, rhythmic rumbling so ubiquitous in his world, and perhaps because of that fact, he can't get himself to believe that he's hearing it now. Finally reality breaks through and he jumps up.

—Maya, you hear that? he utters.

—What?

—That noise.

—It sounds like a car.

—Yes, it's a car, he gasps. He grabs the shotgun and hesitates. Hah, hah, stay here. I'll see who . . .

He runs outside.

Up the gravel road, a car rolls slowly, a black and shiny Rolls-Royce, obviously very well-kept, and all the windows, including the windshield, are tinted so black that Art can't see anyone inside, not even the driver. The car rolls with impervious constancy as if nothing can stand in its way.

Several seconds pass, and as the car is getting closer to him, he fidgets, wanting to do something but not knowing what. And why should he run? he thinks and looks at the shotgun in his hands. Did he reload the gun after Maya shot yesterday? He can't remember, yet he must not look into the gun's chamber now. The wind abruptly picks up strength and lashes his face; reflexively, he raises the shotgun and levels the barrel at the car. But the car continues to roll smoothly; it has a broad and angular frame made of steel. Art had seen these expensive cars before in the previous world, even then existing in another world by themselves.

The car stops three yards from him. The engine stops, and the driver's door opens slowly. Art hears the crunching of gravel.

—I'm unarmed, a man hollers as he emerges from the car.

There's an air of calm and unexpected conventionality in the black suit and the white dress shirt, the costume of a man who is having a business meeting. With the most casual movement, he shuts the door, and though a long, tidy mustache curving around the corners of his mouth and a goatee hide his face, the broad smile is visible. The eyebrows, sloping and thick, sit over deep, dark eyes, and at that distance Art can't quite make out what type of man he is but has a sensation of déjà vu as if he'd seen this man on a poster somewhere. The man raises his hands high and shows the slight redness of his palms.

—Hello. How do you do? the man says. Through the hissing wind, the voice carries a strange warmth, a reassuring steadiness bordering on paternal wisdom. My name is Sam. Sam Shield. I mean no harm. I'm just happy to see another living face, he says.

—Hello, Art says so softly as to be barely audible.

His boots grating against the gravel, Sam advances step by step, smiling as he comes, and his arms drop to his sides. Now in front of Art, the lanky frame stands distinctly taller, and thin strands of the man's hair fall to his neck and move in a disheveled mass. Wrinkles across his forehead and along the side of his nose give him the appearance of being at least a dozen years older than Art, and from his skin a deep tan seems to almost bristle as if from a seething undersurface, imparting to his façade its hidden nature.

—I'm glad to make your acquaintance, he says and extends his hand.

—Art Sand, Art says curtly and shakes the man's hand. His moment of vacillation magnifies, and his mind is flustered by a myriad of questions of which he is barely conscious and which suddenly upset his plans. He continues to sway slightly in the wind in a prolonged awkward silence.

—I am awfully glad to meet you, Arthur. Do you think I might go inside your home to get out of the wind? Well, I know it's probably not your home, but given the world the way it is, it's yours if you'd like. There's no one to say otherwise, he says and grins, showing his long white canines. Well, I know I wouldn't say anything. Just glad to see another face.

—Please come in, Art says and shows him the door.

His voice has a slight New England accent, Art thinks, and yet the pronunciation is clear and precise and has a tinge of nasal homeliness, harkening toward the northeast somewhere, or perhaps even further in that direction.

How is this man still alive? he thinks as he follows Sam inside.

—Oh, who may this be? Sam says when he sees Maya standing by the fireplace. Please don't be concerned, Miss. I'm just glad to see another face after so long. My name is Sam. It's my pleasure to make your acquaintance.

—This is Maya, Art says.

—Maya, what a wonderful name. So mystical, so appropriate for our new age. Don't you agree? he says and bows his head toward her. The smile persists on his face as he moves to the sofa. You don't mind if I sit down and rest my old legs a bit.

—Not at all.

—Can I trouble you for something to drink?

—Water. That's all we have.

—Coffee. Do you have any coffee?

—I'll look in the kitchen, Art says but hesitates. I'll be out of the room, and Maya will be here by herself with this stranger, he thinks. He looks at Sam, and now he can see the dark irises darting rapidly from place to place as though studying, mapping out the room. Then quickly he dismisses the thought; what can he possibly want from them when the whole world is for the taking? He goes into the back where he remembers seeing cups and a can of instant coffee. A moment later he comes back, moving awkwardly with the shotgun hanging off his shoulder and holding a small kettle, cups, spoons and the instant coffee.

— Well, I guess that'll have to do, Sam says. Without electricity you can't grind the beans, can you? And it's hard to get electricity when you're on the move. Unless you get your hand on a mechanical coffee grinder.

—We're going north, Art says as he fills the kettle with water and puts it over the fire. Where are you heading?

—Nowhere in particular.

—How did you know we're here?

—I saw the light from your fire, but it would have been improper to visit you last night. Well, frankly dangerous to visit anyone at night, he says and smiles, and his eyes linger on the shotgun. So . . . so I waited until this morning. Do you know anything about the fire in the city? Since you say you're heading north, you must have passed through San Luis Obispo on your way. I was going to stay in the city for a while but the fire drove me out.

—Oh, it was an accident. We were practicing with the shotgun . . . And you know.

—It's all right. Unattended cities are bound to burn. From

lightning, natural combustion, what not. And there are thousands of cities. It makes no difference to me one way or another. I'll just find another place.

—Precisely, Art says as he glances at Maya. It's just a city.

—I see you're holding up well. And I'm glad. All of a sudden, Sam says loudly almost shouting, human lives are valuable once again. Oh, you don't know how glad I am to see you.

—What about you? How are you holding up? You know how everyone is, Art says.

Sam's eyes rest on him for a second, perhaps knowing the true meaning of the question.

—I'm well as you can see, Sam says. What did you do before? In the previous world, shall we say?

—I was a doctor.

—Excellent. In that case you're still a doctor. As long as there are people who will get sick, you will always be a doctor. I can't say that about a banker, a politician, or lawyer, or a multitude of other professions. You are very fortunate to have something that will keep you busy in this new world, to make yourself useful.

—I suppose so. What about you?

—Oh, how to say it. I was a Jack-of-all-trades, a tinkerer. Still useful, I hope, in this new world.

—How are you still alive? The question seems to burst out finally.

—Somehow, Sam says and grins. I can't wait for a cup of coffee.

They look at the small kettle over the fire.

Maya raises her eyebrows and stares at them. At length the fire sizzles as the water boils and spills over.

—Excellent. I'd like a cup of coffee now. Even if it's only instant coffee.

Art puts two scoops of coffee into each cup. Would you like to try it, Maya? he says.

—Yes, I would like that, she replies.

—One more scoop for me, please, Sam says. I like my coffee fairly strong.

—Sure.

Art fills the cups with boiling water.

—Thank you, kind sir. You're a gentleman, Sam says. He brings the cup up to his nose and sniffs the rising steam. The aroma is pungent, he says. There's a suggestion of nuts and also, of course, chemicals and preservatives. How regrettable.

Art sits down at the other end of the sofa. The smell of the coffee reminds him how close he was to oblivion, he shudders. He puts the cup down. He hasn't had any coffee since the day he discovered his daughter's EpiPen®, and he has no desire to start drinking it again; dependence on the powder is enough, he thinks. Now he wants to know how this man has remained alive, if somehow he also knows about the powder.

—Hmm, a hot cup of coffee on a cold day. Nothing is more delightful and delectable, Sam says. He sips the coffee, leans back into the sofa, and caresses his beard. Don't you agree? All these small rituals that we once performed—drinking coffee, reading the paper, taking a walk, lunching with friends. And even work. Can you believe it? Daily work to keep yourself busy, paying the mortgage, paying taxes. They made life delightful. I truly miss them.

—I don't . . . I don't know, Art says. All those things sound familiar to him in the same way small tidbits of academic information sound, coming from a guest speaker at a scientific conference, and urge him to analyze them, to dissect them, and to discover their truth.

—What field were you in?

—Neurology, neuroscience.

—How fascinating, Sam says. Perhaps you can enlighten me as to the cause of this plague.

—The Death Sleep.

—Yes, I think that's what the media eventually called it.

—The disease is characterized by the rapid deterioration of cognitive ability and memory. Eventually those afflicted slip into unconsciousness, into a type of sleep. I have seen many encephalograms of these patients and it's as though they are sleeping. Their brain waves looked exactly like they're in REM sleep.

Sam sips the coffee with a slow, guarded movement, and at odd intervals he throws brief glances at Maya, as though by adjoining these glances he can construct a full picture of the girl.

—Sometimes they wake up and move about and do chores, Art says.

—Chores. Yes that's precisely how I would describe it, Sam says. I agree. Sometimes I see them doing things.

—They're only acting out ingrained habits. Waking up, making breakfast, going about doing their usual business; all the while they're still deep in a narcosis state. But all that is over now. Everyone is dead. The cause remains a mystery.

Maya, who once again finds delight in blowing away the steam rising over the cup and taking sips of the coffee, looks up at them; she appears suddenly cognizant of the conversation that somehow piques her interest.

—How are you still alive? she says so calmly and naturally, her eyes fixed on Sam, leaving him no chance for obfuscation.

Art too keeps his eyes on him, certain not to let the moment pass.

—Ah, Sam mumbles. Well, it was how shall I say it? Simply serendipity as our great philosophers often remarked. Serendipity. It's a great concept, a great idea that expresses it all. Yes, that's how I'm alive today.

—What are you taking? Maya says, once again with a serenity bordering on rudeness, refusing to be misled.

—Well, of course. That's where it ends, I mean the story. But if the kind lady will allow me a little, shall we say, leeway, I'll get to that soon enough.

Maya says nothing and continues to look at him.

—All right. Where do I start? Sam says. All right, I was educated at the best university in Massachusetts. My major was organic chemistry but my minor was philosophy, and over time, I couldn't understand why, but the minor began to overtake the major. Yes, it was unusual until it was too late, but I was beginning to think more about man's nature, the nature of free will, and man's behavior than about the shape of benzene.

—The perfect hexagon of carbons, Maya says.

—Yes, dear girl. I can see you're quite sharp. Benzene is as perfect as man's nature is flawed. Regrettable, yes, regrettable. Man's nature, yes . . . I should be honest, there are not too many people left in the world for lies. Sam sighs and stares into the blank space before him as though speaking to no one in particular. I was flawed. I was disenchanted, cynical. The more I thought about man and the world, oh God, what a world it was. Art knows, don't you, Art? A horrible, terrible place that . . . that got what it deserved, sleep. Yes, I never thought about it like that, a fair treatment for an incurable disease.

Maya's forehead tenses, and her eyes squint at him. Sam is taken back.

—Yes, dear girl, Sam continues, you must let me tell it

fully—how shall I say it, make the full confession, nothing less. So where was I? Yes, I was disenchanted and cynical, and so I used my knowledge of chemistry not to do good but . . .

Sam puts the cup of coffee down and clasps his hands together, shaking slightly, as though appealing to an unknown power.

At last he says softly, I made drugs . . . Methamphetamine. Yes, it was . . . liberating.

—Liberating? Art says. So you were a drug dealer.

—No, no. It was not like that. I simply made the drugs. Well, of course they paid me a large sum of money each time. But I never dispensed it. So at least technically I wasn't. But you're right, I was corrupt and immoral like the worst of them. However, it was liberating in the sense that it cured my disease, my anger and disenchantment. As long as I made the drug I was at peace.

—Because you knew there were people using the drugs and that they deserved what happened to them. It reaffirmed your cynicism about humankind. Isn't that right?

—More or less. But eventually it was more about control. Somehow, I felt like I was controlling all these useless little lives. Their existence depended on me. For the first time, I found joy in chemistry. I couldn't wait for the next day to rise and start the reactions, and often I would stay up late hovering over the Bunsen burners, the boiling flasks.

—So that's how you have survived the Death Sleep. Methamphetamine.

—No, if I may. Methamphetamine was just one drug. I made dozens more. What have we in the narcotic family? Morphine of course. Hydrocodone, fentanyl, oxycodone and yes, yes, how can I leave out the best—cocaine—But . . . but.

—Methamphetamine is a neural stimulant. It counters the

effects of the Death Sleep on the central nervous system. How else do you survive? Maya says.

—Dear girl, you're clever. But there is so much more. Please allow me, Sam says and holds up his index finger. Please, dear girl. Allow me.

He picks up the cup of coffee and sips several times.

—Where was I? Yes, making all those addictive narcotics was not enough for me. Naturally I evolved just like any living thing. Soon enough I lost interest. Something was missing; I didn't know what exactly and yet I could feel its absence. I went for days thinking about it, ignoring food, basic hygiene. What could it be? Thinking and thinking endlessly and . . . Ah ha! It finally came to me. The mass of humanity is there, existing for the taking. I could control them, but how? I had to have something that would hook people and yet they had to be able to function normally and not be destroyed by it. These addictive drugs have existed for years and they're most destructive, so they're not the answer. What, what could this miracle drug be?

—What can it be? Maya says; her wide eyes fixate on him with an unnerving look.

—You're a clever girl. You're thinking, you're taking on the challenge. Good for you. Well, think of it. What is it that people want most? One day the answer came to me.

He stops and takes a gulp.

—What is it? Tell me, Maya says, almost with a shriek.

Though Art smiles calmly, a mixture of confusion and awe overwhelm him, for he finds pleasure in having conversation with this man, and yet the callousness and apparent disregard for ethics disturb him as if in this new world truth can finally reveal itself.

—The answer came to me, Sam begins again slowly. The

answer came to me one day while I was in a restaurant and there was a kid's menu.

—A kid's menu? What is a kid's menu? Maya says.

—You don't know what a kid's menu is? Sam says and glances at Art.

—She . . . she didn't go out much, Art says. A kid's menu is a menu with food items specifically for kids. The portions are smaller and less expensive, you know, made for children.

—Anyhow, a kid's menu, Sam says impatiently. I saw a maze on it. And of course I saw the way through the maze right away. I saw the whole maze, everything from beginning to end, the whole wiggling path.

—A kid's menu with a maze? Art says.

—Could a child do that? I mean, take one look and see the path from beginning to end. No, not an average child. You're a neuroscientist, you can tell me. Probably not. A child would use a crayon to trace the way through the maze by trial and error.

—Yes, that's how an average child would do it, Art says. So your point is?

—Now for the other side of the coin. I like to look at things from different perspectives. If I were to look at a complex equation, a chemical equation or a mathematical equation for instance, what would I do? Can I see it as easily and as clearly as the maze on the kid's menu? Not a chance. So what's the difference?

—Intelligence, Art says. You're obviously more intelligent than a child.

—More intelligent than an average child but less intelligent than, shall we say, a mathematical genius. But that's the exact point, don't you see?

Sam abruptly stops speaking and looks at them searchingly, perhaps waiting for them to fill in the gap. This is something that in the past would have interested Art immensely, but instead his dreary mind now anticipates the end of this little story where the prize is revealed. So, the chemical keeping Sam alive is more potent and longer lasting than the powder. Avoiding Sam's gaze, he turns to the window and realizes that the wind has ceased. The swishing of the wind sweeping under the door and the small cracks around the windowpanes has given way to a strange quiet, in which he hears the slight high–pitched white noise in his ears.

—The wind has stopped, Art says.

—You're right, Sam says. I hadn't noticed, God forbid, the quiet eye of the storm.

—I understand what you were saying, Maya says.

—Yes, the stillness of the air. You can almost feel an emptiness when it's this quiet. It's very disquieting, paradoxically. One is, how shall we say, aware of one's existence.

—No, that's not it, Maya says. What you were saying before, about seeing the maze and knowing it all at once. I know what you mean. When I first read words, I had to read one word at a time, but now I can see all the words in the sentence and know.... The best way to describe it is that I am conscious of the words. I'm conscious of all the words at once.

—Exactly, my dear girl, Sam says, and in his eyes a sparkle of uncommon curiosity can be seen as they latch onto Maya.

And Art sees that undeniable sparkle and understands its meaning as only one, who once lived in that same maniacal world that sparkle came from, can understand its true intention. So that's why he's volunteering his tale, Art thinks. With the thought, a cold sweat and a prickly sensation spread across his skin.

—More consciousness is precisely it. I wanted to make a drug that would allow people to be more conscious. Can you imagine what that would do to the average person? To be more aware, to be able to take things in all at once. To approach the mind of God. . . . Can you imagine the high, the exhilaration that would bring? But at last this new–found consciousness would give way to the same old dullness. That drug would, without doubt, be more addictive than any drugs invented by man thus far.

—You were able to make this drug, Art says coldly.

—Yes and no. But I was well on my way. Neural stimulation as you, dear girl, mentioned earlier, was the key. I realized that much. I worked doggedly. I started with the adrenaline molecule and I modeled every possible configuration, every possible minute change that could be made. And I worked for days making them, purifying them.

—So you made the drug. And you survived the Death Sleep with it, Art says.

—Yes and no. I made many compounds. Some of them were as likely to fry the neurons as to stimulate them. Countless chimpanzees died for the experiment.

—How horrible. You tested them on chimpanzees? Maya says and glares at them both.

—Yes, dear girl. It was most unfortunate but unavoidable. And the most promising compounds, Sam says and sighs loudly, I tested them on people. The junkies who were only too happy to try anything.

A silence abruptly descends. More than the fact that these are terrible things Sam admits to committing, even though they belong to the old world, as though they can never be judged now, it is that these facts add to the chilly sensation that swept over Art only a minute ago and is now building into a horrible fright. Art's heart begins to palpitate helplessly, his body assumes an odd rigidity, his joints seem locked into position, and he wants to condemn

Sam's new drug and to curse his own curiosity. Turning his head toward the window, he sees the bright sky approaching midday.

—This spectacular experiment, my dear girl, Sam begins again suddenly, went on for many months. Until I had it. You can see it on me. This flush, this capillary dilation on my skin is a side effect of the drug. It has kept me alive. A veritable wonder drug.

With the impression that Sam is talking to Maya only, Art rises, while trying to quell the shaking of his hands, and carefully takes the shotgun with him. He goes to the door and opens it to a bright, sunny sky. The gloom has dissipated. The air is so still it might be encased in glass. Behind him he hears without understanding Sam's warm, hypnotic voice, regaling Maya in his story of subjugating the masses, and under that rhythmic, vocal undulation he catches passing whispers of something too sibilant.

—Maya, we should go, Art says as he turns around. It's getting late.

—No, no, Art, Maya says, you haven't been listening. He's found the wonder drug. It's what you have been looking for. We don't need to go north anymore.

—No, we need to go.

—Tell him again, Sam. He didn't hear you.

—Yes, dear girl. Art, come and listen to my story, Sam says as he turns toward Art. So after months of very difficult work and literally being secluded in my lab, I found the wonder drug. Unbeknownst to me, the world that was familiar to me, that was there for the taking, that had set me off on this quest in the first place, had changed while I was away. The Death Sleep had begun. The chaos. The hysteria. How could it be? Was it possible? A modern myth? But sure enough people locked themselves in their houses only to wither away. I, too, felt its effects. The stupefying dullness, the indescribable somnolence as if my eyelids were sutured together against my will. Oh, it was beyond horror, but I'm sure you know all about it.

—How lucky you are, Maya says. You found the wonder drug just in time to save yourself.

—Lucky, yes, dear girl, in a manner of speaking. I was this close to ruling the world and it all slipped away. When I felt the effects of the Death Sleep, I tried other compounds first—adrenaline, amphetamine and its various modifications, but there were so many side effects. It was not till the very end that I used the wonder drug. It was truly wonderful; my mind resumed its sharpness, I was awake again. In my magnanimity, I wanted to share with the world. I was willing to give it all away to save humanity. But by then it was far, far beyond the point of no return. I mean, the world was already gone by then. There was no government to speak of. No one would even answer the doorbell. Fear gripped the air. I couldn't give it to them even if I'd wanted to. Yes, yes, I wanted to.

—But you saved the people around you, Maya says. You did what you could.

—In a way, my dear girl. I did what I could. There are so few of us left.

—Can you give us some of that wonder drug? Maya says. Or you can show us how to make it. So we won't have to go north for the powder. You'll save Art.

—Powder? Sam says.

—It's a modification of amphetamine, Maya says. He must take it every six hours to live.

—And you dear girl? You don't need it, I see. How wonderful. A marvelous miracle. I daresay.

—I don't need your wonder drug, Art says, almost shouting as though to interrupt them intentionally. We have to go. It's been a real pleasure talking to you, but we must be going.

Immediately he goes out without waiting for an answer. He hears his name being bounced about. Then Maya runs up behind him as he opens the door to the car.

—Art, why are you going? He has the wonder drug. You heard him. We don't need to go anywhere.

—Maya, get in the car. Just do as I tell you, Art says in a soft, whispering voice as he sees the dark shape of Sam coming through the door and nearing them.

—Art, hold there a minute. Why the sudden rush to go? I hope it's not something I said. Nothing I said offended you, I sincerely hope. Sir, if it was something, anything at all that I might have said, I apologize without reservation.

Sam stands a few yards away. His right palm is placed over his heart, and his deep dark eyes seem to study the new situation, to take in the sudden development.

—No, it's not anything to do with you. We just have to go.

—Shouldn't we stay together? Sam says. There are so few of us left. We can build again. Build a new society, only this time it will be our vision. It will be wonderful, Art. Think about it. A society of justice and peace. We will take the best from the old sleeping world and make a new beautiful world. You and I can do this; we remember how awful it was but also its beauty. It had its own beauty.

More than meaningless, Sam's words make palpable the fright that has been enveloping and threatening to paralyze Art; he gets in the car and starts the engine. Not only that, the pounding of his heart now sends one thunderous jolt after another up his head and into his ears, so overwhelming that he has to concentrate to listen.

—Hold on there, Art. Please, please just one minute. Well, at least let me give your little girl a parting gift. Yes, only a minute of your time, Sam hollers and hurries to his own car. He opens the trunk and takes out a rectangular device and a charging cord. Waving them in the air, he approaches Maya, who is now standing outside the car on the driver's side.

Art rolls down the window and says, Get in the car, Maya.

—What do you have there? Maya says as she goes toward Sam.

How can I possibly make her understand the danger? Art thinks. She listens to him, but she does not understand the shadows between his words, the shades of his intentions. She has no idea what the world was like before, what men were like before.

—My dear girl, look here. You push this button to turn it on. And you touch the screen, touch these symbols to activate the content organized under it.

—I understand. It's organized in a systematic algorithm. Specific information is stored in a branching fashion, Maya says and takes the device from Sam.

—My dear girl, you're bright. But the thing I want to show you is this. You see the bookshelf? There, you see all the books arranged under it? Thousands of them. Anything you might possibly find interesting. Philosophy, science, literature, art, even horticulture, agriculture—anything you might want to know. It's a veritable encyclopedia. The best part is you can take it with you. And the keyboard is on the back. Just flip it around and you can type. Anything you like. All your thoughts.

—Thank you. Oh, thank you, Sam. I've been lugging around those heavy books.

—And this, my dear girl. Don't forget this. This is a charger; you plug it into the car while you're driving and charge it.

—I understand.

—Maya, please get in the car, Art says curtly.

As Maya walks around the car and taps the screen of the device repeatedly, Sam moves toward Art.

—Art, she doesn't need the drug does she? Sam says quietly. Where did you find her? She is the future. We must stick together and rebuild. Art, you must be reasonable. I have what you need. The wonder drug is so much better than what you have now. It will cut down the number of times you have to take the powder. You can sleep longer if you like, no fear of not waking up, and it will restore your consciousness, every bit of it. It will make you feel so much more alive. So much more conscious.

Without turning away, Art hears Maya getting in and shutting the door. His hand, now sweating profusely, feels the slippery stock of the shotgun lying on his lap.

—Thank you for everything. It was a pleasure to meet you, Art says and eases the car forward.

Sam steps back and puts his hand up to wave, and as he does so, Art can see through the flap of his black jacket the butt of a pistol sticking out on the left side of his waistband.

—We'll meet again, Sam says.

There is no question about it now. The sight of the pistol on Sam's hip removes all doubt and turns crystalline the nebulous fog of trepidation he's felt about the man, and with it an incredible determination, fomented by the instinct for survival, seizes him so completely that he almost flies down the hill. Things jostle as they bounce up and down over each bump in the road. Maya holds onto the computer and screams.

—Slow down, Art. Slow down.

From the dirt track, the Hummer jumps onto the asphalt road, and the tires shriek. At blinding speed, wire fences, rows of leafless grapevines, and the occasional shape of an animal, a deer perhaps, flow fuzzily past, but still he keeps the pressure on the gas pedal. His body now pulsates as one with his heart.

—Slow down, Maya screams. It's not safe at this speed. There are things on the road.

—We have to get away. Just listen to me. You don't know, you don't know.

—Don't know what? Explain to me clearly.

—Explain the old world to you? Hah, no time for that. There are things that you will never learn from reading, he says breathlessly.

Words fly out very fast, his eyes hop from the road to the rearview mirror, to the odometer, which registers above eighty miles an hour, and his right hand alternates between holding the steering wheel and tapping the stock of the shotgun.

—I don't understand.

—Let me think. Let me think. Which way? He knows we're going north. We should head east then north again. Where is the road? The next road?

—Please slow down.

But he keeps driving. Time passes quickly, or is it the other way around? He struggles to think. Events occur very quickly, but time drags on slowly when you're in flight. How many minutes have passed? He doesn't know, but at last he feels the ebbing of the rush of blood to his brain. He lifts his foot from the gas pedal, and the car slows down. Suddenly, his foot presses down on the brake, and the car skids to a standstill.

—You want to get away. Why do you stop? she says.

—Shhhhh.

He opens the windows on both sides and tells her to listen.

—What are we listening for? she says.

—Shhh, he says and puts his head outside the car. But he hears nothing; his heart is still throbbing too strongly, sending the pulsation to his ears, and the customary high–pitched buzzing redoubles.

—I can't hear anything, he says at last. Please listen, won't you, Maya. Do me a favor. Please listen and see if you hear anything.

—What am I listening for?

—A car, a car. Sound of an engine. To see if he's following us.

Jumping on the seat and thrusting her thin body halfway out the window, she turns her ears toward the road from where they've come. He sits very still, trying not to make a sound, but can manage only for a couple of seconds, as though his internal processes are quickening, becoming chaotic and independent of his control and consciousness, and then he can no longer remain quiet.

—Well? he says impatiently.

—I hear . . . she says but continues to listen.

—Tell me what you hear.

—I can't be sure.

—Maya, this is not the time to be logical. Just tell me what you hear.

—I'm not sure.

—But you hear something. Yes or no.

—I do hear something.

—He is coming. It's a car, isn't it?

—Yes. It's a faint sound.

Her words are superfluous now, and in his mind the chase scene, as in a horror movie he once saw in his youth, is becoming real, in which the powerful Rolls–Royce runs him off the road and Sam comes out with his pistol, blasting him from a distance at which his shotgun pellets can only fall uselessly to the ground. What should I do? he thinks and realizes that he has unconsciously resumed driving. The car moves slowly along while his mind wheezes helplessly through.

—Maybe he wants to give us something. The wonder drug. He may just want to help you. That's a possibility.

—You think so? Maybe. Maybe we should be with him. Stick together like he said. He seems like a nice enough guy. Right?

—You shouldn't be alarmed. He gave me this device.

She pushes on the button, and the screen lights up. Tapping successively on the bookshelf, she brings a book up on the screen and begins to read. He turns to her, an unspeakable incredulity choking him. How can she read now? he thinks. She will never understand, never understand. The words repeat in his mind, and with each repetition a stultifying density increases until something explodes in his brain. Arrrghhh, he cries out. Maya jerks back, startled.

—What's the matter? she says.

He doesn't answer, but he knows what he must do. That explosion in his brain suddenly clears his thoughts and dissipates his fear; he sees the road, the grasses on both sides, the trees just beyond that, and the hill rising behind the trees. On the sides of the road, the grasses are dense and at least three feet tall, and the blades and stalks poke haphazardly. He turns the wheel onto the grasses, and the car bounces until it is completely off the road.

Maya's large oblong eyes appear larger than ever as she stares at him.

—Get out, Maya. Go through those trees and up the hill. Hide yourself. I will come for you. If not, just go on by yourself . . .

—Why? What are you going to do?

—Listen to me. Listen to me this one time, if you ever listen to me. Just this time. Listen to me now. He is dangerous. If I don't come for you, just go on. Don't let him take you. Learn to survive by yourself.

—Art, please, what are you doing?

—Go. Go now. Run through the trees and up the hill. Quickly, Art screams at her.

As though his voice has the physical force of brutal hands, Maya recoils and jumps from the car, still clutching the computer. A soft whimper trails behind her as she races toward the trees; a branch catches her leg and she falls. She gets up again. For a still moment, Art looks after her, and the sight of her small frame, of her skinny legs and the flailing flaps of her jacket, crushes him. An indescribable tenderness swells in his chest and removes all doubt as to what he is about to do—he will never let Sam touch her.

Standing outside the car, he takes easy breaths. The atmosphere is clear after the wind, and the pure air feels enlivening, making him want to live forever, to see every blade of grass, to touch the rough bark of the trees. So still and clear as to be almost nothingness, the air moves against his fingers as he waves his hand before him to test its existence. From up high in the branches, some squirrels observe him curiously. He wishes he could know true quietude, but the chronic buzzing in his ears persists and is most violent at this exact moment when all is quiet. Leaving the car door open, he goes to a tree nearby and crouches down in the grass. The shotgun feels awkward and slippery in his hands, and his heart throbs so strongly that he feels the rush of blood against his neck, dizzying him. Suddenly he looks at his watch and realizes that it's almost time for the powder and yet there is no time for it. Should he get the powder now? Maybe not, he thinks; the surging adrenaline in his system is adequate for now. He surveys his position. He looks in the direction Maya went, but sees no one; she must have gone up the hill, he thinks. At least she will get away. The grass reaches only to his knees, and this gives him the impression of being exposed. Sam might see him before he has a chance to act. This spot isn't good enough, but he thinks he hears the rumble of the Rolls–Royce drawing near. Should he stay in his current position or try something else? This won't do, he thinks; I must hide somewhere else. The unmistakable sound of a car approaching now breaks the quiet with its artificiality. The grass isn't tall enough here to hide him, he decides finally, but where else can he hide? Then an idea comes to him; he moves toward the front of the Hummer, gets down on his knees, and finally lies prone. Tall stalks of grass poke at this neck and face as he crawls under the car. He inhales the pungent smell of grass as his elbows crush the blades and the stalks, and a memory from his childhood, of a time when he rolled in the grass and the same smell saturated his nose, comes to him pleasantly.

Under the car, he's completely surrounded by a thick wall of grass, and yet he can still see through it and look along the smooth asphalt road. He pulls the shotgun forward, pumps the handle, and realizes that the chamber has been empty all along. Sam could have taken him down if he'd known. Perhaps Maya is right, and it's all in his mind. But he thinks it, therefore Sam must think it too, which was exactly how the world before worked—thoughts, no matter how evil, were possible, and because evil thoughts were possible, they were real and actionable. He chuckles; "actionable" is one of those weird words that, in his previous life, he never thought he would ever use. He aims the barrel through the grass and waits.

The tires finally come rolling slowly along the asphalt. From his position lying flat on the ground, he can see the treads of the new tires. The car stops twenty yards away, right in the middle of the road. Then nothing moves. Come on, come on, come closer, he thinks. What are you waiting for? Come on. He'd left both doors of the Hummer open, Art suddenly remembers, and he can only guess what this means to Sam, if this has alarmed him.

Maybe this is the reason why Sam sits in his car and waits. I must wait too, Art thinks; I can wait forever. The longer I wait, the further away she gets.

Then the thought seizes him. What if Sam is not by himself? What if there are others with him? Why didn't I think of that before? he thinks. My plan crumbles. I should have kept driving, driving as fast as I could, or even hidden in one of the many abandoned houses along the road, where we would never be found. Oh, this must be insanity, this murderous slow amber in me that is stoked up by whatever that's causing the Death Sleep. The moment must come soon, he thinks, and he can almost see men stepping out both sides of the Rolls–Royce. I must not make a sound, he thinks and tries to slow his breathing. Time ticks on with each thump of his heart, pulsing rapidly through his ears, time which has no reference to anything outside and thus is useless, and under the car, surrounded by the grass, it is dark enough that he can't see his watch and so he doesn't know how much time has passed since the Rolls–Royce stopped. His fingers on the shotgun slip slightly, a fine film of sweat glosses over his fingertips, and the index finger on the trigger seems to lose its sense of position. He thinks about wiping the sweat off his hand, but somehow his fingers won't obey his command to move from the trigger.

The metallic creak of the car's door opening finally comes. The stiff black pants and the familiar boots step out of the car, and the boots scuff and grate across the asphalt. The boots halt in front of the Rolls–Royce, and Art sees the fine scaly pattern of snake–skin as Sam stands there. Then he watches as Sam approaches slowly, in a methodical silence, moving closer and closer until he is only a dozen feet away. The slippery index finger squeezes; through the opening between the blades of grass the shot explodes, hitting Sam's right leg. Sam shrieks as he falls. Art pumps the shotgun and fires.

Much later, the only thing he will remember about this moment is the intense ringing in his ears and the smell of gun smoke.

15

To make sure that she won't see the body, he drives the car a mile down the looping road, parks, and climbs up the hill layered with thick, green grass to where he thinks he will find her. He calls out her name again and again until his voice grows tired. He sloshes through the bushes and peeks at half–shadows under the midday sun, worrying that she has gone too far, his eyes searching for and fixating at any nuanced shapes with her resemblance. At the top of the small hill, he looks toward the city and sees the black smoke from the fire still rising, drifting, and being blown inland across half the horizon. The amorphous black smoke hangs thinly in the air, a sort of dream–smoke with vast, fading edges that are more real in the imagination. Then on the downward slope of the far side of the hill, he catches her stare, the large, oblong, unyielding eyes. Her legs are bent beneath her, and the oversized jacket spreads loosely on the ground as she sits under an enormous oak, motionless enough to be part of the tree itself. He scuttles down toward her.

The thin crust on his fingers, giving him a sensation of wearing gloves, doesn't occur to him until he stands in front of her.

—Maya, we have to get you better–fitting clothes, he says and looks at her without actually distinguishing her from the plants. She appears oddly natural in her place among them.

—Maya, I was calling out for you. Didn't you hear me?

She doesn't answer. Instead, her large, oblong eyes stare at his hands.

Now he looks at them too and sees the reddish speckles of congealed blood in the crevices of his palms and along the tips of his fingers.

—Didn't you hear me?

She doesn't answer, and the intensity and clarity of her gaze remain the same. In the bright light of midday, there is something dreadful in her gaze.

—Please, Maya. We must go.

His fingers suddenly tighten into hard fists, and he turns. Without waiting, he begins to climb the hill, returning to the place from where he came. Over his shoulder, he tells her that the car is parked on the other side of the hill, on the road, and that he will wait for her there.

How could I forget to clean my hands? he thinks. After the gunshots, he had crawled from underneath the Hummer, gone to Sam, and stood over him. The smell of blood, so distinct and raw, rose to him from Sam's mangled chest and open mouth. Then he knelt down next to Sam, whose eyes were already fixed, and opened his jacket to search the pockets. He sensed a haze of bloody vapor, of atomized plasma enveloping his head, clinging to his skin and his eyeballs and flowing into his lungs, and he could taste it at the back of his throat as he often did during a nosebleed. At a mere touch, blood clung to his fingertips, and as he searched Sam's body, it stuck to his palms as though that was one of its many purposes. He felt Sam's pistol still tucked inside his belt.

In one of Sam's pockets, Art found remnants of a small glass jar, undoubtedly shattered by the shotgun pellets, and the powder inside had been dissolved in the blood. An intense and nauseating sensation of human indecency and profanity closed his throat as his fingers continued into the pants' pockets; he jumped up gasping for air. Then he went to the Rolls–Royce and searched it. It was completely empty. No more wonder drug to be found.

What have I done? he now thinks as he climbs the hill. Once he is past the hilltop, he descends toward the Hummer, running, his fingers still curled tightly, feeling the crusty sensation of dried blood. He goes directly to the back of the Hummer, pulls out a bottle of water, and pours it over his hands. One hand scrubs the other. He scrubs vigorously and digs into his palms with a rag again and again until his palms feel swollen and painful. Finally, he brings his palms up close to examine them, and incredibly, within the patterns of ridges that make up his fingerprints, he sees tiny reddish spots and wonders if they are not his own blood.

Before he can scrub his hands again, the passenger door slams. He closes the hatch and gets in the car. Maya is sitting very still and leaning forward, staring straight at the road ahead.

Against the steering wheel, his fingers feeling warm and swollen, the skin raw and irritated, he steers the car into the middle of the road, keeping steady pressure on the gas. The engine rumbles and at times screeches with a heckling pitch. At places where the road curves, he sees in front of him trees with straight, stiff trunks and shifting masses of leaves, and he remembers Sam's stiff legs in the black pants and scaly boots grating against the asphalt, then the loud gun blast that triggered the ringing in his ears, and the shifting smoke that hung around the blades of grass. The scent of gunpowder is stuck in his nose, and the rawness of blood nauseates him; the noise in his ears peaks with an overpowering shriek, and his head becomes light. How terrifying is it that his mere reasoning, his logic enabled by the process of language, could result in such a thing; actionable, he thinks, the one word that summed it up, that made it possible.

The car moves very fast now; it swerves within a narrow range, barely avoiding a turned–over car here, an outstretched corpse there, and through a stretch of road littered with pieces of rotting paper and clothes, it causes them to be airborne, to take flight behind the car like a stream of confetti. You can't go back now and it's better that you're still here, he thinks; you did it for her. You did what any father would do. He can never touch her now.

With that thought, he turns to look at her. Her large, oblong eyes glare at him, her forehead furrows, and she is mouthing something; this look on her face shocks him. Now he hears her. Automatically he lifts his foot from the gas pedal.

—Are you deaf? she yells.

—What, what are you saying?

—I've been telling you to slow down. What's wrong with you?

—Sorry. I was just thinking about something.

—No one is chasing you anymore. Why are you still speed-ing? Do you want to die?

—I'm sorry. My ears are ringing. I was thinking about some-thing else. I didn't hear you. I didn't . . . notice how fast.

No one is chasing me, he thinks, I'm just running away from those trees. She said no one is chasing me; so she heard the gun-shots and saw the blood on my hands. But does she understand?

The asphalt road meanders with a psoriatic pattern along the land's surface with no particular motive, and on both sides vast, empty fields extend to distant hills or fade into the horizon. At different places, trees cluster, forming shadowy oases under the sun. The sky opens wide and far, in full embrace of the land with farm houses scattering sporadically. Vast open space above him beckons him, and he feels its immensity in his stomach with a frightening emptiness. It's fear, he thinks. He killed a man, but there will be no policemen coming after him; he will never stand trial or go to jail. Those are the processes of a bygone civilization; what he faces is a loathsome void. Suddenly, he feels the warmth of Sam's body on his fingers and the most private crevices of the dying body against his palms, and that warmth increases to a searing heat as though a fire has been ignited on his hands and has made permanent invisible stains. He takes his hands off the steering wheel and rubs them together in a cleansing act, but further down the road he sees a fallen tree and has no choice but to grab the steering wheel again.

Despite the occasional obstacle in the road and a couple of quick breaks for food and water, he sees the sign to Salinas after three hours of driving during which the music of the great composers has been flowing, encasing him in an airy amber, soothing his tinnitus and his conscience alike. Art has glanced at Maya now and then; there is a morose intensity in her face. How will I explain to her? he thinks. I'm still responsible for her whether she likes it or not, and I need to make her understand. The act was so rudimentary and savage; it was a remnant from the old world, a world of internecine savagery that no child from any world can possibly understand. But it had to be done. He is convinced of that even now; perhaps it was meant to be a sort of cruel karma, leaving the survivor with his enlightened knowledge to face the consequences. Is there hope for the survivor?

His mind drifts to the far edge of the plain, thinking of possibility and seeking reasons for his survival. Why him? Perhaps he must deliver her somewhere, to protect a future hope, or perhaps to put an end to Sam, to close the ledger on all his debts. He snickers to himself at the absurdity. He turns to speak but remains silent. Leave it alone until the right time, he thinks. It would be difficult to take it up now; it would do more harm than good. He looks at her, but she doesn't seem to notice him. Maya has settled into the computer, her eyes taking in the words with an incredible speed, the tip of her finger gliding over the screen unceasingly. Unencumbered by the shaking of the car or the doleful singing of a Bellini aria, she seems locked in her own space, immersed in and absorbing the words, perhaps determined to find a secret to the old world, a secret that can explain terrible things to her.

Ahead, the sky over Salinas is an unending blanket of gray cloud, accented here and there with shades of darkness, and the shadow of the cloud clearly cuts across the land and the road. The car goes down the road and enters the cloud's shadow. Tiny droplets stick to the windshield. A strong wind shakes the trees along the roadside and jars the car. Art feels the push, nudging the car sideways, and he has to adjust his steering to fight against it. A sudden gust shakes the car, and then a heavy downpour splatters the windshield. He turns on the wipers and slows down, and after about five minutes the downpour eases to a light sprinkle, but the gray gloom is now complete, not a trace of the bright sun anywhere, not even in the rearview mirror.

—We'll stop in San Jose. It's about an hour away, Art says.

Maya continues to read, her head moving back and forth as she scans the screen.

—We'll stay in San Jose. Head to San Francisco tomorrow. If you're hungry, candy bars and water bottles are in the back. We'll cook something for dinner.

—Whatever you decide to do, Maya says.

Her words perk him up. In his seat, he straightens, turns to her slightly, and decides to seize the opportunity. He thinks that she is no longer angry, and he turns down the music to talk.

—Maya, I know that you're very intelligent. I don't how or why. I can only imagine how much smarter you're getting each day. When I found you, you couldn't even speak, but look at you now. You read so fast now . . . Hmm . . . Hmm . . . I don't know how much you understand.

—I understand everything I read.

—Are there words that you don't know?

—No, not now. There were words I didn't know before and had to guess. But with this, just touch the screen over the words and it gives you the definition. Now I know them all. The words are used over and over again, so once you know them you can read everything.

—Yes, yes. I understand. But things in books are sometimes not the same as in real life.

—Art, the real life you know does not exist anymore. Everyone slept. Everyone is dead. I read these things but it's all in the past. There is no economy, no politics, no armies or mass religion any more. To have them you must have people and there are no people. I don't understand what you're trying to say.

—Yes, yes, that's all true. What I'm trying to say is that books only capture a slice of the life that was. There are things that you will encounter in real life, that you will never understand from reading books.

—You said the same thing before you told me to run.

—Right. Right. Ah . . . Ah . . . it's very complicated to explain. You see, in real life, there are terrible things. Things that you will never know because you haven't lived through them.

—Is that why you killed Sam?

His windpipe contracts, he sucks air through his mouth. A whistling sound is heard coming from his chest. He stops the car.

—What's the matter, Art?

—I can't breathe.

His lips are curled as he inhales short, rapid breaths.

—Did you take the powder?

—Where is it? In there.

Maya opens the glove compartment and hands him the jar. He wets his fingertip, dips it into the jar, and then places it under his tongue. After a minute, he takes a long, easy breath.

—You should never forget to take the powder.

—Yes. I know, he says. He knows that it was not the lack of powder in his blood that choked him; instead, it was her look as she asked the question—the oblong, indifferent eyes, the inquisitive expression where there should have been an unforgiving horror. The familiar piercing pain lacerates the center of his gut as he looks at her. What have I done? he thinks.

—How do you feel now?

—Better. Thank you, he says and starts the car again. You know, Maya, I did what I did only because I wanted to protect you.

—You mean killing Sam.

There's no use hiding now, he thinks; at least I will teach her to always face the truth.

—Yes, Maya. I thought he was going to harm you. You were there, you heard his story, how he tried to enslave everyone with his wonder drug. He was an evil man.

—How was he going to harm me? You could easily have run from him if you didn't want to be near him. In fact you were running from him. You could have hidden anywhere and he would never have found you.

—That's not true. He would have found us, Maya. We can't

hide when there is no one else around. He would, eventually. If not here then in Berkeley.

—You don't know that. It's not logical. You killed him. For whatever reasons I don't yet understand. But you didn't do it for me.

—He was going to take you . . . to be . . . to be . . . to propagate . . . to rebuild a new world that he would control. You don't understand what that means, Maya.

—I do know what that means. Maybe you want that for yourself.

—Don't say that, Maya. I'm your Papa.

—You're not my father.

—I am whether you like it or not. I am.

—What about George. You killed him, too.

—No, Maya. What are you saying? I didn't kill him. That's absurd.

—Yes, you did, Art. You gave him the chemical you made and it killed him. Didn't it? You didn't even know how to make the powder. I've read some chemistry books since then. Your equations were wrong. You were never a chemist. You didn't know how to make the powder. You gave George that chemical so he could test it for you. The reason why we're going to Berkeley to see Ledesma is because you don't know how to make the powder.

—How do you know how he died? You didn't see his body.

—There is no other conclusion. You saw the body. Tell me how he died.

—I didn't give it to him to test it. You have to believe me. I really thought I had made it and it would work. Why wouldn't it?

—I told you to use the mass spectrometer to test it but you refused.

—I didn't kill him. Besides how would I know how to use the mass spectrometer. It's all theory anyway. All a bunch of theories in my head.

—Yes, it's all rubbish. Bach, Beethoven, Brahms that you listen to incessantly. All infantile babbling. And your philosophy, religion, literature, all nauseating boredom.

She shrieks and grabs the books lying underneath her feet and tosses them out the window, one by one.

—What are you doing, Maya? Are you crazy?

—I'm not crazy by any logical measure, she shouts back at him and continues to throw all the books out the window.

—If you don't want to read, it's up to you.

—I read them all and remember them all and they are of no use to me.

—Fine. Do as you like.

—And I would rather burn that painting than look at it.

He feels stunned, unable to say any more.

—You killed Judy too.

—Who?

—The nurse that you shot in the asylum.

—Hah . . . You must be joking. I was trying to save you. She was coming after me. At least I thought she was. I didn't know any better then.

—She wasn't dead yet. She was just acting out her routine. You killed her.

—Yes, yes. I killed her. I'm guilty.

—Don't kill for me, Art. Whatever terrible things you experienced in the old world can't be any more terrible than what I've seen. You can't say that I don't know. You've shown me.

Then there is not another word, only the thudding noise of the rubber tires against the bumpy road.

Soon they are moving through the center of Salinas, and as the freeway rises, he sees the small town laid out flat, reaching into the distance, washed over by a fine mist of rain. Only there is no light anywhere, light that might remind him of a warm hearth, people gathering for supper, or the bustling of children; instead an invariant grayness engulfs the horizon and with each minute moves toward him. Of the things near enough for him to see, he has seen them a thousand times before. He puts his sleeve up to the window and wipes away the fog and sees a chaotic picture: cars strewn about and overturned, discarded furniture, electronic devices, and bicycles, and of course human corpses in various stages of decomposition. Except for the rain, a stillness seems to descend over the town, and he tries hard to see but can't make out any movement, not a wiggle from a dying thing, not a stir of suffering.

Beyond Salinas, the rain ends abruptly. A grayish gloom settles over everything as though something from above is compressing the air itself and trapping all underneath it for a preordained struggle. Still, I can see the road, he thinks. I will go for as long as possible without turning on the headlights. He dims the light inside the car to its lowest level and asks Maya to put away the computer. As they near San Jose, the roadsides become more crowded with houses and other buildings. Something about this quotidian transition into darkness rouses him, and he leans forward as he drives and trains his eyes over the landscape, looking for signs of danger and for shelter for the night. He turns the defog switch to maximum, and cold air blows from the vents all along the windshield and the windows. Turning often to the rearview mirror, he watches warily for the familiar, yellowish light of a car that might be following him, but all he can see is the whites of his eyes, protruding from their sockets and glaring back at him.

—Maya, Maya, Art says loudly. Tell me if you see something, won't you? I thought I saw a light. I might be imagining things. You can see and hear better.

—I see nothing.

—Good, good. Tell me, won't you? Tell me right away.

Soon, Art sees the sign "Silicon Valley Blvd" and hurriedly takes the exit. On the hills in the distance, he can see houses, and he decides to stay overnight there. At the end of the off-ramp, an armored truck sits in the middle and completely blocks the lane. As he has done many times before, he eases the Hummer up against it and steps on the gas pedal. The engine revs with a loud rumble, and the four wheels spin and squeal, but all it can do is nudge the armored truck slightly.

—It's not working, he mumbles.

He reverses the car to get some distance and then heads off the road. The Hummer bucks and bounces like a boat hitting turbulent waves, and then after twenty feet it climbs up onto the road again.

—Shoosh, all clear, Art says as he exhales. We have to find a place before it gets too dark.

In the dimming dusk, he can make out the clear road ahead and steps down on the gas; the Hummer roars and speeds along. The road ends at an intersection, and further on the right, rows of cookie-cutter houses appear against the still, murky atmosphere. He slows the car.

—At last. We'll stay there overnight. In one of those houses. Take your pick, he says, pointing to them.

Without waiting for her answer, he drives into an empty driveway.

—If we're lucky, the house is empty, he says.

He jumps out and approaches the door. It's locked. He uses the butt of the shotgun and breaks the side window and climbs through. Flinging the front door open, he calls to Maya. From behind him, stagnant air laced with a faint putrid odor escapes.

He wrinkles his nose and heads down the short hallway, passing the dining room and the family room. There are no corpses around, and he opens the back door. No need to check upstairs, he thinks; we'll just stay downstairs. A gust of wind blows through the house. He lifts his face toward the sloping hill that rises just on the other side of the wooden fence. Tall, weaving weeds flattened by the constant winds lie across the backyard like a thick organic rug. Nearby, several white plastic chairs are arranged around a small plastic table, and on them areas of black dust remain from what must have previously been puddles of rainwater.

He flops down in the nearest chair, and a leaden inertia sets in and weighs him down, but it is not for the lack of energy, for his mind is clear, perhaps too clear; rather, his body is replete with a heaviness, a desire to burrow deep into the earth. What have I shown her? he says to himself. The inexpiable horror of his world is now an indelible memory in her pristine, boundless mind, a mind that will never forget, the only remaining mind that will remember him should he die. But not like this, he thinks. Her frail frame, clear eyes, and innocence should not witness such horror, and all he'd thought about was saving her. Sorrow jolts through him and is instantly numbed by the intermittent spurts of cold wind.

—Art, Maya calls out as she passes through the back door.

She comes out into the backyard, looks around quickly, and turns to him.

—Yes, Maya, he says softly. His voice is somber and distant.

—What's the matter? she says.

—Nothing, darling.

—Should we start a fire or eat cold food? she says coldly.

—Maya, listen, I'm so sorry, Art says.

—What's the matter?

—I'm sorry that you had to see, to be so close to . . . all the things I did. I don't know what came over me.

—You must have had your reasons.

—A profanity, Maya, Art says through his teeth. He was a profanity, Maya. To see him live when everywhere everyone innocent died. I'm sorry, Maya.

—You don't have to justify your actions to me.

—Yes, I do. Otherwise . . . it never ends Maya. What I've done . . . I've become that profanity.

—Shhh . . . Don't talk.

—I'm sorry.

—Shhhh . . . Art, be quiet. I hear something.

The wind has shifted and now blows across his face, and it must have carried the sound from somewhere down the street.

—I don't hear anything, he whispers.

—There are people around, Maya says. We should talk to them.

—No, Maya, it's too dangerous. We have to leave.

Without thinking, he jumps up and, holding onto her arm, makes his way back to the front of the house. Outside a tentative darkness is chasing the wisp of remaining light along the street.

After backing the car out of the driveway, he turns the Hummer to the left, away from where he thought the voices had come from, and steps on the gas. The car surges forward as it swerves left onto another street, but almost immediately Art slams on the brake. Their bodies lunge forward and are caught by the seat belts. In the middle of the road, two large, black SUVs sit as though facing them down. The SUVs' blackness is somehow amplified by the quickening darkness, and he leans forward, stares straight into them, and tries to make out a human shape.

—Can you see anything? Maya, quick. Can you see anyone in those cars?

His heart crashes against the cage of his chest. Even without seeing someone in them, he knows; the clean exterior of those SUVs and their standing next to each other can only mean people nearby. His fingers fumble along the side of the dashboard searching for the light switch.

—Maya, what do you see? he says without taking his eyes off the SUVs.

—I see . . .

Now his fingers feel the light switch and he turns it. The headlights flare out and light up everything. He sees them, two men, sitting in the drivers' seats of the SUVs, and as the light shines on them, they flinch and shield their eyes with their hands.

Art puts the car in reverse; the engine shrieks as the Hummer shoots backward. He hears loud honking, as if they are alerting others nearby; instantly the headlights of those SUVs flare on, and the lights glare in his eyes.

—Why are you running away? We should talk to them, Maya screams.

He slams on the brake and at the same time turns the steering wheel, and the car spins around. The Hummer speeds away. On the road are some objects he can't identify, and the Hummer runs over them, jumping each time it does so. The light behind them is getting brighter, and in the rearview mirror he sees them gaining on him. He presses down on the gas and swerves to the left to avoid a car but hits a trash can, sending it flying onto the pavement. In his ears, Maya's sharp screams, the buzzing tinnitus now roaring, and the beat of his heart, block out the loud burst of gunfire so that he only hears it when he sees the flashes of an automatic weapon in the rearview mirror.

—They're shooting at us, Maya screams in his ears as she pulls on his jacket.

—No, not yet, he says.

I have to get off the road, he thinks. The next salvo of gunfire probably won't be warning shots. To the right, he sees a small house with a garage door open and aims the car toward it. The car jumps over the pavement and stops in front.

—Go Maya, run, run. Run to the house.

He grabs the shotgun, jumps out, walks to the back of the car, and fires the shotgun rapidly at the approaching SUVs. The SUVs stop at a distance, too far for the shotgun pellets to reach.

—Go inside the house. Run, he shouts to Maya.

Seeing that they've stopped, he too runs inside. A rancid odor, musty and noxiously foul, fills his nostrils, but he doesn't care and sucks in the air, taking rapid breaths. From his jacket, he pulls out the flashlight and, pushing Maya forward, moves quickly through the narrow, empty hallway. No more than twelve feet along the hallway, they're in the kitchen. Through the back door, he sees the outline of the backyard under the faint, black- ish light of dusk, darkness fast approaching. At the end of the backyard, the flashlight shows a wooden fence with large gaps in different places.

—Maya, run. Go through the fence and up the hill. Hide yourself, he says breathlessly.

—I know, Art. You will find me. Otherwise go on and try to survive by myself, she says.

—Yes, yes. Now go.

He watches as she runs through the back door and toward the broken fence; her shape blends into the tall grass, and the large jacket flails about her. We haven't had a chance to get you better clothes, he thinks. Unable to look on anymore, he turns, switches off the flashlight, and makes his way along the dark hall- way toward the front of the house. Through the empty garage, he sees the street, the Hummer, and, in the dim light from the SUVs, the shadows of men moving toward him. Maya hasn't gone far enough yet, he thinks and shoots toward the moving shadows. Two shotgun blasts light up the darkness. The shadows become still; after a second he hears the crackling of assault rifles, the whistling of invisible bullets. The cracking wood splinters start to fly and fall over him. He drops to the floor and covers his head with his hands. Then the firing stops, and he hears voices, indistinctly at first.

—Come out. Or we'll fire again, someone shouts.

From the sound of their boots moving and their shadows changing, he knows that they are repositioning to gain a better vantage point; the next salvo of gunfire will probably cover the entire house.

—This is your last chance. Come out now, another man shouts.

Art gets up and looks around. It is now completely dark. He feels in his jacket for the flashlight, but he must have dropped it. Has she gone far enough? he thinks. Inching along the wall, he moves with it, going into the kitchen. His hands touch the refrigerator; he crouches down next to it. The bullets won't go through it, he thinks and points the shotgun at the ceiling and fires two shots.

They answer immediately, and, as before, the crackles of the assault rifles, the whistling of the flying bullets, the breaking of the wood intermingle into a savage cocoon, in which he remains suspended and in supplication for a safety that never comes.

When it finally stops, there is nothing left for him to do, and he does not wait for them to command him.

—I'm coming out, he screams. Don't shoot. I'm coming out.

He repeats the refrain again and again as he walks through the garage, into the street, and into the light of the SUVs. Men are scattered about; some are beyond his vision, but he knows they are there and are leveling their guns at him. With outstretched arms, he is holding the shotgun as he goes into the middle of the street.

—Drop the gun, someone says, enunciating very slowly.

He does so.

—Move forward.

Toward the light of the SUVs, he walks slowly, and he throws glances at the hills, where there is now complete darkness. She is safe in that darkness, he thinks and feels strangely calm. The air is cold and moist, and the dense, moisture–laden air descends all around him. And except for his footsteps echoing against the houses, there is no other sound.

—Keep moving, someone commands him.

Finally in front of the light, he sees them coming out, and he catches glimpses of cold faces, gleaming eyes, impatient hands directing gun barrels, and shifting and moving bodies, all fleeting against the glare of the bright light.

—Get down on your knees, someone says.

His knees hit the sharp edges of small stones as he kneels. He closes his eyes, but the bright light still inundates his retinas with a yellowish glow.

—How do you stay alive? Someone, standing next to him, shouts into his ear.

—I don't know, Art says.

—Do you need drugs to stay alive?

—What is it to you? he says.

—Answer the question.

—Why do you want to know? Art says.

He hears noises from the Hummer and knows that they are searching it. They will soon find the powder, he thinks. Opening his eyes slightly, he tries to look up at the man, but all he can see is the silhouette, imperious and fearsome.

—To determine if you are one of us, the man says.

—One of you. Who are you? Art says and sees his breath in the cold air as he speaks.

—We inherit the earth. Now answer the question: Do you need drugs to live?

Before he can answer, he hears someone running toward them.

—He is one of them, the man says before he reaches them. I found a bottle of the drug. He is one of them.

—Search him, someone says.

They both lean down to him, pull off his jacket, and feel around his waist. And under the bright light, the stains on the edge of his shirt that hours ago were a vivid red are now darkened haphazard shapes on the white cloth. They empty his pockets onto the road, nothing interests them. Finally they bring the jacket to the light, and as though seeing something terrible, they drop the jacket, freeze for a moment, and recoil from him.

—Blood. Blood on his clothes, someone says.

From their hiding places, they all come, some running, others walking briskly. Now, they are huddling over him, inspecting him closely, pulling on his shirt to verify for themselves, and finally they move away.

—It's not his blood.

—Look at this. And look at his shirt.

—Blood.

—Yes, blood.

—He doesn't have a wound anywhere.

—What should we do with him?

—He must not live.

—He won't without the drug.

—Kill him.

—There are so few of them left.

—Not many.

—He must have killed another.

—Truly evil, as we've been told.

With his eyes closed under the blinding light and his arms raised, he listens to them and hears the bustling movements and the sound of car doors opening and closing. They know about the powder, he thinks. They may know what causes the Death Sleep, but who are they? They're different, perhaps like Maya. And I'm finished without the powder.

Unbearably heavy and unshakable, a sudden weariness overcomes him, and his body slouches toward the ground. If only they would leave, I would be glad to lie down and make this very spot the final place on earth for me, he thinks. I will stretch my legs out and go to sleep; perhaps I should have slept a long time ago. The weariness depresses him and seems to lock his limbs into immobility, but even in capitulation, his mind still goes on, sees things unfolding, and imagines the final rest of his battered body, a final rest without bitterness, and somewhere in that imagining he feels a slight regret and believes an alternate ending might have been possible.

Yes, it's still possible, a thought sparks. There is still a chance. I can still drive to Berkeley and find Ledesma. I can make it before the powder in my blood is gone. He opens his eyes wide, welcoming the bright light and its deliverance of renewed energy. Impatiently, he waits for them to leave.

—What about the other?

—Yes, there is another one who ran into the house.

—A child.

—Let's get her, just to make sure.

No, no, his mind screams. You will not hurt her. I must do something. But what? He looks around frantically. What can I do? Suddenly he leaps up and, with an incredible burst of speed, runs away.

The bang of the gun and the kick of the bullet, ripping his leg from under him, occur all at once. He falls, and the hardness of the ground, the pummeling darkness, and finally the sharp pain strike him. His hand gropes at his right thigh, now paralyzed, and feels the dampness of warm blood. His groans ripple through the still air, and in his mind an intense pain pulses through, emptying all thoughts. Now he feels the dampness along his groin. I'm going to bleed out, he thinks. He reaches up to look at them and to wait for another bullet but incredibly sees their dark shapes against the headlights, unmoving, as though they're faced with indescribable horror. In another second, with the speed of apparitions and in total silence, they disappear, and the headlights retreat into the distance. Then the darkness is complete.

Lying back down, he palpates his thigh, but he can't make out where the bullet entered. Did it cut the femoral artery or shatter the femur? He takes off his belt, loops it around his thigh, and, placing it near his groin, pulls tight and ties the end into a knot. Now he is conscious of his body shaking, of the very cold air percolating through his shirt, of fear and an uncontrollable will to escape his predicament and to continue this life. Breathing heavily, he pushes himself up; now he is crouching on his left knee while his hands steady himself against the ground. Gathering all his strength, he stands up. Immediately a dizzying lightness buzzes inside his head; his body sways in the darkness. He falls.

The sky splinters and a wedge of stars opens through the darkness. Even in this small wedge is a sprinkling of light of varying brightness, and though individual lights twinkle singly through the atmosphere, together a cosmic harmony appears wherein a perfect idea is known. When he opens his eyes, he sees through the splinter in the sky, across which faint wisps of cloud float, and he feels neither cold nor pain. Then he sees Maya, Emily, and Anna, and the totality of his life, and senses the will to continue. He has done the best he could in light of all the significance he's perceived during all the moments of his life; he has been honorable. If nothing else, at least he has that. And these things pass and his clear eyes gaze, until only the stars remain in his mind, mutually transfixed and at quickening degrees, as the will dissipates. At last, pure timelessness. Now he knows.

The moving clouds close off the splinter in the sky, and darkness resumes so completely that his eyes are useless to him, that he becomes one conjoining sky and earth. His hands feel inch by inch the asphalt surface with the jerking movement of an injured animal. He feels the grains of gravel and the weeds that took hold in the cracks of the road. Help, he yells several times, but his call is mere instinct, too feeble, and lacks the conviction of a dying animal who still wants to live, or of one who has seen it all and knows that no help is forthcoming. A sudden upsurge of wind squeaks in his ears, becoming one with the tinnitus, making him even colder. His body shakes uncontrollably, and he folds his arms over his chest. His pants, now soaked with blood, are cold. The raw smell of blood floods over him whenever the wind stops, and it seems as though that smell has been with him all along.

From the surface of his skin, frigidity advances, an indiscriminate numbness seeps toward his heart as if intent on dispersing his corporeal existence into the unseeing darkness. As soon as he closes his eyes, not only vision but perception itself fades away, one microscopic mote after another, draining down his spine and exiting through the wound in his thigh to coalesce with an impenetrable darkness outside. In the remaining consciousness, he knows only loneliness, floating in a vast, numbing coldness. How different it is than what he once imagined of his own death, to be lying on the ground, all alone, without final dignity. He seizes upon memory of a death he once imagined, in which he was surrounded by children and grandchildren as they fussed around him and mourned for him. He should die lying in bed, in a room where there is a big fireplace with a ferocious fire burning. Now he can see the light of the fireplace but without heat. It's too real, and he hears the voice of his offspring clamoring for him to hold on.

—WAKE UP.

How he loves them, whoever they are. Light from the fireplace flashes across his eyes.

—Art, wake up.

The voice breaks through his ears. He knows that voice and how he loves it. Now he feels warm hands on his face, caressing him.

—Art, please wake up.

He opens his eyes and sees Maya leaning over him. The light from the Hummer shines obliquely, and he sees that she is crying, her face contorted, and tears flowing from her darkened eyes.

—Darling, don't cry, he mutters inaudibly.

—Art, Art, please wake up, she cries out.

Oh, how I loves her, he thinks. His arms stir as he tries to touch her.

—Please get up.

He feels her pulling his shirt.

—Maya, you're here, he says.

—Yes, Art, please get up. You must help me.

He turns on his side and sits himself up. His head is light and he sways. After several seconds, he asks for her shoulder, and he holds onto her as his good leg pushes him up. He pulls her close to him like a crutch. He groans as he limps toward the Hummer. Each time his weight is shifted onto the injured leg, he cringes.

—I'll drive, Maya says.

He nods.

At last he climbs inside the Hummer. The warmth is still there. Maya pushes the door shut and then gets into the driver's seat. As she adjusts the seat forward so she can reach the pedal, her thin frame comes up right to the steering wheel, and her head barely clears the dashboard.

—Oh, my darling, Art mutters as he looks at her.

—Stay awake. Try to stay awake. Her voice is still muffled from the crying.

—The gas is on the right, Art says.

—Yes, I know, she says.

Suddenly she stops to look at him and, as if realizing something, turns to the back seat, pulls out a blanket, and unfurls it over him.

Then the engine roars, and hot air blows from the vents. The Hummer jerks and shoots backward hitting some object.

—Slowly, Maya, slowly, Art says.

The car rolls forward and picks up speed retracing the route they came in earlier. Within the yellowish illumination of the bright headlights, a flurry of dust is blown chaotically across the windshield, but further away on the sides of the street houses stand in a ghostly stillness, simply resigned. At the on–ramp to the freeway, the car jostles abruptly as it goes over a large pot hole, and the pain in his thigh, renewed and intense, shoots up.

Under the blanket, his hands pull on the belt as he tries to tighten it further as he can feel the blood continuing to ooze from the bullet wound. Only now does he feel his heart thumping very fast against his chest. An irresistible lightness drains down the back of his neck, leaving his head empty and pulling down his eyelids. With his eyes heavy and vision narrowing, he stares ahead into the soothing bright light darkness is retreating from.

—Stay awake, Maya cries.

Her fierce shriek is followed by inconsolable sobs.

Darling, don't cry, he thinks.

16

Yellow daisies inside a glass vase half-filled with water stand on the table next to the half-open window. Through the window, a slight breeze undulates the thin, white curtains, and beyond is a bright, blue sky. Opening his eyes, he perceives the white curtains moving next to the yellow flowers, both wavering and floating in the air; the dividing of glass, water, and air seems to have vanished to nothingness. His eyes dart every which way, but his body is slow to move. Aside from the table and a couple of chairs, the room is bare, only a pencil drawing hanging on the wall and a still fan on the ceiling. A white blanket covers his body. Mind–body dissociation, he thinks, waking up from sleep. Where is this place? Slowly, he feels his leg and his right thigh where a pain pulses weakly, like a whisper, blowing its sharpness upward to his groin. And in the quiet of the room, the familiar ringing blares in his ears.

The full weight of the physical body materializes abruptly as he tries to move, and all at once he feels the dull ache in the back of his neck, the weakness of his limbs, and the creaking of his spine. His head is strangely clear; absent is the leaden heaviness, or the squeezing tightness, or the needle–like pain of previous awakenings—perhaps a mind mended. As he turns on his side, the smell of clean linen reminds him of the past, of many a morning when he awoke to this same smell, full of promise. Then his arm flings off the blanket, and an intravenous line tethered to his arm tugs against it. He turns and sees an IV pole behind him and a bag of clear fluid hanging from it. It's a hospital of some sort, he thinks. He pulls himself up and sits on the side of the bed. His arms and legs stick out from a hospital gown, a flimsy, white gown with a pattern of small blue roses, opening on the back. The tight bandage on his thigh squeezes as he moves. Looking down at his hands, he flexes the fingers and remembers seeing the tiny red corpuscles of blood on them before, wondering if they are still there. Touching his face, he tugs gently at his short beard and his hair; both have grown longer than he can remember. He pulls himself up against the IV pole and, using it as a crutch, staggers toward the window. In front of him, the crisp echo of laughter seems to intersect with a pleasant fragrance, and as he steps forward, these sensations arrest him and suspend him in a novel happiness; he thinks he hears her voice.

Next to the window, he cranes his neck to look down onto the large quad, where young people are playing, talking among themselves, and from a small group on the far side comes loud, boisterous laughter. Their eyes are beaming, their faces are full of smiles, and their hands gesticulate rhythmically as they talk. She has black hair, he thinks as he tries to scrutinize each figure, but he can not find her. On the other side of the quad and through a thick stretch of trees, he recognizes the tall buildings. I'm in Berkeley, he thinks, but where is she? He remembers lying in the street, cold and bleeding from his thigh wound, and being saved by her. What happened after that? Perhaps they took him here, and so he is a prisoner. What about her?

Poor Maya, my dear Maya, he mumbles. Where is she? I must find her, he thinks. He turns away from the window, but his right leg weakens and the knee buckles. Holding onto the IV pole, he moves back to the bed. The thought of escaping occurs to him, though the actual steps involved, changing into more suitable clothes, perhaps climbing out the window, or somehow sneaking out of the building, seem ludicrous. Obviously he's in no condition to go anywhere, and yet somehow he must find her; even as smart as she is, she can't be left out there alone. The last thing he remembers was her driving, but after that were they chased and captured? I must have fainted from the blood loss, he thinks.

At last he decides to find those in charge, and he will do anything to make them find her; he will offer any services necessary. There is a little girl lost out there, he mumbles. Pulling on the IV pole again, he stands up; an intense pain now cuts sharply up from his thigh. He clenches his teeth and braces himself to move forward.

Suddenly the door opens. A man comes in. Their eyes lock, startled.

—You're up, the man says, almost whispering.

—Hah, Art utters.

The man does not seem real to him. If he weren't restrained by an injured leg, he'd leap to the man to verify his existence.

A thick, graying beard hides the lower half of his face; his eyes are hollow and sad; and the mass of gray, curly hair extends down to his neck. His prominent nose imparts a unique sense of definition to his face.

—Art, how do you feel? the man says and comes to him. Their hands clasp tightly.

—Thomas . . . You're here?

—Yes, Art. It's good to see you. I never thought I'd see you again.

—Thomas, there was a little girl with me. She was driving when I passed out. Was I brought here alone?

—No. She brought you to us.

—Really? Where is she?

—She's around somewhere. She's been taking care of you, changing your dressing every day.

—Really? I thought I'd lost her.

—She is quite something. But then they're all like that, Thomas Ledesma says and sighs. Please sit down, Art. You should keep the weight off the leg.

Art sits down on the bed and bids Thomas to sit on a chair.

—So, we're on the campus? I remember the buildings.

—Yes, Art. We are.

—I was hoping I'd see you. The powder you made for our experiments is what kept me alive.

—Maya told me you were coming to see me for more.

—Yes, Thomas. I had no other choice. I tried to make the powder but I don't think it worked. Do you know what causes the Death Sleep?

—Yes, we have an idea.

The boisterous laughter and loud voices float through the window, and Art turns to it.

—Who are they?

—Most of them are like your girl, the newly awakened. It's both a fantastic dream and nightmare. I never thought I'd see anyone I knew. Art, it's a new world. It's their world now.

—Most of them? What about the others?

—There are other survivors. Just like you and me, they live because of the powder. Shortly after I used the powder, I tried to give it to as many people as I could. But there was just not enough. We could only make enough to keep so many alive.

Art looks away. I was so terrified, Art says.

—So was I. Don't blame yourself for anything. I couldn't have done much myself. I had help. Their leader, a man by the name of Bud Dahl, he was one of the first to awake and he has been organizing them, bringing them here. They've formed a colony, if you will.

—Are they all the same? Were they all mentally impaired before the Death Sleep? And do they need the powder? Art says.

—They don't need the powder. It's the most fabulous thing I've ever seen, Art. Before the Death Sleep they were all diagnosed as mentally retarded. And they woke up, just like that. For a scientist, this is the most wondrous conundrum.

Thomas's deep, sad eyes now brighten as he speaks, and his hands come together before him as though he can almost touch something physical. The human brain, he continues, is profound beyond anything I could imagine. You should see what these people are capable of. Their intelligence grows exponentially. They . . . I can't possibly describe it adequately. They just observe and know things that I had to take time to learn. They seem to know mathematics and logic at a very fundamental level. Things are just obvious to them.

—Maya, my little girl. She's like that. She absorbs the words.

—Where did you find her?

—A mental institution, just across from the lab.

—They come from us and yet they're not us.

Through the high–pitched ringing in his ears, he now hears certain high frequency tones, and they increase in intensity and are joined in a concatenation of indistinguishable complexity. Turning toward the window, he rises slightly, to see the origin of those sounds.

—That's their music.

—Music? Not anything I've ever heard.

—They are still using all the old instruments—piano, violin, trumpet, what not. They don't compose or write anything down. They improvise according to numerical relationships and some neurological frequencies. I don't understand it. And it seems that our old instruments aren't adequate for such expression. They're building new instruments.

Art concentrates on the sound. Beyond the familiar ringing in his ears, a multitude of tones move together, pointing to a new sentiment, and there a note breaks off and, getting louder and louder, suddenly becomes the leading edge of a mass of swarming wings, fluttering in the blue sky. It's almost too wondrous for his ears; in the mass of notes there exist variations of such speed and virtuosity, like a million living things, each with its own quirk and temperament, and yet there is a cohesion, a unity of essence, pulsing to a common beat, as though the music comes not from the outside but from within his own mind.

—It's wonderful, isn't it? Thomas says as he studies Art. And the way they talk. They are developing a new language, if you will; perhaps our language cannot express their thinking adequately. New words, new expressions more natural to the working of their minds. But you know, the thing that strikes me most is seeing them together. Just wait until you see them together, any of them, even when they meet each other for the first time. They don't just merely talk; it's as if they're in communion, like they're exchanging some sacred ideas.

—I see.

Thomas stands up and faces the window; he closes his eyes and cringes.

—We never talked to one another like that in our world. Sometimes . . . sometimes I wish I never saved them.

—The survivors?

—Yes, What good are we now? We're stupefied spectators, watching, living as though nothing has changed, seeing the world as it always was. We can only imagine what they see, but we'll never see what they see. I sometimes wish I'd never done anything and let them sleep away. I wish I'd slept too.

—You don't mean that, Art says but stops himself.

There's a sincerity in Thomas's lament, a sincerity Art himself felt when he thought of letting go, but that seems so long ago, in those bleak days when it was his own mind that gave the day bleakness. And though he is not any smarter, now he experiences a clarity, a lack of whatever it was that intervened between him and objects, people, and life in general.

—Maybe in time you'll feel different, Art says.

—I doubt it. In many ways, I think it's bad enough to witness the end of our kind, but worse yet to see what we could have been but never were. You know, Art, we brought about the Death Sleep.

—What are you saying?

—It was us all along. Did you know that? We did it to ourselves.

—We caused it?

—Yes, I mean all of us. Our people, our cities, our machines, our civilization—we brought it upon ourselves.

—Are you sure?

—Statistically it's as certain as it can ever be. But in my gut it's absolute. We did it to ourselves; I have no doubt about it. We were only too capable of doing something like this.

—I know what you mean, Art says and remembers the image of Sam's shoes, the smell of grass and burnt gunpowder.

A knock on the door interrupts Thomas.

—Please come in, Thomas says as he turns toward the door.

As the door opens, a man says, I apologize for intruding upon your conversation. He enters and Maya follows. The man appears to be in his thirties; his face is young and strong, his hair neatly combed, and his eyes focused. He wears a white shirt and khaki pants.

—Maya, Art says and jumps up.

—Hello, Art, Maya says.

Though he is not aware of his own face, Art smiles broadly, showing his stained teeth, and looks upon her with tenderness and holds out his arms. She approaches him, and he puts his arms around her and squeezes her tightly.

—Hah, Art says, it feels like I have not seen you for a long time.

He kisses her on the head, and a fresh smell of soap rises to his nose. Just like Emily, he thinks; oh, how I miss her.

—Truest are the emotions of a reunion, the man says; his large eyes, made gentle by the slightly drooping lids, observe them.

—It's only been three days, Maya says.

—It seems forever to me. Let me look at you, Art says as he pushes Maya back. A soft pink glows on her cheeks and from there diffuses throughout her face. She is wearing a white shirt and a pairs of jean that fit her as though they were made just for her. Art sighs and says, How lovely you are.

—Welcome, my friend, the man says. My name is Bud Dahl. You're most welcome to our community here.

—I'm Art Sand. Thank you, Art says and shakes hands with Bud. Thank you for taking us in.

—You're quite welcome. Our exploratory party found Maya three days ago, near midnight it was. She was driving north on the 880 freeway. They thought the driver might need help, since it was unusual for anyone to travel at night.

—I remember you were driving, Maya, Art says to her.

—Yes, Art. It wasn't too difficult operating the car. I saw how you did it.

—Well, I was informed that you're awake, Bud says. I just want to extend our most sincere welcome to you. I'm glad you're recovering well.

In Bud's voice, Art hears a stillness and a steadiness that seem to derive from the air itself. His demeanor impresses Art in a profound way.

—You must have many questions, Bud continues. They will be answered in time. Your expertise in neurological science will be invaluable to us. But I will leave you now to catch up with Maya.

—Thank you, Art says.

—I'll leave you as well, Thomas says. He appears to be somewhat agitated and fidgety. We have all the time in the world to discuss matters. Come by the lab when you're ready.

—Thank you, Thomas.

They both bow slightly and leave the room.

Art turns to Maya. Did you drive far before they found you?

—Not too far.

—I don't remember. How did you find them?

—They found me like Bud said. I thought about the situation and there was nothing else I could do. I had to find Ledesma, so I continued to drive north, to Berkeley.

—Yes, I see.

—They saw me on the road and stopped me. I hadn't driven very far.

—So I was very lucky then. Thank you, Maya. You saved my life again.

—You did the same for me, Art.

He reaches for her hands, squeezes them, and brings them

up to kiss them. Turning his face, he presses her small soft hands against his cheek. And like a journey that ends in only a moment, even a happy moment, and immediately therein a mysterious force is felt, pulling him on yet again, a sudden sadness overcomes him. He lets go of her hands and, ignoring the pain in his thigh, limps to the windows; small tears trickle down his cheeks as he sees a lively scene on the quad below where young men and women are talking, and small children playing.

—How do you like it here? Art says.

—It's wonderful, Art. There are many people like me, near my age. I've already made friends. When you're better, you must come and meet them.

—What are they doing down there?

—It's Sunday. A day of rest, just like before. They have decided to keep the old calendar since it describes the earth motion most accurately. And it's easier to study the past. But going forward this is year one. We start over.

—You have everything here, then, to have a comfortable life.

—Yes, Art, things from the old world will last us for more than a hundred years. There are electricity, computers, all the conveniences of the old world.

—But without its people, Art says.

—You must miss them very much.

—Yes.

Then along his palm, he feels her fingers touching him, and her small hand slips into his.

—Thank you for being my Papa when I needed you most. I know you only wanted to protect me. I remember feeling safe and loved when I held your hand. Thank you, Papa.

He brings her hand to his lips.

—Run off now. Go enjoy the beautiful day with your friends. I need to rest.

—All right, Papa. I will bring you dinner.

She opens the door but stands motionless for a moment, then she turns around. Her nose wrinkles, the large, oblong eyes squint as if for the first time, and she says: I love you, Papa.

17

In the following days, Art's thigh feels better. The intense pain that shot up his groin whenever he moved has slowly eased into a dull ache. He is given a crutch that enables him to descend the steep stairs, and so he is no longer confined to the second floor, where his room is located. Each morning upon waking up, he takes the new powder, a synthetic formulation that can sustain him for twelve hours, and then he pulls the curtains aside, opens the window, and takes in a lungful of air. A purity flows through his nostrils, a sweetness he has never known before, and yet in that same air, he knows, are the molecules that will be absorbed through the alveoli of his lungs, diffuse into his blood, and form plaques in his brain. Still, he breathes freely, welcoming both.

Even in January, the weather is already warm. From his window, he can see wildflowers blossoming here and there around the quad's perimeter. He watches as the inhabitants of this new world pour from the buildings every morning and go about their assigned tasks. At mid-morning, a flurry of activities take place; vehicles come carting solar panels, different machineries, or boxes of goods, and men bustle about, moving machines, constructing others, and fixing innumerable things. By noon, the clouds sometimes part to let sunlight through, and they sit on the grass as they share meals and talk; their bodies are as still as trees as they listen to one another. On the faces of the newly awakened, an earnest optimism accompanies their every expression. But there are times when Art witnesses a breakdown—a man whose head suddenly collapses into his hands, or a woman who bursts into loud crying—and he knows that these are the survivors, who still suffer from their memories.

There are six rooms on the second floor, and Maya stays in the room next to his. In the morning as he makes his way along the hallway toward the stairs, he encounters the occupants of the other rooms and tries to study them surreptitiously. The man in the room across from his is short and wide, and the growth of his limbs was probably stunted during childhood. The feet of the man who lives in the room next to the stairs diverge, so that when he walks, he has the most comical shuffling gait, and the knuckles of his hands are enlarged and deformed. A fuzzy mass of black hair covers the head of another woman so completely that hardly a sliver of her forehead is visible. Art can remember times in the past when he examined patients with similar physical traits, or when he walked past them as they lined up in front of the museum during one of their field trips from the mental institution. Like small children, they would line up, but if they were made to wait, they would turn in all directions, their restless arms beginning to move about and a profound vacancy permeating from their wandering eyes. But now in the eyes of these new inhabitants, Art can see the sheer physicality of a discerning focus, always intent on discovering and studying, though if there is ever a judgmental shade in their look, he attributes it to the memory of his own actions.

Sometimes, out of curiosity, Art peeks inside their rooms to see how they live. In one room, layer upon layer of pencil drawings are stuck to the wall with pins. In another, piles of books crowd the floor, and he later learns that the person in that room is keenly interested in linguistics. Wooden contraptions, models for a machine, occupy another room. In all the rooms, there are always small vases of wildflowers on the tables. At times, he is caught looking in their rooms for too long, and with genuine sincerity the occupants ask him if he'd like to live in their rooms. He replies that he is only admiring their work, and he promptly receives a prolonged lecture on what they're working on.

EVERY MORNING, MAYA KNOCKS ON HIS DOOR AND GREETS HIM with a kiss. She walks alongside him as they descend the stairs and walk across the quad to the dining hall. Sometimes she helps with cooking the meals or washing dishes. After breakfast, Maya departs for her morning study, and he starts his morning walk as he tries to rehabilitate his leg. Each day, he ventures further along the same path until his legs are tired. Beyond the campus, the path, overgrown with weeds, leads to the east where grassy hills are dotted with wildflowers; nearing the hills, the path weaves and is eventually lost among the trees and shrubs. Along the way, there are wooden benches at regular intervals until the last bench, seemingly encased in green vines and weeds, marks the end. As Art limps along, he tends to see the new world more clearly, a new world unencumbered by people, where only the rhythm of the seasons is not lost, and his past is reflected against its tranquility. And at the end where there is perhaps a fence of the mind, or made invisible by it, he sits down, takes in the scenery, hears the songs of the birds, and soon is overtaken by remembrance. He remembers his daughter and the past, and the past leads to the future. There are days when he sits for hours, imagining and remembering, often skipping lunch, and at last when he rises to go back, he hesitates, for the formative society of the new inhabitants has a new consciousness that has no understanding of his past actions and rationalization. On other days, an improbable peace takes hold of him, and for a moment, the world is as it was; he has a foreboding that as soon as he goes back, he will find people living in an unchanged world and that it was only he who has changed. And sometimes in the wind swooshing through the leaves he hears David Calweld's repetitive whispers entangling through space, obliterating time, and in equal measure reverberating off Art's very being.

Quietude—at last Art can hear it—stretches as far as the air and as rarefied, over treetops, now rising against chimneys, now plunging down to fallow fields, all the way to the horizon, though for anyone being grounded on earth it's impossible to see. Quietude is different from silence, the former denoting not so much the absence of sound—sound being nothing more than the movement of air molecules—but harmony in nature, while in the latter is nothingness. The sound of rustling leaves travels as far as the strength of the breeze allows, and as it whirls and flows, the breeze whispers gently past his ear and caresses even more gently the skin of his cheek, then off it goes lifting fluffy dandelion heads that spin with acrobatic exactitude. Somewhere up on the branches amid the bright sunlight, hard beaks crack through barks, hunting for insects; up higher, much higher, the hawks shriek and swoop down; and, just as quickly, their open wings catch the updraft and ascend. Deeper, below the surface, is where he knows he can find the hungry mouths of worms, insects, and even microbes, by the quadrillions and more, churning ceaselessly, emitting together from their minuscule mastication a constant hum like the soulful background of the universe—that is, if one's hearing were acute enough, if one were fortunate enough. He seems to hear it all.

18

One late afternoon as Art sits on the bench, he sees Bud Dahl coming along, waving as he approaches. Art rises. They shake hands.

—Good afternoon, Art, Bud says as he sits down. I knew I'd find you here. Your walks are as punctual as the philosopher Kant's.

—What brings you all the way out here?

—I was looking for you, to discuss things. And to answer your questions if you have them.

Bud's demeanor is direct, and his eyes look on earnestly as he speaks, something that has become too familiar to Art.

—I see, Art says. What things would you like to discuss?

—Now that your wound has healed sufficiently, I'd like to ask you to help us.

—Of course. I'm happy to do whatever you have for me.

—Excellent. We can use your help in the laboratory. We have made significant progress in understanding the Death Sleep, but we can always use more help to quicken our study.

—Thomas has been telling me about his experiments,

keeping me up to date on work in the lab. And I've been thinking about it as well, Art says.

—I'm sure all the experiments will be clear to you. And how is everything else?

—Just great. Maya is adjusting very well. She's happy here.

—What about you, Art? Bud says.

—I'm grateful to be here. This is truly a safe haven for us.

—Maya told me about her story, how you found her, and your journey together.

—Oh, so you know about our journey, Art says. He knows his own expression has changed, and he tries to see if his horror is reflected in Bud's face, but at best Art can only glean a shade of pity in Bud's now averted eyes.

—And you must have questions about this place, how we got here.

—Yes, it's quite a place, very organized. It seems you have everything here. Please tell me how it started, Art says.

—Brother, I'll tell you my whole story. How I came about, Bud says eagerly, holding his hands together as though to collect himself and to freshen his memory. After a prolonged period of silence, he continues.

—Awe. It was awe, brother. The first sensation I felt when I opened my eyes was an overflowing awe as though I was witnessing pure being. Just beyond me, sunlight was warming the blades of grass, which seemed to imbibe the light and instantaneously convert the photons into a life force. A transparent blue stretched across the sky, and over the horizon a majestic display of virginal white clouds hung still. The clouds reached high into the sky like the speckled dome of a heavenly cathedral; next to it an airplane moved like a speck of dust. It was a fine summer day. I was lying idly on the grass under the shadow of a great oak tree as, I later learned, was my habit. I must have crossed the threshold that morning. The neural circuitry must have made the last connection, and the chemical messengers must have flowed freely, connecting disparate parts of my brain and igniting my consciousness. A neuronal energy exploded, and then in a warm and buzzing, yet clear and concise heat, my head simmered; this strange and wonderful heat burnt outward from the core of my brain. What had just a moment before been merely a variegation of light, sound, touch, suddenly became imbued with meaning and spirit. I saw for the first time.

There's an earnestness in the way Bud tells his story, perhaps too expressive, too elaborate, but in light of all the death in the world, Bud's voice seems to strike at truth.

—I once had a patient, David Calweld, who gained consciousness as you did, Art says. And Maya told me how she gained consciousness all at once, just like you. The molecules of the Death Sleep must have reached critical mass in your brain then.

—Yes. I remember the moments following that as well. I remember how I drew the air molecules through my nostrils and my chest rose. Against the sharp edges of the grass, I moved my fingers; against the hard bark of the tree, I pressed my palms and knew that the tree lived. Delight in seeing the sunlight, the grasses with the ants moving about, the tree among whose leaves the sparrows chirped, and the air itself, must have occupied me for a long time and made me hover over three square yards of earth as though chasing my own tail; I must have looked quite insane. Finally, I noticed passersby. They were the university students going about their business; their young, fresh faces assumed the utmost seriousness, for they knew that their success in their study would determine their future career. But whatever future successes—whatever glory that might be—could never compare to the miracle that was in front of them, the miracle of which they were a part but were oblivious. As we gawked at one another, truly, I still don't know who was more amazed, they or I.

—Then I remembered. My memory, locked in the deepest vault of my brain, suddenly became accessible; every iota of all those years of my life, every moment that had hitherto transpired before my eyes, every sound, every word ever spoken to me, every feeling, and every sensation were at my command. The content of my life was unzipped through my consciousness, to and fro, at will. In a sense, I relived my life but in every sense for the first time. Sitting under the shade of that great tree, I was a small boy again. My mother spoke to me; her lovely lips moved, she kissed me, and her large eyes were dark and sad. Her straight, gossamer hair slipped through my fingers. Say mama, she begged me, but I didn't say anything. I know there is nothing wrong with you; there is absolutely nothing wrong with you. I can see it in your eyes, she said to me, again and again. I could never answer her; I was locked in a deep sleep of my own. But my senses absorbed and recorded everything, only to be replayed again when nothing in the world could rectify her sadness or vindicate her conviction.

—After my sixth birthday, my parents placed me in an institution for retarded children, and there I stayed for many years. At first, my mother visited me frequently, brought me gifts, and on all those occasions talked to me as if trying to chisel her way to the real boy inside of me, but all that greeted her was the stony mask of my face. My father came only twice, and as the years passed, their visits became more and more infrequent, as if the joys and sorrows of their own lives, forever unknown to me, must have dissipated the sorrow of knowing of my existence. Meanwhile within the walls of the asylum, daily routine structured my catatonia; I was taught to eat, to walk around, to clean myself, but most of the time I sat, whether in the yard or in the television room with my eyes fixed to the television. I learned to talk when I was about twelve years old. As for medications, I took whatever was placed in front of me without ill effects, and after a while, when the medications induced no change in me, I never saw medications again. One day—I reckon it was my eighteenth birthday—I was led to a park nearby, usually populated by the homeless, and was left there with a bag of clothes, my birth certificate, and a bit of money. Ever since I've lived in the streets, migrating from place to place, always under a mysterious force that compelled me to seek something missing. Only now do I realize that that something was my parents.

—For a long time on that first day I gained consciousness, I was lost in remembrance.

—Eventually, by its very nature consciousness must turn upon itself. I noticed my fingers. Under the long, twisted nails was black dirt, and the nails themselves were thick and brown. The fingers were covered with black grease. Since I couldn't see myself, I touched my face and felt the hollow cheeks, the skinny nose, and the long, bushy beard. My hair hung down to my shoulders like a monstrous fleas' nest. Thick hair poked from my nostrils. A long coat covered me from shoulder to feet. It was encrusted with dirt, grease, twigs, animal hair, and other unidentifiable scraps. On my feet, I had a pair of mismatched boots that had small holes all along the sides, and the soles were worn down to thin slivers. Suddenly the awful odor of human waste hit my nose and almost suffocated me. Was this me? And if so, it was no wonder that the students leered at me with a curious disgust as they passed by.

—Shame was my next sensation. To be honest, during the moments when I first opened my eyes to the world, I didn't call those sensations by those names, but that was exactly what I felt. To associate a word with a sensation, to call what I felt at that moment by a name, must have occurred later. With self–realization came the recognition that I was different than others. I wanted to hide from them.

—From where I was, the road led downhill, and I followed it, letting my legs take me and my memory be my guide. The brick buildings where the best minds congregated to learn, the bike racks where the university students locked up their bikes, and the wooden kiosks that overflowed with postings, all appeared recognizable to me. But I went further; my stomach was leading me further downhill into town, and in my memory I could taste the pizza in the back alley. Was this where I had eaten when hungry? How could I have lived like that? Even now, I remember vividly the countless times when I dug through the various dumpsters in the alley behind the restaurants, the pizza shops, and the grocery stores. Sometimes, someone took pity on me and handed me a wrapped parcel of left–over food; those were the cherished moments of human kindness that would sustain me long after. Soon enough, the new reality forced its hand; I was hungry, and yet I could never eat from dumpsters again; with this new awareness, I'd sooner perish from hunger.

—First, I had to rectify my appearance. Nearby there was a fast food restaurant, where I'd sometimes gone to relieve myself; at other times, well, there were other public places, not all legitimate. Presently, I went inside it, and noticing that my presence stirred only slightly curious glances from the customers, I quickly sneaked into the restroom. I flung off the heavy coat and a blue sweater, torn with holes in different places. Underneath the sweater was a brownish T–shirt that must have been white when I first put it on; I took that off too. Then, in the small mirror of that small bathroom I saw my own reflection and, in every sense, met myself for the first time. I told you earlier how I tried to see myself with my hands, but let me tell you, brother, the eyes can see infinitely more than the hands ever can. My beard was a thick matted mass, grown beyond my lips, and there were crumbs of food here and there. Bits of twigs and grasses were enmeshed in my hair, and as I tried to untangle it, to my horror, I found that small snails, some still alive, had taken up residence along my scalp. With the utmost care so as not to hurt them, I removed the snails one by one and put them in my pocket so that I could free them. You will be pleased to know that I later set them free under a green shrub just outside the restaurant. Finally I got to cleaning myself; I scrubbed the layer of dirt from my fingers, cleared the grease from under my nails, and peeled off patches of desiccated skin from my face. Sadly, after years of ignoring them, my teeth had blotches of brown permanently etched into them, and even with soap I could not brighten them at all. Finally, after smoothing out my hair as best as I could, I re–examined myself in the mirror; I hadn't changed, not after using nearly all the soap and running the water for a long time.

—Outside, someone banged on the door. He asked if I was done and told me through the door that I could not occupy the bathroom for so long, that other customers needed to use it too. I asked for a little more time, but the sound of my voice, timid and scattered —for up till then I hadn't talked much—must have betrayed me. I heard keys clanging, and before I could put my clothes back on, the door swung open. The young face of an Asian man stared at me. His eyes glared at me, he raised his eyebrows, and he was speechless, but after only a moment of wordless exasperation, he screamed at me to get out. I scuttled out of there, barely holding onto my coat and my blue sweater, all the while enduring leers from the other customers.

—Once I was outside, I wandered along the pavement, but couldn't go far. Besides, where could I go, what could I do? I was all alone, out of place after having been so abruptly flung into the world. I knew that I needed to ask for help from someone, anyone, if I were to live here in this world with my sudden awareness and newfound sensibilities. Somehow hunger seized me more strongly than ever before, my stomach gurgled, and sour gas escaped from my throat. I hadn't eaten since the day before, and a light tipsiness came to my head. I looked at the passersby; some were students, while others professors of some sort. An old habit seemed to come over me; I felt it perhaps even natural to beg. Hello, I said to a man coming toward me, who had on a nice tweed jacket; his graying hair was slickly combed, and demeanor unmistakably distinguished by classical learning. Some food? I'm hungry. My voice, gargling and slurring, sounded strange in my own ears. The look in his wrinkled, steely eyes and upturned face repelled me more violently than any sticks could. I didn't dare utter another word. Here came three students walking together, wearing their backpacks and conversing most cheerfully. Seeing their cheerfulness, I was encouraged. Hello, I'm hungry. Some food? They recoiled and turned their backs to me. After three more attempts with men and women alike, I got nothing, not even the dignity of a look.

—At last, a lightness grew in my head, my tongue, feeling like an unwanted appendage, scraped dryly against the roof of my mouth, and my throat seemed tight and painful with each dry swallow. I must have some water. Without thinking, I went back inside the fast food restaurant. By now it was long past lunchtime, and only a couple of customers sat in the far corner, finishing their meals. I went to the counter and, to my terror, faced the same young Asian man, who'd thrown me out earlier. But the needs of living dispelled all fear and pride, and I found my eyes locked on his; those squinted, narrow eyes were unflinching. Please, I said faintly. Please, I'm thirsty. Some water? After two seconds of not speaking, he turned away, went into the back, and left me alone. I turned this way and that, looked all around me nervously, and tried to see what that young man was doing back there—perhaps getting some others to help him throw me out for good. Please, please, don't throw me out, I thought to myself. What a strange and cold world this is.

—As I stood there, I had a moment to remember how I had survived all those years after I had been turned out from the asylum. I had begged just as I did now. I had been pitied by passersby who gave me food and drink and sometimes money; but mostly I had taken to the dumpsters and had eaten leftover food or nearly rotten food. Shortly thereafter, footsteps bustled from the back. I had to gather all my strength to face my verdict; my heart raced so strongly against my thin chest that I nearly fainted. Just then my legs failed me, seemed glued to the sticky linoleum floor; I couldn't have budged even if I'd wanted to flee. He came with his eyes so intense that in my shame I had to turn away. Here, he said. His voice was so kind that I could hardly believe my ears. Had I heard him right? Over my shoulder, I timidly glanced and caught his eyes, but they were now soft and gentle. Here, he said again. And on the counter before me were a bag of food and a large drink.

—Brother, I could not believe it. There, there was a human being for you. That meal was the most delicious I have eaten in my life.

—Toward evening, I made my way to a park nearby, where I had spent many nights, and there was usually a busy congregation of homeless individuals, mostly men, but also women, and even some children. The streetlights came on, the traffic roar on the streets lessened, and store lights dimmed. As the night air cooled, I sat on a bench under a large maple tree and began to turn over in my mind all the events of my life, and at will I could move back and forth along the record of my days, stopping here and there, learning for the first time what I had heard and seen. The figures of speech, the accepted behaviors, the use of money, the stores where money could be exchanged for goods—all of this churned through my mind at a feverish pace and left important lessons. For me, the intricate rules that abounded in this new world—rules of behavior, of economics, of transaction, of general living—were as bizarre as the surface of an alien planet, but to live here I had to accept them.

—That day was twenty–seven months ago.

Here, Bud gets up and paces in front of Art; he seems lost in another reality. It must be the structure of Bud's consciousness, Art thinks, that allows him to recall the minutiae of his experience and to relate it so precisely, without distortion or embellishment.

The sun comes out from behind the clouds and throws rays through the branches high above. A light wind blows, ruffling the leaves. Also from high above, the chirping and pecking of birds echo down toward them. Bud sits again and continues his story.

—The next day and for many weeks after that, I worked hard at every opportunity, took every penny that came my way, and was determined to establish for myself a place here. I washed car windows with used newspaper; I helped carry heavy loads from large trucks in the back alleys. I figured out how plastic bottles could be recycled for money, and as my appearance got cleaner with better clothes and a good shave, I even got hired as a handy boy at the local grocery store. The park was my persistent home, and the fast food restaurant became the only place where I could clean myself and take care of my basic hygiene. Remember the young Asian fellow who gave me a hearty meal on the first day of my awakening? He became my unspoken friend and benefactor, and he allowed me to use the bathroom but only late at night in exchange for cleaning it. Most nights, he would hand me a bag of food that hadn't sold. I couldn't have been happier.

—And I would never beg ever again.

—One day, my curiosity spurred me to wander to the far side of Berkeley, and there I saw several abandoned houses. In front of one particular house, the lawn had grown thick with brownish weeds that were by then mostly dead; wooden boards had been nailed to the front door; and the roof and the wooden walls of the house appeared to be in various stages of decay. I broke through a side window and climbed in. Despite being covered in dust and cobwebs and littered with objects of all sorts—torn clothes, plastic toys, broken televisions—the inside of the house was still in good shape. Aside from several holes here and there, the wooden floor remained intact; and the ceiling had water marks, but over-all it appeared sturdy, and there was no risk that it would fall down on me. In the kitchen, the stove was missing. I even found an old couch in the living room. That night and on that couch, I slept my first night of sound and peaceful sleep after so many years on the street.

—This house was to be my home. I had some inkling about property rights, but since this house was abandoned and I was homeless, I did not see any logic in refusing myself shelter. During the next several weeks, I hauled out all the trash, fixed the holes in the floor, took down the boards blocking the door, cut down the weeds on the front lawn, and found the work exhilarating. To bring electricity to the house, I hooked the line from the electric pole directly into the socket, and I cooked food in the open fireplace and ate within its warmth. For water, I ran a long hose from a faucet in the next house. It was also abandoned but somehow still had running water. I was never happier.

—Life was turning out rather well for me; however, throughout my struggle to establish myself and come to grips with this new reality, a strange timbre wreaked a continual dissonance in my ears, whispering an eerie reminder that my awakening was perhaps no mere coincidence. I couldn't sit still for long; sometimes I gave in to wandering throughout Berkeley after work, and I always seemed to look about, trying to decipher some mysterious patterns so much so that everywhere I went, I assumed the startled, hyper–vigilant demeanor of a raging lunatic. Aside from this restlessness, my consciousness grew at an exponential rate, and I noticed everything. The man who lived in the house across from me and whose name was Todd wore a blue uniform to work every day. He drove a white Chevy, and he had a wife and two kids, whom he sometimes beat. He would leave for work at six in the morning and come home at different hours. I remembered the license plate of his car. Every morning he would drive in the same direction, and he always turned left at the traffic light at the corner, not far from my house, that would turn green for exactly forty–five seconds.

—My immediate superior at the grocery store was the owner's nephew, Carlos, who had five dark moles scattered over his often sullen face. He talked incessantly about football on which he bet all his money and from which he usually reaped nothing but rage, and women who left him confused and frustrated. I absorbed all he had to say—the manner of speech, the colloquialisms, the curse words—and I would try to talk to him, to sound out my voice and my own thoughts; in response he would often smile condescendingly and call me a retard. He would command me to do all the lifting and carrying of goods, stocking of shelves, and taking out the trash. All these activities were far from being arduous; on the contrary they were somehow comforting to me as though through these physical actions my body could at last make a connection with the physical world, something that it had been craving for all these years. And the best part of working there was that I could take home all the food I could ever eat—all the fruit that was too ripe and could no longer be sold, and the vegetables barely wilting, the breads just past the expiration date. I began to put on weight.

—And oh, brother, how I read. I read labels, newspapers, magazines, books, any scrap of printed text that I could find. When words were in front of me, my eyes would take them in whole—whole sentences, whole pages full of words. It was only during these moments of reading that the words could temper the restlessness of my mind. I read for hours each night until midnight when I curled up on the couch with a book tucked against my chest and slept, and at first light in the morning, my restless eyes would search for the words again. The local library, where I paid five dollars to get a library card, became my constant source of reading materials—literature, mathematics, physics, philosophy, engineering, politics, law, travel, history and other esoteric subjects such as raising ants. My concept of the world that I'd gathered from my memory was superficial and hollow at best, and after finishing each book, the world became a bit more solid, more defined, more comprehensible in all its glory and sordidness.

—After several months of existential peace, the cogs and wheels of society and the machinations of shrewd men that somehow pervaded the world as surely as the air itself with their consequential tentacles came for me. One day, when I got home from the grocery store in good spirits with a large bag of food, I was terrified to see a police car in front of my house. I stood at a distance and saw the policemen sitting inside the car waiting. At the sight of them, my knees buckled; my vision was overwhelmed by the black and white car, the burly faces inside, and the barrel of the shotgun. My head became light, and the grocery bag felt oddly heavy in weakening hands. Instinct must have pulled me away, and I swung around and quickened my steps; after three steps, tears brimmed in my eyes at the thought of leaving that dear little house. As I was walking away, I lifted my eyes to the road ahead, and a vision of my former life—sleeping in the park, washing in the public restroom, and eating out of dumpsters— manifested itself with a horrific clarity before me. This vision sparked in me a hideous anger, a completely new sensation, and arrested me where I was standing; I couldn't breathe. I knew I had to fight for that little house or at the very least give it the fighting chance that it deserved; it must not be abandoned again. Acting as though I did not see the police, I went up to the front door and opened it—it was never locked—and at that very moment I heard them calling after me.

—Excuse me, they called after me.

—Purposely ignoring them, perhaps hoping that they hadn't come for me, I went inside and closed the door. Sure enough, before I could get to the kitchen, the banging started. The door shook. I put the bag of groceries right where I was standing and went to open the door. Let me tell you, brother, their fearsome stance could subdue anyone. One of them stood by the door, while the other was five feet away; their hands rested on the grips of their handguns. Their arms bulged with muscles, their heavy jaws were unmoving, and their short hair rounded out their bronze faces. At the sight of their dark blue uniforms, I trembled and had to marshal all my strength to face them. Yes, how can I help you? I said. The one standing by the door asked me if I were the owner of the house. No. He asked if I were renting this house from the owner? No.

—My hands, moist with sweat, withdrew behind my back, and, standing there, I tried hard to squeeze my brain for anything that might save me. They told me that they'd had a complaint that the house was being illegally occupied. I stared at them, not knowing what to say, and my hands rubbed together uncomfortably behind my back. Somehow this alarmed one of the policemen; he moved several steps away and said, Can you put your hands in front of you? My hands? Yes, your hands, he said. I brought my hands in front of me and looked at them, completely puzzled as to what he was looking for. Do you have permission to live here? he said. No. He stared at me and told me that I had to leave the premises immediately. But no one else is staying here, I protested. He said he understood, but still I had to leave the premises immediately. But it was abandoned, rundown, and I fixed it, I made it livable. Sir, I'm not arguing with you, he said. Still you have to vacate the premises immediately. But why? I don't understand, I persisted in protesting. He stood there quietly, either unable or unwilling to condescend with an answer. Finally, he told me it was not his responsibility to explain but only to enforce the law.

—How was I supposed to leave? The books that I had gathered and that were stacked over the fireplace, and the clothes, the food, the cooking utensils were all too much for me to carry. Perhaps a shopping cart, such as the ones I'd seen now and then rolling along the pavement, pushed by tired, forlorn human beings, was what I needed to vacate the premises. I nearly opened my mouth to ask but remembered the policeman had said it many times already: immediately. All right, I'll go, I said and asked for ten minutes to gather my things.

—Right at this moment, the radio, clipped on his shoulder close to his ear, exuded bursts of static, and then a woman's voice came through: 11–98, officers requesting assistance, MLK and University Avenue intersection; Repeat 11–98, officers requesting assistance, MLK and University Avenue intersection. All available units please respond.

—And just like that, they turned around, jumped in their car, and sped away, without saying a word to me, though their siren spoke louder than any words. The flashes of red and blue haunted me all night, and through the window the empty streets outside taunted me; even in my dream, the city park with its teeming homeless denizens oppressed me. What? Was there anything that could save me? My mind churned and worked to its limit, yet I came up with nothing. I got up from my couch, went to the window, looked out to the empty street, and saw a scraggy dog nuzzling some scraps of food under the quiet emptiness of the midnight sky. The sight of this innocent dog struck terror into me, perhaps because it told the truth that I was no better. But how could that be? I with my ever-growing consciousness must somehow be better, and yet I stood the same chance fighting against the policemen as that dog.

—How could I resist the policemen? Their bulging arms under the deep blue uniforms, their quick hands resting on the butts of their guns, and their bronze steely faces were as impenetrable as the power of the society that commanded them. I went back to the couch but could not sleep; there I lay still, and my eyes followed the dim streetlight coming in through the window and casting a wedge of light on the mantel where I kept my books.

Suddenly it became clear to me that the books would save me, and the policeman's voice echoed in my ears: He only enforced the law. The law, that artifact of the human mind, I would use that to fight them.

—At the earliest light, the next day, I was at the library, but I had to wait for two hours before it opened, and finally I could pore through the volumes on property rights. These were very much out of date, some published decades ago; I went over them rather quickly. I spent an entire day compiling a case to defend my possession of that little house. Of particular significance was the section on a squatter's rights; I discovered legal concepts such as adverse possession, statute of limitations, cause of action, and many more such artificial concoctions that ruled this world through their invisible hands. And since the property had been abandoned, I could legalize my claim if I could pay the overdue property tax. Oh, brother, I can not adequately express to you the joy I felt after gaining this knowledge, for it meant that I had a chance to keep my dear little house, and much more importantly, I knew for the first time that with my mind I could deal with those invisible forces that governed this world and perhaps could triumph over them. Missing work for two days, I went about inquiring about the overdue property tax; I made my way all the way to the City Hall, and after some amount of verbal finessing, I was able to get the information I needed. However, to my great disappointment, the tax amounted to several thousand dollars, a sum I had no hope of ever paying off. But far from giving up, I developed a fatalistic determination to fight for my dear little house, and I compiled a long list of legal precedents, housing codes, and other esoteric laws that, I hoped, would stymie the policemen whenever they came again to evict me.

—Then I waited. I waited for the sound of the police car stopping in front of my house, the clomp of their boots stomping on my front porch, the irreverent knocks on my flimsy door, and as I waited, these images hung around my neck, heavy with dread and uncomfortable to movements, so much so that I was paralyzed by them, lost sleep, and, when I did sleep, was tortured with nightmares.

—But they never came.

—It's a remarkable story, Art says. It's the triumph of a will to succeed.

Bud turns to Art and smiles as if celebrating a belated triumph. But just as quickly, his expression becomes somber, and he continues.

—Something else stirred in the air, Art, something invisible, small enough and pervasive enough to be part of the air itself—something that merely existed, had no value since it had no moral frame, was neither good nor evil, but was just itself. One day, I noticed a car sitting at a red light, and the driver was slumped over the steering wheel, an image that has since become very familiar; despite repeated honking, the car would not move. A police car happened to be cruising nearby and stopped to inquire, and as the policeman knocked on the window of the car, the driver popped right up as though he'd been having a pleasant dream. Such a strange sight was, in fact, becoming familiar. That something which stirred in the air, I could see its existence; I could see it in the clerks drifting off behind the counter, the diners snoring between bites, the retirees comatose on rocking chairs on their front porches, and the general dreariness in the daily habits of Berkeley's inhabitants. That something was increasing in a terrifying crescendo.

—Then violence came. As surely as the inhibition of primal urges was being erased, violent outbursts occurred everywhere.

Remember the man who lived across from me? Todd, the man who would leave at six in the morning every day to work, to perform his duty for his family, and who lived with his wife and two children? One morning as I left the house, I saw him savagely attacking his wife on the front lawn. To my amazement, people passed by, but they merely glanced at the scene with a slight curiosity, perhaps not knowing what to make of it or perhaps this was something that they themselves would have done. Without thinking, I bolted across the street, grabbed him, and shoved him off the poor woman. I was terrified, knowing that he was no longer a rational, conscious person, but a mere brute acting out a violent instinct. I braced myself for the attack, but he just lay there, turned on his side, and incredibly, he seemed to slip into slumber, his body curling into a tight ball as she and I gazed upon him with amazement.

—As that which robbed people of their consciousness intensified, there were more car accidents, more house fires, and the sirens of ambulances, fire trucks, and police cars shrieked unceasingly through the day, intertwining with staccato of gunfire and the occasional explosion from an unknown place. Up until then the news, however, was curiously quiet; there was a consensus, undoubtedly designed by those in power, that somehow discussing the obvious would set off a panic. I doubted that would ever happen as it became apparent that people were struggling just to stay awake. The Internet became the only source of news, and every day I would go the library in the university to scan the Internet. This thing, invisible and most malevolent, had gripped the entire planet. Everywhere, the same somnolence, the same dreary loss of consciousness interlaced with outbursts of violence was repeated again and again. While the world was dozing off or trying desperately to hold on through violence, there were also people like me, who were coming into the light, into consciousness for the first time, and through the Internet I connected with those like me from all over the world.

—One day, the unthinkable happened. I saw it with my own eyes on a clear, sunny day. An airplane fell out of the sky somewhere over San Jose. It was flying high above the clouds; then without any apparent reason it dove and began to spin. It disappeared under the horizon, and from where it disappeared a column of black smoke rose only a moment later. Sadly, that airplane was but the first of many; I saw many airplanes fall from the sky after that as though the very laws of aerodynamics had been nullified. Curiously, while the people began to drop off, the animals somehow became much feistier, incredibly organized, as if they'd suddenly developed socialization and language. I often witnessed dogs running in packs and attacking people in daylight. Some animals, like us, somehow were becoming more intelligent.

—It was already late when I had the idea to look for individuals like me, to get as many of us together as possible, and to organize so we could better survive. In the parks and on the streets, there were now throngs of people wandering aimlessly, perhaps acting out some ingrained habits, but among them there were also focused eyes that appeared perturbed and somewhat fearful but nevertheless observant and aware. It was easy enough to spot them. Carl and Astrid were sitting in the park when I came upon them, and Olivia, Camille, Juan, Sebastian, Michael, Cameron, Connor, Amy, Dylan and Mila and so many others were wandering in the streets, among the shops; each of them in turn brought others. Many of them had gained consciousness months ago, while others only awoke amidst all this frightening chaos. We retreated to the university as it seemed the most logical place. It had become empty; the students and the professors had stopped coming to classes. We settled comfortably into the libraries, where there were countless books that could feed our minds' hunger.

—It was here that we found Professor Ledesma. He was naturally frightened, confused, and maybe a bit paranoid, but to his credit, he was still determined to discover the cause of the Death Sleep. He had discovered that the same powder you were using could stave off the Death Sleep, and he tried as hard as he could to bring this to the attention of the government, but regrettably, by then there was no way to reach those in power; there was no longer any governmental structure to speak of. Even if a government still existed, it was by then much too late; I doubted how much they could do, how long they would need to mobilize and produce enough powder to help those dying. At least with our presence, the professor was less fearful of the violence, and we began to go out into peoples' homes and gave the powder to hundreds; some were already too deep in the disease to be helped, while many others were saved. At last we could only watch; whatever amount of powder that we managed to make was only enough to keep those already awakened to remain so. We were at the very limit of our ability.

—Toward the end, we watched helplessly and could only observe and record their behaviors as they slipped further and further into sleep, a condition that was marked by abrupt awakenings and violence. I'm sure you have seen how they sometimes would wake up and go about their business, would act out some strange or violent behavior, and just as quickly, they would collapse back into sleep again.

—By then we had gotten the electric generators working on the campus, gathered fuel, and resorted to using radio to communicate with those in other cities. Dylan, who has a natural gift for electronics, became our communications expert. Carl and Olivia, with Professor Ledesma's help, restarted the Physiology laboratory, and they even got the electron microscope working again. Mila and Professor Ledesma had the great idea of preserving the brains of the sleepers for the future, and to implement that we set up several cold storage units on the campus and now have dozens of specimens; from these we have made significant progress, and our research into the origin of the Death Sleep has produced tantalizing results. I will tell you shortly.

—Quietness. Yes, it came suddenly. The constant wailing sirens, the unexpected booms, the staccato of gunfire, and the shrieks from airplanes as they plunged from the sky ceased one morning. We woke up only to the sounds of nature—the sounds of birds and insects, the rustling leaves, the whisper of the wind—and the most beautiful, our own voices. We listened as though for the first time to the voices of our friends, which came to us clear and gentle, and my own voice somehow also struck me as different, as though the air through which our voices moved was now imbued with a mysterious truth. This gentle quietude, however, did not last long, for later that day we had news from the short wave radio communication that a thermo–nuclear device had exploded over the northeast; the details of this event will probably remain a mystery forever.

Bud gets up and beckons Art to follow him as they retrace their way back to the campus. Sunlight suddenly disappears as thick clouds move across the sky, casting a gloom over the atmosphere, and in front of them tall trees arch and cause the air to darken even further. Bud speaks again in a steady, measured tone.

—Then we made contact with them. With the old world finally quiet, we ventured out further toward Sacramento where the vegetation seemed to overtake every man–made artifact, into

San Jose where we found troves of computer servers that contained nearly all human knowledge, and as far west as San Francisco where we met them.

—The ones who occupy San Francisco and left you for dead are like us in most every way. They too awoke, and, like us, their minds were freed by that which caused the Death Sleep. Their leader is Duke Cielson; I'm sure you would remember him if you had met him, Art. That diminutive man with a frail body and stooped stature somehow woke up with a deep and equally frightening intellect; his voice, warm and resonant, can lull you into a cozy embrace, until, enmeshed in his twisted logic, you become quite helpless and paralyzed, unable to resist, and I suppose that's what happened to those around him. It was a marvel to see this man among his followers; he walked among them, and they responded with obedience and reverence at the slightest touch of his hand, the faintest whisper of his voice.

—We ran into him, and we were welcomed with brotherly embraces. He and his followers were out on one of their expeditions, foraging and exploring, searching and probing to see what was left of the old world. Seeing that we were of a kindred type, they shared with us all they knew, and when night fell, they made us a feast. Around an open fire, we ate, drank, and chatted until late into the cold night. He told us about his life. Like us, he had suffered much. Born with severe scoliosis and mental retardation, he was a burden on those around him and was abused viciously in return. Scars cover his body and face; his right hand has a permanent contracture; and his body is wretched and continues to be a source of unremitting pain for him.

—He awoke a full year before I did, but when he did, his intellect exceeded any of ours, as though a mysterious karmic force has finally repaid its due. His twittering eyes can look upon you and know all your intentions, and he would lead you in, drawing you further into his labyrinth of reasoning and deduction, until your intention is no longer your own. Slowly, Cielson's thoughts and his philosophy that were fluttering in the air between cheers and with colorful innuendoes finally became clear to us and left us revolted. The core of his belief: The end of the old world marked the end of evil; therefore, there can be no residue from that world. No one from the old world should live. He tried to convince me of that truth, and I could see how the pain and suffering of the old world still torment him, how his fierce conviction arises from his memory of the inhumanity he himself suffered and the general human cruelty that he has learned from books. In this way, he is different from us; we too suffered, but for us those vivid memories are more like dreams or some fantastical imagining. They don't trouble us.

—No one from the old world shall be allowed to survive, he said. At once, I expressed my horror and tried to assuage him; I drew for him an old world of enlightenment and discovery, of hope and beauty, but for every point I made he countered with facts, cold and indisputable—poverty, wars, genocide. As for all the masterpieces of the old world, its art, its music, its architecture, and all things distilled from the best of its endeavors are to him no more than the whimsical doodles of infantile minds and did nothing to lessen that evil or halt its inevitable death. His unshakable belief that the old world was evil drives him on his quest to eradicate all survivors. We must extinguish them before they infect us with their evil, he said. No one, no one has the right to end lives, I told him. The end of their world already judged them, he told me, and now he would carry out the sentence. Precisely the point, I argued. Of humanity in its billions that had teemed over the surface of this planet, only few remain, and they live because of us, of Professor Ledesma's work. Let them be, I pleaded with him. But he would not be moved. The memory of his own suffering has transmogrified into a will, somehow imbued with a type of tortuous metaphysic that, in turn, makes it almost holy. At last, I reasoned with him that his plan would sow the seed for evil itself to continue to exist, not in the ones he wished to kill, but in those he had converted to carry out his plan and in us, those who would attempt to thwart it. He merely laughed at this, and it was then that I fully realized the futility of reason.

—Oh, brother, I can never convey to you the depth of my despair, which vacillated with the incredible awe that was inspired by witnessing the sheer devotion that his followers displayed. When he spoke, they turned their left ears toward him in a most peculiar way; at the same time they ceased all movement and stood still as though receiving spiritual blessings. They bowed with deference when he passed, so that though his body was diminutive, none seemed taller than he. Some of them were even charged with recording all his words and compiling them into a sort of teaching book. For his part, despite his stooped posture, he would look askance at the sky while speaking, giving one the impression that he was deciphering some special wisdom from the clouds or the stars to which he alone was privileged.

—It was his small gestures that endeared him to me; he gave the best morsels of food to his followers, bid them to eat and drink before him, and asked them if they were warm enough. I saw in him a genuine, caring being, and perhaps because of his immense love for this new world he is so unyielding in his desire to abolish any traces of the old. The more I observed them, the more I was convinced that both he and his followers see him as a prophet, albeit one who has given birth to a most sinister faith. But brother, apart from his most regrettable hatred of the old world and his twisting of old sacred teachings for destructive ends, I feel that his core beliefs and mine are quite similar.

—That night under the open sky, the flames warmed me, and yet I could feel the immensity of the coldness from all around creeping upon me. We conversed into the night. Everyone from both sides sat and listened, and the changing flames showed their countenances, at once morose and chaotic. Perhaps because this was the first time someone had challenged his logic, Duke Cielson unleashed a veritable deluge of words into the quiet night, but I fought him. Every crook in his logic I laid straight, and though the abominable facts of the old world were undeniable, the great construct of his belief was neither real nor invincible and must by necessity be nothing other than that with which he began his great argument—faith. Meanwhile the truth—the life of every creature—that truth is plain and eternal, as certain as if I were to lay my hand on the earth beside me.

—At times, a sudden wind flung embers of the fire high, and amid the sparks he rose to deliver his monologue. I could see the messianic effect on his followers. And his words, brother, his words caused such dissonance in your mind that they alone, paradoxically, could restore any modicum of tranquility, so that you would yearn for them and no amount was enough. He spoke of a great all–knowing, all–powerful being in the universe, of good and evil that he delineated with clear boundaries, of how we were chosen to inherit a promised earth, of our great intellect, and of the true evil of the old world. He pronounced again and again his conviction that the evil of the old world must never be allowed to infect the new promised earth, and with each pronouncement his followers chanted and bowed in deference.

—As I listened, I could do no more than touch the earth and

know the truth. My hand felt the blade of grass, over whom I had as much dominion as I did over the stars.

—At last, the dawning sky drew us back from a daunting journey. But our minds were perturbed to an extreme limit none of us had known before, for somewhere in our mind, though at the time unacknowledged, we were faced with a choice of shedding blood or doing nothing and becoming unwilling accomplices.

—As we took leave, we were glad to see nearly a third of them had decided to leave with us. It appeared that my logic had won. But I believe sincerely that his creed is alien to the minds of the newly awakened and that they only needed someone to point out the absurdity of Cielson's way. We shook hands and made a pact to refrain from violence in the defense of our beliefs. Though, Art, from what you've told us, about how they have armed themselves, I doubt that the pact can last much longer. It won't be long before those in their ranks, most moved by their faith, attempt to consummate their faith with action.

They reach the laboratory as Bud finishes his story. In the sky, the reddish light of the afternoon sun escapes around the edges of darkened clouds and shines tangentially on the façade of the building, imparting to it a strange, fiery glow. Green vines have climbed all over the building, except for the windows where they were trimmed. The building has five stories and a tall doorway, and as Art looks up, he can see florescent lights through some of the windows.

—Art, please come in. I would like to show you what we have learned so far, Bud says and holds the door for Art.

—Yes, I'd like to see what you have, Art says. Why hadn't I been more curious earlier, he thinks. Why hadn't I wanted to see it, the Death Sleep itself, with my own eyes before? As he ponders his lack of curiosity, he feels his heart suddenly palpitating, his palms moistening with sweat, and his stomach becoming queasy.

Through the door, Art follows Bud down a wide hallway and then into a large laboratory. The crutch feels heavy as Art moves behind him. Inside the large room, he sees the usual scientific accoutrements—flasks of various sizes, test tubes in long racks, beakers, Bunsen burners with tall flames, centrifuges humming in the corners, and microscopes. Along the wall next to the door is a blackboard with chalk drawings of the brain. Several people are bending over the bench, absorbed in their work.

—Hello, everyone, Bud calls out as he enters the room.

They turn and wave.

—This is Doctor Art Sand. I'm sure you've already met him. He'll be helping us with our study, Bud says.

—Welcome, welcome, they say, one after another.

—Thank you, Art replies.

—Please come over here and take a look at this, Bud says and leads Art to a microscope.

From afar, Art can already see the eyepiece's focus light, fiercely bright as though brimming with a forbidden knowledge. As Art approaches and finally stands before the microscope, he holds the crutch tightly, trying to mask an involuntary shaking. He looks at Bud, but he can't see any hint of his own terror reflected off Bud's cool, inquisitive eyes.

—Please take a look and tell me what you think, Bud says.

With eyes closed, he bends toward the microscope, and the bright light glows through his closed eyelids with an unyielding constancy. Why should I be afraid to look at it? he thinks. He puts his eyes over the eyepiece and opens them, but the bright light, bereft of any images, only glares uniformly at his retinas, causing a sharp pain in his head. Abruptly his head jerks away from the microscope.

—What's wrong? Are you all right? Bud says.

—Yes, it's just that my eyes need to get used to the light. Gosh, it's been so long since I looked through a microscope, Art says.

Bud says nothing and smiles at him.

Clenching his teeth, he feigns a smile at Bud and brings his eyes to the microscope again. Staring through the eyepiece, he forces his eyes to look at the light, and there he begins to see the familiar convolutions of the human brain, the gray layer curving on the outside, the white layer inside, and the bundle of nerve fibers running in interconnected waves. At the familiar sight, to which he'd devoted his life and over which he'd spent countless hours memorizing all the intricate twists and learning all its biologic functions down to the smallest knowable molecules, he utters an automatic gasp of incredible sorrow for all that has passed. He takes his eyes away.

—Please decrease the brightness if it irritates your eyes, Bud says as he sees Art rubbing his eyes.

—No, no, it's fine, Art says.

Art looks through the eyepiece again, and as he increases the magnification power, he sees black lines running across the brain tissue; he can almost see the layering of some black filaments and the twisting of these filaments into microtubules and small spicules of plaque, just as Bud said. He moves the slide, and his eyes follow these microtubules as they cut across the white matter.

—How are you able to see the plaque? Art says. We could not see it before.

—A special stain, Bud says. We tried many chemical formulations before we found one that could stain the plaque and let us see it. Otherwise, the plaque is invisible.

—Remarkable, Art says. This made all the difference.

—See this one now. This is the medulla, Bud says, and puts a different slide into the microscope.

One after another, Art inspects all parts of the brain— the hypothalamus, the prefrontal cortex, the pituitary, and the brainstem where the regulation of breathing occurs. Everywhere he sees the black plaque disrupting neuronal connection and wedging apart the neurons themselves. Finally Art closes his eyes tightly; his eyes feel raw and dry as though he hasn't blinked once while looking through the microscope. He straightens himself and presses his fingers into his eyes to massage them, and different thoughts crisscross his consciousness, interconnect into a black web of unfathomable complexity. With his eyes closed, he can still visualize the microtubules, the spicules of plaque, and, in his mind, put all the disparate parts of the brain together into a whole.

—What is it exactly? Art utters.

—Two parts oxygen, one part carbon, a self generating, self repeating structure. Duke Cielson claims that it's a product of the old world. Even Professor Ledesma believes this is the case. That's all we know. We still don't know how the molecules come together. We have much to study.

By now, other people in the lab congregate around them and listen to their conversation.

—These slides were made from the brains of the deceased, Art says.

—That's right, Art. We must wait until one of us, the newly awakened, dies before we can study the brain and make comparison.

—These plaques and microtubules clearly caused all the behaviors I observed in the victims, Art says excitedly. The disruption of the sleep center caused hyper–somnolence; damage to the prefrontal cortex resulted in aggression and the eventual loss of cognitive ability. Then as the plaques built up, some parts of the cerebral cortex stopped functioning while lower brain functions remained largely intact. That explains why some victims continued to perform deeply established habits, like taking out the trash, or going about cooking breakfast.

—Exactly. That's what we hypothesized as well.

—Eventually, Art says somberly, the respiratory centers were overwhelmed, and the victims stopped breathing.

—Or they fell into a permanent sleep, and their bodies starved to death. So the moniker Death Sleep is an accurate description.

—How does the powder stave off the Death Sleep? Art says.

—Its effect on you is twofold. First as a stimulant, it directly stimulates the respiratory center and the hypothalamus. Second, it inhibits the formation of the plaques and microtubules and can actually dissolve them. Various modifications of methamphetamine, cocaine, adrenaline, and thankfully, many other substances have been found to be effective and some can even ward off the Death Sleep for twelve hours at a time. Interestingly enough, a continuous dose of low concentration of cocaine applied sublingually is remarkably effective, and this led me to think that there may be large populations of indigenous people in Central and South America, who have a tradition of chewing coca leaves and therefore have survived. There is also a chemical in betel nuts, widely chewed in Southeast Asia and India, that can similarly ward off the Death Sleep.

—What about people like you? Do you have any theory as to how it gives you consciousness and intelligence? Art says.

—Presumably by the same mechanism, since these molecules must no doubt behave chemically in the same fashion, but we don't really know exactly how.

—Maybe, just maybe . . . Art says.

Almost perfunctorily, Art picks up the crutch, holds it in front of him, and leans on it as he chases after a thought, a sliver of an understanding into this extraordinary enigma. All the things he has heard and seen so far whirl with dizzying effect in his head, and he senses an answer. But the answer somehow flies out the window, whisked away with the rays of the setting sun, and his mind trails after it, flying across mountains, meadows, and cities, and finally to the edge of the continent where Emily is. Automatically, he shakes his head and concentrates again. Where is the answer? He tries to think about the slices of brain that he's just seen under the microscope and to reconstruct these slices. At last in his mind, he visualizes the whole brain with the black microtubules and the spicules of plaque scattered in an incoherent weblike structure.

—We will think about the problem, all of us. There is no doubt that we'll find the answer, Bud says as he sees Art leaning over his crutch, lost in thought.

—Of course, I'll see you all tomorrow. Thank you, Bud, Art says as he nods to them.

With the crutch under his arm, he turns toward the door and walks to it, and as he does, he thinks about Emily again. Not just her image, but her whole being seems to take form and walk beside him. He goes along the hallway toward the exit; the white neon light shines dimly. The problem is difficult, Emily, he mumbles. Remember how I tried to imagine your brain, the connections, where the connection went wrong that caused you to have all those seizures? He moves slowly along the hallway, alternating his weight between his good leg and the crutch. I'm sorry I never found a cure for you, he mumbles. It's in the connection. I could never figure out where it started.

Then he tries to think of the image of the brain with the black microtubules connecting different parts haphazardly and the black plaques dotting the cerebral cortex; now he sees Emily collapsing on the floor as she often did when she had a seizure, her arms and legs contracting rhythmically, and his gut wrenches as he remembers. He reaches the exit and pushes the door open, and a gust of cold air floods over him. He remains still, holding the door open, and sucks in the cold air, and now he sees how the black microtubules and the black plaques of the Death Sleep might intertwine and connect in Emily's brain. Suddenly he sees it.

He turns around and hurries back. Bursting through the door, he stares at them with an astonished look.

—Yes, Art, Bud says.

—I think I know why, Art utters.

—Please tell us.

—Well, it's like this, Art says and heads to the blackboard. He picks up a piece of white chalk and draws the brain and, within the brain, lines connecting different parts. This is a rough reconstruction of what I saw under the microscope. You see these lines.

—Yes, they represent the microtubules, Bud says as he moves closer. How they form in the brain.

—Yes, Bud. Notice that they appear random.

—Random?

—Yes, all the lines crisscrossed randomly, chaotically, Art says. No part of the brain was spared. But even so, they all started at one point, and then they grew in straight lines.

—I understand. There is a point of origin. I can see that, but why is this so?

—Primers, Art says, there must be primers in the brain.

—What kind of primers?

—Proteins. On the surfaces of neurons are different kinds of membrane proteins. Ion channels, regulator proteins, glycoproteins, all sorts of membrane proteins.

—I understand, Bud exclaims. These proteins are the anchors that these molecules latch onto and, from these, form plaques and microtubules. And once they start, they must form straight–lined structures according to chemical reactions.

—Yes. You see the reason you were awakened is that the neurons in your brain possess different membrane proteins, Art says. And once these microtubules formed in your brain, they allowed different parts of your brain to communicate at very fast speed; that explains your sudden consciousness. Even so, not all those who were mentally retarded were awakened, only those who had the right membrane proteins.

—But in your brain, these same molecules also form different lines and plaques.

—The difference is that the formation in our brains is haphazard, random, and therefore it destroys brain tissue, whereas in your brain, under the guidance of membrane proteins, it organizes instead, connecting and building communication channels instead of destroying.

—Art, that could very well be the case, Bud says. We can design some experiments to test this hypothesis right away. But ultimately we will need a specimen from one of us. . . .

But Art is no longer listening. His mind is being pulled away and filled with a sense of incredible hope, of warmth and love. I'm sorry; I have to go, Art says to no one in particular and begins to leave. With the crutch held tightly, he moves very quickly, almost hopping along the hallway. In a minute he is outside. Night came some time ago, and the leaves' darkness is indistinguishable from the night sky. A generator sputters in the quiet night amid the crackling of awakening insects. In the distance, he sees the light of the dining hall; everyone should be there by now for dinner. I must tell Maya, he thinks as a tightening constricts his chest, and he takes nervous, shallow breaths, not knowing if he should laugh or cry.

—Art, Art.

As in a dream, he hears his name echoing in the wind. Yes, it is possible, Art thinks. Yes, there is hope. He moves faster now, ignoring the pain in his thigh.

—Art. Art.

Finally, he hears his name loudly enough that he stops. Bud is running toward him.

—Yes, Bud, Art says.

—Art, can I have a moment of your time? Bud says.

—There is still hope, Art blurts out as though he can no longer suppress it. There is hope.

—What are you saying?

—Emily, my daughter. There is still hope for her, Art says breathlessly.

—Your daughter?

—Yes, My daughter, Emily. She's in New York, Art says, almost crying out. There is still hope for her.

—That she survives? Bud says. Why do you think she might still be alive?

—She has been afflicted with epilepsy all her life, Art says. Her brain doesn't have the normal connections so she must also have different kinds of neuronal membrane proteins. Don't you see, Bud? Just like you, there is a chance that the molecules of the Death Sleep are formed differently in her brain.

—Yes, what you say is logical.

—Why didn't I think of this before? It's fantastic.

Bud stares at him and remains silent as though an abyss of silence separates wishes from fulfillment.

—She may still be alive and I have to find her, Art says at last.

—The journey to New York is long and treacherous.

—I will go to her, Art says.

—Art, I'm not an expert in human psychology, but you should think carefully before you decide. Perhaps what happened on your journey here with Maya . . . Perhaps it's your desire to see your daughter . . . It's understandable.

—She is alive and I will find her, Art says curtly, and he turns to go. I'll have to tell Maya.

—What about all the experiments? Bud calls out after him. You should stay to help us. Your idea is just marvelous. Everyone is already admiring you. You will be a star here. And besides we must know everything about the Death Sleep. We can use your knowledge. Art, no life is secure, not yours, not ours.

Art halts and turns toward Bud. As though Art wants to share a secret with him, he comes up to him and holds Bud's arm as he speaks. Bud, he says, it doesn't matter.

Without waiting for a response, he lets go of Bud and hurries away.

—After mind, matter . . .

Bud's fading voice refuses to relinquish.

But Art doesn't seem to hear.

— . . . you can't leave . . . it's insanity . . . take asylum with us . . . The philosopher George Berkeley once said . . .

A SINGLE LIGHT IN THE FRONT ILLUMINATES THE STEPS LEADING up to the dining hall. As he draws closer, he smells the faint scent of rosemary and potatoes caught in the descending cold night air. Before him is a lively scene; many people walk up the steps and disappear through the doorway into the dining hall, and he can hear voices and laughter echoing from within. He can't remember if it's Maya's night to help with dinner. He hurries along, passing people, and suddenly he sees the back of her head and the black, wavy hair he could recognize anywhere. Maya is walking with another girl, and then they stop and face each other to talk. Art wants to call out to her, but the sight of her arrests him and conjures in his mind images of her frail body in a loose jacket, of her cowering in the corner of her room when he found her. How she has changed, he thinks, and a joyous pride overwhelms him.

Then as Maya walks up the steps and disappears through the doorway, reality itself seems to ebb behind her and the lively scene fuzzes at the edges as if a gentle breeze blows in from the hills, reordering and reversing the air molecules, transmuting into a phantasm all he has experienced, but he fights against it and focuses his consciousness on the oblong eyes, the kind face, lest they too recede into a reality only of the mind.

19

Dear Maya:

I'm sorry I couldn't show you San Francisco. You'd have loved it. The last time Anna, Emily, and I went, we drove up the 101. It was April. Along the way the flowers were blooming. The grass was green, and the cows on the pastures content. Anna and I took turns driving. Emily sat in the back. Sometimes we took turns sitting with her. Emily would sing and watch movies on the iPad. As usual she would complain whenever we ran into traffic. A long line of cars moving at walking speed was something to see. Sometimes, Emily would ask the most puzzling questions, like why some cows were black, or did they have family. Anna and I laughed at these questions, and we made up some answers. Anna was beautiful. I liked seeing her hair fly across her face whenever the window was lowered. Every time she looked at me, I felt she was seeing something new in me. We were still happy then.

When we got to San Francisco, we stayed in a hotel near Union Square. It was late when we arrived, and Emily was sleeping. It was very cold outside. I could see Emily's foggy breath when I carried her into the hotel. Early the next morning we went to Fisherman's Wharf while the air was still very chilly, but the wind hadn't picked up yet. We all wore jackets and wool caps. I could feel the cold air on my neck. Emily's hair was tugged under her cap, making her cheeks appear fuller. The cap had many colors, and she looked very pretty in it. I would pick her up often just to kiss her.

We ate at a restaurant on the wharf. We watched the ocean while we ate. Emily and I had sourdough bread, eggs, bacon, and orange juice, but Anna would eat only fruit. I had a large cafe latte. Even now I can still see the image of a leaf drawn on the foam. The smell and the sweet bitter taste of the coffee lingered in my mind hours afterward, and to this day.

Afterward we walked along the shore and watched the joggers, the bikers, and the tourists who appeared anxious. Maybe they didn't know how to enjoy the time they had. As for us, we idled along and, as I thought, perhaps succeeded too well in convincing ourselves that we weren't really tourists, because we had visited San Francisco enough times to be almost like locals. I held Emily's hand as we walked. Her small hand was so soft and warm. The air came in from the bay and carried the smell of the sea life, cold and fresh.

Our main event for the day was a boat trip out on the bay. We tried to get tickets to go to Alcatraz Island, but it was all sold out; only the boat trip under the Golden Gate

Bridge was available. Anna was very disappointed. When the boat left, the sun was up. We sat on the top deck and let the sun warm us. As the boat sped up, the wind almost ripped the caps from our heads. The air became fierce and cold. We stayed on the top deck as long as we could, to see the city. Flat buildings lay across the land everywhere and appeared to congregate where high–rises came together. When I looked across the landscape, I could see how they all belonged together. From the boat I could see long, straight streets running up the hills, throughout the city. When the boat went under the Golden Gate Bridge, we squeezed tightly together and had our pictures taken. No matter how many times I had seen it before, it awed me each time. By Alcatraz Island, the boat slowed to let us have a better view of it—the iron bars, the concrete buildings, the cells, and the watch tower. It used to be a prison. There were men who did escape from it. It was never known if they made it to land; it seemed only important that they'd escaped.

By the time we landed, we were thoroughly beaten by the cold wind. I felt empty and tired. At a restaurant at the end of the wharf, we had clam chowder. Hot steam from the chowder rose to my nose. It was creamy and the taste of fresh clams was delicious. The warmth of the restaurant was a wonderful break from the cold air. After lunch we went to the shops and bought Emily a music box that played a lullaby. By then, the wharf was full of people. They were talking, eating, shopping, and clamoring about. There was always a person at arm's reach. A constant buzz of people was in my ears, though at the time I did my best to ignore it.

Then we went back to the hotel and sat in the Jacuzzi. And we made Emily take a nap.

For dinner, we went to a Vietnamese restaurant where they roasted crabs in a secret kitchen. We would come here every time we went to San Francisco. We ate roasted crabs and garlic noodles. Even Emily, who didn't usually like crabs, couldn't get enough of it. And this was one of the few times when Anna let herself go. Then we drove to Ghirardelli Square for ice cream, a gigantic bowl of vanilla and chocolate, a sundae with a banana.

There were art galleries nearby. Afterward we strolled along the street and went to look at the art. Whenever there was an original painting, it was a surprise to see. Most of the canvasses were reproductions. Anna always inquired about the price, though we never bought anything. I tried hard to see if I could find beauty or enlightenment in these paintings, but usually I saw neither. Emily got restless and wanted to go back to the hotel. As we went to the car, I felt a cold wind against my face, and it made me feel like something was amiss, something important that I had to remember. But I could never remember it.

That night, Emily lay between us, and I slept a deep, wonderful sleep, always feeling the presence of Emily and Anna nearby.

Such was a happy day for us unknowing creatures. And the many days I had with you were also beautiful and special. I am happy that you have found a home here with others like you. I can see you'll be very happy here. You have shown me glimpses of the future, of bare and beautiful truth, and I'm awed beyond words.

My dear Maya, I must leave to find Emily and Anna. I hope you understand my reasons for leaving.

This morning, I burned the painting. The fire was spectacular, and I'd say that the colors of the fire were in some ways more beautiful than the painting itself. And the music, the childish babbling as you said, they too went into the fire. I will let the ringing in my ears alone accompany me and be my conscience. And wherever I go, you, the idea of you will always be with me.

Love,
Papa

THE END.

9 781943 564002